The BMX Kid

& the River Cult Murders

The BMX Kid

& the River Cult Murders

Paolo Sedazzari

NEWPULP PRESS

NEW PULP PRESS

Published by New Pulp Press, LLC, 926 Truman Avenue, Key West, Florida 33040, USA.

For information contact:
Publisher@NewPulpPress.com

ISBN-13: 978-1945734007 (New Pulp Press)
ISBN-10: 1945734000

Cover design by Gavin Sanctis

Printed in the United States of America
Visit us on the web at www.newpulppress.com

The BMX Kid

& the River Cult Murders

Part 1

Chapter 1

My First Proper Homicide

Wednesday 14th May 2014

IF YOU DRIVE AROUND the Walton on Thames area as often as I do, you would have seen him. I call him the BMX kid. He is late teens, rides a big-wheeled garish purple mountain bike, and has long, light brown hair brushed over either side like earmuffs. He appears to be trying to grow a beard, but instead can only muster tufts of bum fluff. He is regularly in the shopping center pulling stunts to half a dozen teenage spectators. Other times I'd pass him on the dual carriageway. I'd look at him getting smaller in my back mirror pedaling furiously, trying in vain to keep up with the cars. Then when we're are all gridlocked he'd get his own back on us motorists by gliding in between us and off into the distance like the master of the road.

Is he still at school? Does he work? What's his story? I am a copper – it's my job to be rational and levelheaded, so why was I so intrigued by him? Did I somehow instinctively know that he was going to play such a key role in my first ever murder case?

So Day One of my first proper homicide case started off brightly. On my morning drive to Kingston nick I clocked the jacketless pedestrians strolling about under a yellow sun among a host of cotton wool clouds. This was the sort of day that would have had an ex-colleague of mine who liked a bevvy insist we go on an all dayer, and I would have been mightily tempted.

Today I was feeling unusually pleased with myself because through my amazing will power I had just completed the seven-day egg diet. (*You will find this diet in the glossary.*) Now of course once you start eating normally again you put the weight straight back on. But for the next few days at least I was going to be noticeable slimmer and less jowly than usual. With the seven-day ordeal of abstinence over, I could now go back to consuming olive oil, grease and alcohol. I was looking forward to lunch big time.

At just before 1 p.m. I drove to my favorite Italian restaurant on Hersham Green and ordered a Fracosta di Manzo all'Albese (that's a Rib eye steak topped with a red wine, garlic & mushroom sauce). With expectant taste buds and my mouth watering, my phone rings – it is Matt the Stat my trusty assistant. I let him leave a message. Whatever it is, it can wait.

For the last five years my partner in crime has been Matthew Wolgrove a/k/a Matt the Stat. Matt is humble, polite, and studious. His hair is greasy and his glasses are massive, and you would never guess he is a copper. But he is, and a damn good one too. He's been instrumental in all of my big cases, rigorously checking the data (hence the nickname) and finding those small but all-important anomalies that will get a successful collar.

Ten minutes after rejecting his call Matt storms into the restaurant, his face molded into a worryingly startled expression. As he got closer I noticed his glasses were steamed up and he was foaming at the mouth. I was about to make some wise crack about rabies when Matt blurted – "Ferdy! They've found a body, washed up by the river."

"Dead?" Stupid question I know.

"Yes – she's dead. WE HAVE TO GO! NOW!" My thoughts were of the chef garnishing my Fracosta di Manzo all'Albese. "Hang on. What's the rush? She'll still be dead when we get there."

Matt gawped at me open-mouthed as if I had just turned into a giant two headed paisley patterned Alsatian. But to me, I was calmness under pressure. I was Francis Drake and his game of bowls. "Look, Matt – why don't you race ahead and I'll join you?" Matt now scowled with deep disapproval, I could sense he was now planning to apply for a new partner. He scribbled down the riverside location for me and made for the door. By the time he had reached the door I had stopped thinking of Francis Drake. I was now thinking of George W. Bush and that footage of him after he'd been told about 9/11, and he remained rooted to the spot, listening like a dullard to the school children singing.

"Matt! Wait!" I called out. "I'll drive."

As I stepped on the gas and sped along the river I was naively thinking in terms of – let's get this done and then I can get back to my lunch. "So, what do you know so far?" I asked Matt. "A woman, unclothed, found when the tide pulled out. She's fixed, strapped to the riverbed."

That sounded fucking nuts. "It could be an accident." I was hoping.

"This is no accident."

The crime scene was on the riverside slip road that links Sunbury on Thames to Hampton Court. Here the row of smart riverside houses clear to give the public access to the riverside. Concrete steps that lead down to the bank framed by arching willow trees that reach over to stroke the shimmering water. It was the sort of spot where you might run into Ratty and Moley messing about in boats.

The steps were sealed off by yellow crime scene tape, watched by three uniforms. A crowd of thirty people were hovering around the tape, craning their necks, staring and muttering. Some had their phones out, snapping away.

There was no place to park so I mounted the curb just by one of the attending officers, and Matt and I jumped out. I didn't need to flash my ID. The uniform recognised me and pulled up the tape.

I looked over to see the crowd gawping at me like I

was a VIP stepping under the velvet rope. I felt a glow of pride. I am doing a job that everybody is interested in. Feeling their eyes on me I charged towards my murder site to get a proper look.

Ahead of me in the shallow water, a group of four yellow plastic garbed CS (Crime Scene) were hunched over a shape that was flat on the floor of the riverbed. A few inches of the form protruded above the water, it was grey tinged with green.

I was up to two inches of water before I felt shivering cold seep into my shoes. I stopped walking as my eyes processed the images to my brain. A face stretched and distorted by the water like a badly made mask. When I registered that I was seeing a human face above the water – I noticed the bloody craters where the eyes should be, and then a large porous dent in the skull above the left eye.

As the stench of decaying water logged flesh filled my lungs I felt myself jolt back and look away. Then I felt a pair of hands grip my shoulders. Matt's was pulling me up. In my shock I had fallen to my knees.

"You okay?" I nodded and got up. It took me a few moments to summon the courage to look again at the waterlogged corpse. I could see that each wrist and each ankle was fastened to the riverbed, before I immediately looked away again. I tried to suppress the tears but I felt moistness on my face. I quickly wiped at my eyes, hoping no one would notice.

"It looks like the body was placed there when the tide was low, to be revealed when the water was at the same level 12 hours later. I've ordered a chart of the tides," Matt told me.

So we are looking at the body being dumped at around 1am, was my glaringly obvious deduction. "That's why I got one of our video people to cover the crowd," Matt continued.

"Good thinking," I said without thinking. Why did he do that?

"If the killer has timed it so the body would be revealed at this specific time, he may be here to watch everybody's reactions."

I scanned the crowd. A motley bunch, young and old, smart, and scruffy.

As I continued to stare, the head CS Guy came out to me and pulled down his yellow hoodie to reveal a solemn expression and a distinguished mane of grey hair.

"What have you got?" I asked.

"Cause of death – almost definitely a series of traumas to the head, and consequent blood loss. She has ligature marks around her wrists, indicating she's been strung up. She's had her eyes gouged out." "Before or after death?"

"Can't say at this stage. There had been considerable bleeding but it had stopped since she's been in the water so it's almost certain the murder was not committed here."

I peered over his shoulder in the direction of the body, but not at the body itself. Instead I was looking at one of the yellow-garbed CS people – the e-fit artist. I could hear her remark how difficult it was to do a useful job without eyes. You could hear the distress in her voice. Even a woman like her who sees disfigured murder victims on a regular basis was shocked.

"She was hammered onto the riverbed, hands and feet, by metal fasteners. They look like snaffle bits," continued the head CS guy.

"Snaffle bits?"

"It's for horses. They go in their mouths for riding." A clue perhaps? Was she killed in a stable or somewhere connected with horses?

A police van pulled up next to my car and four uniforms came out carrying sandbags.

"The tide is coming in fast. We're losing our crime scene," I heard someone say.

Matt sprang into action. "We must get that picture from above the body immediately. We need to get those footprints," and Matt raced off searching for the photographer.

As the men from the van began sandbagging around the body, vainly trying to stem the tide as the water streamed above and around the bags, Matt had nabbed the photographer by the wall of graffiti. "I am waiting for the crane to arrive," explained the shaken lensman.

"We can't wait. We need to take the photograph now. Get on my shoulders."

So Matt gave the photographer a hurried and shaky shoulder carry towards and over the crime scene.

I grabbed the senior grey haired CS Man again – "any distinguishing marks to help us ID the victim?"

"None so far. No tattoos, or even piercings. She may have some birthmarks. Will let you know." I felt the chilly tide coming in around my ankles. I was out of my depth. I just hoped everyone else was too focused on the body to notice.

Twenty foot away from the body, raised up on the road was a bus stop that would mostly be used by school children and pensioners. Was that why the body was dumped there? Timed to be revealed to them?

Did someone want to deface this picture of idyllic Old England charm? Plant a vile picture into the minds of those innocent nearby school children? The sandbags were not holding back the crime scene sufficiently and the body was now covered by water. The CS team lifted the body up which brought loud groans from the crowds. One of the CS prized open the corpse's mouth like a goldfish and took something out with tweezers.

I stared hard at the faces in the crowd, was somebody

enjoying this? Did I see an evil smile on someone's lips? My nausea gave way to anger. Thinking about the gouged eyes, the blinding, the loss of blood. I dare not even imagine what this woman went through. I was repelled and yet it was my duty to delve into the deepest detail of this horrible crime.

I felt a tap on my shoulder and the silver haired head CS guy showed me a folded card in a see through plastic bag.

"This is what we found in her mouth," he told me.

It was a playing card, folded into a V, the picture on the outside. A medieval illustration in black and white of the Devil standing over two smaller naked figures. The number 15 in the bottom left hand corner.

I gave it back to him. We had our first solid clue. But leading to what?

The Thames was very narrow here, just twenty foot from bank to bank. So I turned to look at the other side of the river. I could see more houses, dowdy flat roofed bungalows, not wealthy and well to do like this side. Over there are the gas works, an oil terminal, reservoirs, desolate stretches of road and open remote spaces. Highly likely killing locations.

I called the station. The door to door on this side of the river was already in progress. I ordered that the other side of the river be covered just as thoroughly.

From behind the crime scene tape I saw the ruddy cheeks of a familiar friendly face. It was Jane Barrow the young blonde reporter at the *Surrey Star*. She had been working on me as her police contact for some time. Now local newspapers, especially in sleepy Surrey, have a tendency to be a bit boring with lots of reports on Boy Scout jumble sales and school harvest festivals. So my crime stories are very welcome to the ambitious Jane Barrow, especially when she can get me to add some juicy lurid detail to make the story come alive. Alarmingly Jane had called over one of the CS boys in yellow and was funneling questions into his ear. I had to jump in.

"Don't tell her anything!" I ordered.

Too late. "A tarot card? What...?" Jane was saying as I pulled the CS guy away from her.

"Jane, I need to hold back details of the crime for reasons you well know"

"I promise I won't tell anyone else until the time is right. Until you've decided."

"No, Jane." I went to walk away. She called me back.

"So it was a Tarot card?"

"I can't tell you, Jane."

"I promise, promise, promise I won't tell anyone else until you're ready to go public."

I pulled at her sleeve and locked into her eyes, she looked back cooperative.

"Listen, Jane. The last thing I need is loads of spurious confessions and witnesses. You must keep this detail to yourself for now. I promise to give you an exclusive if you hold this back."

"So it's a Tarot Card?"

I gave an uncertain nod.

Jane's eyes widened. "What? Like the death card?"

I nodded again and walked away. "Remember." And I covered my mouth.

Trusting a member of the press? What was I thinking?

I lost track of the time I was at the crime scene. But I stayed there long after the CS people had taken the body away.

I walked around not knowing what I was looking for, tracks, a dropped match, something that would open up a path to the perpetrators. Finally I decided it was time to go back to the station and go over with Matt what we had. As I walked along the pavement towards my motor, I heard a whizzing sound and felt a whoosh past my trouser leg.

It was him – the BMX Kid – on his bike as ever – "Excuse me? Are you the head investigator?" he asked, fixing me with a blue-eyed stare.

"I am in charge of this case. Yes."

I looked at him hard, could it be him? He's pinpointed me as the lead investigator and he's fucking with me.

"Have you clocked that satanic looking graffiti nearby?"

"Satanic? What are you talking about?"

"Yeah it's a symbol. A globe with tentacles – it's done with a stencil art. Come take a look."

The BMX Kid glides over to the wall with such elegance, it was as if the kid was born on two wheels. I held back for a bit, just to let him know who's boss. But then joined him to look at the low concrete wall between the river bank and the road, twenty feet away from the body."

"This is what I mean." In among all the usual hip-hop tag graffiti was a distinctive black globe with eight pointed tentacles reaching out. It was clearly done with a stencil, and recently as it was on top of the more colourful hip-hop tags. "So we think we should be going after Banksy then?"

"I think you should find the person who did this graffiti."

"Why not go for everyone else who's daubed this wall?"

"There's something unusual about this though, and it's pointing in the direction of the body."

"Yeah, it's pointing in every direction so it would, wouldn't it?"

"It's unusual graffiti that happens to be by a murder scene. I would have thought it's worth following up."

"And we will. I will get our cameraman on this wall

and we will find the person behind it."

The BMX Kid then turned to me, his eyes glinting with mischief. "Do you know about the satanic rituals on Brooklands Park?"

Chapter 2

A Farewell to the King Edward Suite

Wednesday 14th May 2014 – Late Afternoon

THERE WAS NO RESPITE. From the grizzly horror of the crime scene we drove straight to the nick to wrestle with the gathered evidence. What with my watery eyes and the falling on my knees, I know I had dealt with my first proper murder scene like a pathetic big girls blouse. Matt the Stat on the other hand was unbelievably together – on fire with those quick important decisions.

Normally my police work is conducted under the flickering strip lights and surrounding battered filing cabinets of the King Edward Suite. So called because it is situated right in the middle of the third floor and so gets as much natural light as a King Edward potato. But because homicides are so rare in Surrey, a dedicated incident room was going to be set up for this one.

So Matt and I stood in a large glass partitioned space as the handy men beavered away putting together the incident room around us – white boards, cabinets, desks, computers. The investigation was well truly off, and it was all hanging on me. So what do we have? The door to door had so far yielded nothing useful – just one resident hearing a splash that may have taken place at around midnight. He was half asleep and saw nothing, and wasn't even sure of the time. But according to our tide charts we were estimating that the body was fastened to the riverbed at around 1 am, so 12 hours from the time it was revealed by the tide again.

But the door to door was ongoing, moving further out, but then going back to make sure that no valuable witnesses had been missed.

With the incident room set up, next came in a special unit team of four men and women who would input the info into the fabled investigative computer system known as HOLMES 2 – (this stands for Home Office Large Major Enquiry System). Holmes also being the name of the world's most famous fictional detective. What are the chances of that eh?

Two of this newly formed team of young helpers set about scrutinizing the CCTV around the area between the hours of 11p.m. and 1am, taking down any vehicle number plates and tracing them. They may not be the killer or killers, but they may have seen another suspicious vehicle. Maybe somebody on a night shift who routinely drives down that riverside road saw something unusual in the early hours.

The CCTV on the river locks yielded nothing. Apparently no boats had been on that part of the Thames that night. But maybe a dinghy, something that dipped under the CCTV. That's why I stressed the importance of speaking to every resident on the other side of the river.

The medical team was wrestling with the unenviable job of trying to gleam information from a decomposing waterlogged body. That would take time, but for now we had this basic information on the victim:

Age – 18-30,
Height – 5 foot 4,
Weight – 137 lbs.,
Hair Colour Dyed– Black,
Hair Colour Natural – Light Brown,
Ethnicity – White Caucasian.

But it was Matt the Stat's shoulder carried photographs of the footprints on the muddy riverbed that offered the most revealing, yet tantalizing, view of what happened. The original photograph is best described as a "fucking mess" just a pattern of bumps and impressions in the mud. Many of these footprints would have been caused by the CS people who had spent so much time in the water around the victim. However a wizard on the special crime team was able to take this inkblot of a photograph and digitally remove all footprints that would have been created by the CS team's distinctive police regulation footwear.

Once they were removed, he was able to give us this digitally reconstructed picture:

Can you spot the two sets of footprints facing each other walking sideways – approximately 5 foot apart? Were they carrying the body? These were the heaviest footprints of all – indicating that they were carrying their own body weight plus one half of a 137 lb. load. Their footprints exiting the river are not so heavy.

In amongst the footprints of the CS people were a number of impressions that we perceived to be knee prints. Was that from the person hammering in the horse snaffle bit that fixed the body to the riverbed?

I felt we had been given the briefest glimpse of our killers, and it would indicate that we were looking at least two perpetrators.

Now closer photographs of those foot prints suggested they are both size 9 Wellington boots. So that would indicate two men. It also gave us an entry point into the river and the direction of where the vehicle would have been parked. We need to get CS back there and go over that area again. Those Wellingtons would have surely left a muddy residue on the pavement.

Those whiteboards above our heads that dominated the incident room were looking very bare, so Matt did a photocopy blow up of his rather sketchy drawing of the crime scene and stuck it up. (He's better at charts and graphs than he is at drawing.)

~ ~ ~

As it got dark, Matt got the email with the artist's impression E-fit of the victim, so that too went up on the white board. Though the girls' face was heavily disfigured through being twelve hours in the water, the e-fit drawer was able to work out the shape and size of the face, the jawline, the cheeks, the eyebrow ridges. We also had a hairstyle. But with her eyes gouged out there was no way the artist could speculate on the size and shape of her eyes, so they were left blank. Without the eyes she looked ghostly and tragic. Without the eyes we didn't have a person. Forensics came back with a report on the Tarot Card in her mouth. It obviously had the victim's saliva DNA, but it also supplied a partial fingerprint. That of the victim. Was that significant? Did she put the card in her mouth herself? Was she a fortuneteller?

The forensics revealed that her stretched tendons indicated that she frequently wore high heels. She was sexually active, but no evidence of being sexually assaulted before being killed. Sexually active? So does that mean she had a boyfriend or boyfriends? Or was she a prostitute? Toxicology came back with the contents of the victim's stomach. My hopes were raised here. In TV cop shows this where they discover an herb that's served in a pizza exclusive to one restaurant.

Sadly no – "In her last four hours she had ingested something that may or may not have been a Ginsters pasty," the Toxicologist dryly reported.

Fucking marvelous! Have you seen this woman? We don't know what her eyes look like and she may or may not have eaten a Ginsters pastry on Tuesday evening. I tried my best not to look disappointed, but I couldn't conceal it and the toxicologist went away in a huff. Maybe the victim had been hanging around a petrol station. We would check them all, along all with all the other cheap convenience stores. Forensics supplied an isotope test from the victim's fingernails to establish genetic nationality. Some dismiss this as junk science, but it could give us a pointer as to where the victim originated. The report was that she is of Slavic origin.

As you can see, the E-fit picture looks eastern European. But then again maybe not. It was getting impossible to conclude anything definite. Every time we appeared to be establishing a fact, we were forced to reconsider and undermine it.

One of the first things that CS did on finding the body was put her DNA and fingerprints through every database we had. She was on none of them. Most prostitutes when arrested are sampled up, so maybe she was new to the country. Trafficked perhaps. We would extend the DNA search beyond the UK and contact all the eastern European agencies.

So Matt gets on the dog and contacts each and every missing person agency in the UK and Europe for a list of missing women who fitted our criteria. The UK police get around 900 missing person reports every day, of which approximately 300 are adults. So we were expecting a deluge. Sure enough, within the hour the emails start coming through. Three hours later we had been sent photographs of 600 women.

Of these 600, those with DNA and fingerprints on their record were matched against the girl in the river and this way we eliminated 200.

Though we had been allocated a team of four back room boys (and girls) to sift through the data, Matt and I personally looked at the remaining photographs – all 400. Trying to match the e-fit picture with the missing person picture.

I sat through a revolving slide of women, all with a variety of expressions, some smiling, some sad, some blank – and yet all with an underlying pervading sadness. There were so many reasons why these women would disappear or leave home, willingly or unwillingly. But there was a common theme – a betrayal of trust, an abusive parent or stepparent.

Through this method of eye balling these missing women Matt and I had narrowed down the list to a possible 150, without totally discounting the other 250. But it was quite possible none of these was our woman in the river. Nevertheless we got the back room team to log them all into HOLMES2. Now I need to provide you with a map of the crime location: As you can see a main road, the Staines Road, is nearby to take you quickly out of the area – and that's where my line of thinking was taking me. If you are going to go to the trouble of putting your body in a car to dump it, why dump it somewhere on your doorstep? You wouldn't dump it in an area where you and your victim are known. No you would dump it somewhere as far away as possible.

But why there? Why that spot, at that time? This led Matt to show me his tide chart.

With this data Matt put together this graphic of the tide and the body. As you can see the nose tip of the body would have first been visible at between 9 a.m. to 11 a.m. Next was our analysis of the cause of death. It is attributed to blood loss from a series of traumas to the head. But we needed to establish how she was actually killed. Squeamish people look away now (or skip over this bit).

There were ligature marks around the wrists, but not the ankles. Indicating that she had been hanging by the wrists. The eyes gouged out. Was this before or after death? And why?

The uneven shapes of her head injuries indicated that they were created by a rock. Was she stoned to death? Maybe it was a punishment – an honor killing. And why were the eyes removed? Where are the eyes now?

Matt suggested a medicine murder. She was killed for her eyes so they can be used in an eye transplant.

The hand and feet were affixed to the riverbed by four horse bit snaffles that were nailed into the riverbed. This had got us all excited at one point, we deduced that the murder was committed in a stable yard or somewhere connected with horses.

But in the end we had to concede this as a non-lead. Those snaffle bits could have been obtained from anywhere and at any time in the last 10 years. A car boot sale perhaps. This killing had a distinctive MO, maybe this was part of a series, so we both trawled through the UK records of previous murders – anything jump out? Stoning to death, eyes gouging out, fastening to a riverbed. We looked through the unsolved murders, and then we looked through the solved murders. Maybe they got the wrong guy, or he was out of prison, or we had a copycat. Nothing. So we needed to look overseas.

At 8p.m. and after several hours of headache inducing number crunching fact sifting, I called my reporting officer Chief Constable Hinton to tell him where I was. I told him about the press conference I had arranged for the following morning which I thought was a "proactive" way to get the public to help us identify the victim. Hinty commented, "You know if you made public the tarot card in her mouth, the press would go into overdrive."

"I know, Sir. But that's actually the reason I am holding it back. I don't want to be on the receiving end of loads of bogus information from cranks."

"Okay, Ferdy. I support your decision. But it does give this murder case a different spin which needs to be investigated."

We had an unusual formal/informal relationship, I would call him Sir and he would call me Ferdy.

Finishing off the conversation Hinton said – "Listen! Ferdy, I heard you got yourself in a bit of a state at the crime scene today. Totally understandable. But it's very important you live up to your billing with this first proper murder case. We are all totally behind you and you have my fullest support. Make sure to put all your warrants through Philip Montgomery. He's our best magistrate and has given his word to fast track everything for you in this investigation. Anything you need with this case, you only need to ask. Okay?"

"Thank you, Sir. I won't let you down." I put the phone down feeling supported and reassured. No seriously, I did. But most of all I felt sick – and out of my depth.

Chapter 3

Beware of Apophenia pal

Thursday 15th May 2014

I DIDN'T PROPERLY WAKE UP the following morning, because I didn't properly go to sleep. I drifted off intermittently but those images would jar me back to consciousness. I sensed my wife Cassie beside me, but there was no way I was going to share with her what I was going through. She would dismiss me as weak and not up to the job.

But my sleepless troubled mind had reached a definite decision. Once I had found the people responsible, I would tell the top brass that I would never do a homicide again. My background was fraud and the fraudsters that I understood. But this level of sickness was totally alien to me. I knew this would limit my earning potential at the force. But fuck it, Cassie was going to leave me eventually anyway.

Most of the time in my job, I walk around with a cocky self-assurance. But my swagger often belies that on my tougher cases I am deeply anxious. This displays itself unseen to the outside world with an itching just above my elbows and in the middle of my right thigh. It has been diagnosed at various times by various doctors as ringworm and eczema. But I know it's triggered by anxiety, and this morning my elbows and right thigh were red raw.

I got up and washed my face over and over with hot water. I needed to somehow revive myself for my morning performance.

The press conference was called for 9 a.m. at Kingston Station and I was expecting a flotilla of OB Trucks, and a room full of jostling journos. Instead I walked into the room to face a paltry showing of three people sitting in the rows of chairs and one of them was the ever-earnest Jane Barrow.

Fortified by several cups of black coffee, I began my prepared speech. I went over the facts of the case. The ones I was prepared to go public with where these:

– She was killed by repeated traumas to the head.

– She had been tied up.

– We believe she was dumped there between midnight and 1am.

– She was nailed to the riverbed by horse bit snaffles.

I held back the tarot card in the mouth and the Wellington boot prints on the riverbed. The important bit came next. I pointed to the eyeless E-fit displayed to my left and said:

"The public must play their part in this investigation. Somebody somewhere knows who this woman was. Was she a friend, a neighbour, or a coworker? Someone you are used to seeing in your daily routine and haven't seen for a while?

"Somebody somewhere knows the people behind this. You may have direct knowledge of their guilt or have reasons to suspect them. If so, please come forward." I had spent the last two hours learning the final appeal to the public by heart, and so did not need to look at my notes. Instead I looked straight at my audience – all three of them and I finished off with this – "This is a horrible grizzly crime, and I will not rest until we find the killer – or killers. We will bring them to justice."

That last bit was poxy cop show stuff, but you could see Jane Barrow lapping this up, while the other two press people actually looked up from their mobiles for the closing salvo.

I opened the floor to questions. Jane naturally had a question, and a good one:

"You sound as though you believe there to be more than one perpetrator."

"I remain open on this. To move a body into the river is easier with two people than one, but that doesn't mean one person couldn't have done it on their own."

The second question was also from Jane – "Do you think it's likely the victim is someone under the radar – a homeless person or a sex worker?"

"I think that's very likely, in fact the most likely scenario, but again just speculation. We are going through the list of missing persons that fit the criteria in this country and beyond, and it's quite a list."

I continued – "That's why it's so important this E-fit goes into your papers and websites. We must identify this woman. From there we can work out her final movements, and from there find the killer ... or killers."

And with that I called the press conference to a close. Like an after show groupie, Jane rushed up to me to say she was going to persuade her editor to hold the front page of tomorrow's edition. This was quite possibly her first proper mystery flavored murder reportage, and she appeared to be in hog's heaven. I wish I could share her enjoyment but my feeling was very different. I wanted this solved and finished with as soon as possible.

Chief Constable Hinton collared me as I was at the main door. I was hoping for a big congratulation on my spellbinding press conference performance, but instead he told me there were two people he wanted me to meet. The look on his face indicated that they were important people. He led me into one of the stark grey meeting rooms. I thought I had walked into a Star Trek convention because the two men sat at the table who jumped up for a handshake didn't look like coppers. Instead they had a decidedly sci-fi geek look about them. One was beer gutted, real ale probably, and bearded. He was introduced to me as Terry Bowell. The other man was tall, pale complexion, with a hairstyle that looked as though it had seeped off an oil spill. He introduced himself as Vince Machin.

Instead of challenging me to a game of dungeons and dragons they launched into a spiel about the 'satanic trappings' of the case and how this could be linked to some of the 'satanic' activity in the area – most notably from among the youth. Bowell is a youth probation officer who had noted disturbing activity among his boys and girls. He had taken his concerns to Machin who is a university lecturer and a self-proclaimed expert on Satanism.

I was not impressed – "So you haven't got anything useful for me then. You just want to speculate that these murders are of a satanic nature?" This took the wind out of their sails. I was about to call the meeting to a close but I turned to Hinton who sat next to me. He maintained his deadly serious countenance, he obviously wanted me to continue listening to these men.

I needed to change tact – "Forgive my skepticism. But please tell me how exactly this murder is satanic and how this satanic line of enquiry will lead me to identify the victim and murderer."

Machin launched forward – "The victim was tied up, she appears to be stoned to death. Her eyes gouged out"
"How does that make it satanic?"

"It's a human sacrifice ritual, it's referred to in many books. If thine eyes offend thee – pluck them out," said Machin.

I jumped in – "Hang about – isn't that a line from the Bible? How is that satanic then?"

"That's what Satanists do, take things from the Bible and twist them."

I did not mention the Tarot Card in the mouth, and I was hoping they were not aware of it. That would of course have added fuel to their fire.

"But what set off the satanic alarm bells for me" chipped in Bowell "was how the body was found. The tide revealing the body, the way it was fastened to the riverbed, positioned as if," he paused for dramatic effect "it was to conform to some ritualistic guideline."

"You have a motiveless crime. Unless you consider that the murderer or murderers are interested in Satanism and performing their hideous rituals," added Machin.

I remained unimpressed, I came back with: "Or we could just be talking about a sadistic psychopath who enjoys inflicting pain and death on people."

"And we know that many sadistic psychopaths chose a satanic path specifically to give them an outlet for their horrible urges," Machin said with an air of triumphant authority.

"And find like-minded accomplices," Added Bowell. I thought he was going to finish off with a touché. Remembering the BMX Kid, I offered – "Do you know anything about the satanic rituals in Brooklands Park?" Bowell looked over to Machin who spoke, "I read something about that on the Pagan Surrey website. You could do a lot worse than investigate. It could have something to do with your murder."

I did not like this case being referred to as my murder. Even though it was my murder.

Bowell lifted up a large manila folder overflowing with paper. "This is a dossier I've compiled on the local Satanists and their activity. I think you should especially look at some of the youngsters who have been desecrating churches. One has been killing animals and nailing them down in a way similar to your murder."

It's not my murder, you git – it's my case.

Machin then gave me his book on satanic cults. "You can do a lot worse than read this; it will give you an insight into the motivation of these people."

"I could do a lot worse eh?" I said sarcastically, noticing his repetition of that phrase.

I took the book and looked at the cover – the title UNDERSTANDING SATANIC CULTS surrounded by pentacles, a goat and other satanic associated symbols. There was a picture of Machin looking especially pompous as the author on the back.

"Thanks. I'll show this to the wife, she loves this kind of stuff."

Machin gave me a stern look – "Are you taking this seriously?"

"I am taking this case extremely serious. Are you?"

Friday 16th May 2014

As every armchair sleuth will tell you, the first 48 hours are critical to the homicide enquiry. Our 48 hours were up and what did we have? Jane had come good with her front page of the weekly *Surrey Star*, hitting the newsstands Friday morning. The other two nationals carried the story, but elsewhere in the paper. The E-fit picture was now up on a number of websites, including our own Surrey Police site and our twitter feed.

So the incident room boys (actually half of them are girls) sat at their desks hoping for some hot telephone activity, and the problem from there would be sifting through the time wasters and nutters.

In the meantime Matt hit the Gog (as in doing web searches) on "eyes gouging out" and "stoning to death." He got stuff on political prisoners, honor killings and medicine deaths. That would keep him occupied for a couple of hours. So perhaps against my better judgment I hit the Pagan Surrey website. Sure enough I found a thread on the satanic rituals on Brooklands Park. I have to admit I found some it intriguing – but relevant to the case? Trawl through some of the highlights if you like, you may see something that jumps out.

<u>Subject: Strange goings on In Brooklands Park?</u>

Virgin Prune – *Does anybody know about those rituals going on in Brooklands Park? Who's doing them? Are they devil worshippers, or one of us?*

Dion's Fortune – *WTF is this stuff about Satanic Rituals doing on this web forum? How many more times do I have to spell it out? WE ARE PAGANS – we have nothing to do with Satanists. I am sick of outsiders thinking that Pagans worship Satan. We do not even believe Satan exists. We worship Nature, Mother Earth.*

Shibboleth – *Amen to that brother*

Liberator X – *@ Shibboleth, Amen? Are you coming all Christian on us?*

Shibboleth – Joke

Virgin Prune – *@Dion's Fortune. Why are you jumping to the conclusion that they are doing satanic rituals?*

Dion's Fortune – *Because I heard about them too. It's a fucked up S&M scene, just a bunch of perverts role-playing.*

Ace of Wands – *Sounds like fun. When's the next one?*

At 10.30 a.m. the incident team got their first phone call. A nice old lady thought she may have seen our girl on a bus to Addlestone on Monday. That was it. She was thanked for her call and the info was added to HOLMES2. Twenty minutes later we got our second. A girl looking like the E-fit was seen jogging in Hampton Court yesterday. Of course it couldn't have been her, she was dead yesterday. Nevertheless we thanked the person for their call. Some people just want to help, even though they are not helping at all. I called Jane Barrow to express gratitude for the front page, but I also wanted her take on this satanic cult angle. She had reported on a series of church desecrations in and around the Weybridge area, one involving a dead sparrow nailed to the door, which had deeply traumatised the vicar's wife. Jane had written about the local character believed to be responsible – a teenager by the name of Roger Farrady who had obviously watched the Lost Boys or Buffy too many times, as he had decided that his name was really Versago and he was in fact a 500 year old vampire.

Roger a/k/a Versago first came to Jane's attention the previous year when he had entered his school's creative writing competition. His submission was so shocking, full of "sadistic pornography" that the school expelled him just for writing it. Jane told me she had read it and was not able to reproduce any part of it in her article, not even a consonant. Versago was part of a gang and also a love triangle, which was reported on by Jane when this story hit the magistrate's court. It was like "a Goth Jules and Jim" commented Jane. Versago got jealous and the girl in the triangle received increasingly menacing threats that involved torture and death. Could this girl be the victim in the river?

I looked through the dossier that Bowell had given me, and sure enough there was big file on Roger Farrady a/k/a Versago. Have a butchers, if you like:

> *Roger Farrady (dob 2.4.1994)*
>
> *Expelled from school for submitting sadistic pornography to a creative writing competition.*
>
> *Extensive mental health record – described himself as a homicidal, suicidal, schizophrenic, manic depressive, sociopath*
>
> *Assaulted Classmates*

Set Fires at School
Believed he was possessed by a spirit named "Josey"
Believed he was a God/Christ
Believed he "got power" by drinking blood
Reports of cruelty to animals.

I then went back to the Pagan Surrey website and found this thread:

Subject – Versago
Shibboleth – *I saw him today. Walking through Weybridge High Street. He was looking pretty fucked up.*
Virgin Prune – *Did you speak with him? I hear he's made peace with his Mum.*
Shibboleth – *I crossed the road to get away from him.*
Liberator X – *He's not Versago any more – he's going by his real name. Rodney I think.*
Where's Wally – *Anybody who can hurt an animal is a TOTAL CREEP. That's how serial killers start out – on animals.*
Virgin Prune – *Listen I know Roger and he's a sweet guy. Yes you read that right. He's actually a sweet guy.*
Mortimer Bear – *That girl they found in the river. Has anybody checked out what Versago was doing that night?*
Where's Wally – *I hear the creep has a Hannibal Lecter tattoo. Why would anybody have a Hannibal Lecter tattoo?*

So I had my first "person of interest." But I was not encouraged, he was merely the local nutter, Surrey's own Barry George with no proven direct connection to the crime yet. I am sure with deeper digging I would uncover some more people who would equally fit the bill. Nevertheless I would be having my Interview With A Vampire in the days ahead.

By the time I had come up for air from my dossier reading, I discovered we had six more sightings – all vague and all of not much use. We needed the public to come forward with some positive IDs. Until then we had no hard leads. I felt impotent. Not something I'm used to feeling you must understand.

Saturday 17th May 2014

Saturday morning, and while the rest of Surrey was deciding what they were going to wear for their jaunt down the shopping center, I had arranged a secret meeting in the garden of a caff in Addlestone. I had chosen a remote location for this rendezvous because I knew that I would be severely reprimanded if Hinty knew who I was meeting. I was meeting my mentor, Bremner – the disgraced cop I mentioned before who liked a bevvy. It was me that first started calling Detective Chief Superintendent William Naismith – Bremner. This is because he's short, Scottish and has a fiery temperament, like the legendary Scottish football player Billy Bremner. The nickname spread around the force like wildfire and before we knew it, he was Billy Naismith no longer.

Though Bremner had a notorious bad temper, he was ... sorry is an excellent laugh. He inducted me on my first day at Kingston nick. After introducing me to some of the muppets in IT, he turned to me with a contagious smirk saying "we get more than our fair share of jerks in this nick." Now it's not that funny in itself, but the way he said it – with that drawling Scottish accent. I cracked up. Bremner did that to me often, he's the best guy in the world to go for a drink with.

Drink. Ah! Yes that was poor Bremner's downfall. Bremner drank to celebrate winning a case, he drank when the case was going badly, he drank when the case was devilishly hard, he drank when the case was boring and routine – and he drank in between cases to pass the time.

With that kind of schedule you're on a collision course with the gutter. It was heart breaking to see. When I first met him he was a genial raconteur and the life and soul of every party, but his wit gradually dulled till it eventually withered away and his company became tedious. I tried talking to him about it, maybe I should have tried harder, expressed myself better. They were problems with his wife that he didn't want to talk about, and I was uncomfortable going there.

But the Bremner I was meeting in the caff was a different Bremner. A Bremner rebuilding his life and trying to get work as a security consultant. A Bremner with a cappuccino and a croissant in front of him, instead of a pint, a chaser, and packet of pork scratchings.

I couldn't help giving a smirk when he told me he was on the wagon. "Is that funny, pal?" He said with his best Glaswegian alehouse menace. He hadn't lost that.

"Why give up drinking now? Now you've got all the free time in the world, and your pay off money, you're finally free to spend days on the lash and not get into trouble for it." "Because I am trying to rebuild my life you bastard." I hadn't seen Bremner so apoplectic since I started a rumor round the nick that he wasn't really Scottish. "And if you're going to be like that. I am off."

I was out of order and I instantly apologised. But this new Bremner was going to take some getting used to.

I told him about the case, all the facts that I deemed relevant, but still holding back the tarot card. I even told him about the BMX Kid and Bowell and Machin – the two 'satanic experts'.

Bremner shared my misgivings – "I know them two, Hinge and Bracket, just two batty old women trying to get in on the investigation. See this is where you've got to be careful. It's called Apophenia."

"What's this got to do with parkas and scooters?" "You'd be a much better copper if you gave up the attempts at comedy. Let me explain about Apophenia. Listen and fucking learn, pal. Apohenia is the deadly trap for every homicide detective. It's where you go over the facts again and again until you start finding patterns that aren't there, and concocting mad theories based on fairy tales. It happened to me with one of my gangland killings. I went all JFK – until I had to step back and look at everything with fresh eyes.

"And that's your big danger with a case like this. Sure it has a ritualistic angle to it, but if you go down this satanic panic path, next thing you know you'll have Hinge and Bracket getting you reading the book of Tholzar about the prophecy of the fallen siren, and you trying to work out the killer's next move from that.

"That's all fucking nonsense, and I hope you're a better copper than that. Let's be straight and smart about this. Your perpetrator is a sicko. This kind of violence didn't come out of nowhere. Your man must have previous – and that's why I kept my weirdo file. That file is still at the nick. That's where you'll most likely find your guy."

I remembered Bremner mentioning the weirdo file. A collection of the local nonces and violent offenders. People who had the form that indicates that they are committed to a life of the worst imaginable crimes. Sexual violence, torturing animals, necrophilia, all sorts of sickening antisocial behavior.

Bremner went on – "My advice to you – question every one of those nasty people in the weirdo file. Some of them may have tortured an animal like they tortured this girl."

This was good advice though, like I said before, I didn't think my perpetrator (or perpetrators) are local.

Sunday 18th May 2014

Sunday was no day of rest for Matt and me. I called him to arrange an emergency meeting at the station's incident room but he was already there at 8 a.m. and had pinned the 27 most likely women pictures to the second white board.

It felt eerily isolated with just us two in the large room and the images of the 27 lost women looking down on us.

We decided on our course of action for the day, I went to the filing cabinet upstairs to pull out Bremner's Weirdo file, while Matt got onto HOLMES2 to look for any patterns or corroborations on the vague sightings so far. Reading the Weirdo File was majorly depressing. It made me realise how sickening prison must be when you get a collection of these people together in one place. How their individual sicknesses would cross-pollinate, feed off each other and multiply, learning from each other. Roger Farrady a/k/a Versago was in the weirdo file, with his previous, but there were also older, more likely candidates – with cars and driving licenses, places of their own, and long track records of real shocking violence. I picked out a top five persons of interest that I will be interviewing in the days ahead.

But I do not like this style of detective work, looking at all the local weirdos and trying to make them fit the crime. I would much rather build a trail to the suspect based on the facts of the case. But I had so little and so I was reduced to this.

After several hours in the weirdo file, I looked up to find Matt the Stat comparing his tide chart with the bus timetable of the nearby bus stop. Had the killers timed the body to appear at the precise time of a certain bus's arrival? I thought of Bremner and his Apophenia.

Monday 19th May 2014

7.45 a.m. I took the phone call before I even sat down. The male voice was elderly, troubled.

"That woman you found in the Thames. It's my daughter."

"You sure?"

"She would be that age now."

His daughter had disappeared when she was five. Snatched from her home while he was asleep fifteen years ago. But the man had no other reason to believe the girl in the river was her apart from that.

I reassured the man that I would get his daughter's file and check every detail against the body found and get back to him.

While I was on that phone call I opened the top letter from the pile on my desk. "THIS IS NOT A CRANK LETTER" was scrawled in black biro. There is no better way to announce a crank letter. This person was grassing up his work colleague – who was "very weird," and murdering a woman and dumping her in the river was "just the sort of thing he would do." He had caught him staring at him at work in a way that was "ultra weird."

This is the big problem that the public don't get. It's all very well to say the police should follow up every lead, but what about this? It's almost certainly a waste of time, but should we follow this up or are we wasting precious and increasingly strained police resources? You have to prioritise.

Later when I got the file on the missing five year old, the DNA did not match, the father would or should be relieved that his daughter was not murdered in this way, but his torment of not knowing would go on.

Matt the Stat had spent the morning pulling out the data from HOLMES2 to put together a handy spreadsheet listing all the credible sightings so far. Matt is the Lionel Messi of spreadsheets, he can do things with that program that us mere mortals can only dream of. But this one is modestly straightforward:

Friday 10th May, 11:00 a.m. – Newsagent, Feltham. Buying a Kit Kat. (Mr. Ahmed Ziad)

Saturday 1th May 10:00 a.m. – Walton Bridge. Looking lost staring over the bridge. (Ms. Tomasz Malinowski)

Saturday 11th May 12:00 p.m. – Walton Leisure Center. Playing Tennis with another woman. (Mr. Trevor Jenkins)

Saturday 12th May 2:00 p.m. – The Admiral Hawke Pub. Having Sunday lunch with a man. (Mr. David Rudkin)

Monday 13th May 9:00 a.m. – On the train to Weybrdige. Going to Waterloo. (Miss Laura Quintero)

Monday 13th May 3:00 p.m. – Waitrose Weybrdige. Check out girl. (Mr. Abdullah Al-Faraj)

Tuesday 14th May 9:00 a.m. – Bus to Chertsey. (Ms. Glenda Helm)

"Have you checked out whether the victim is a local working girl? Please try all the nearby places." (Simon – Surname Withheld)

Thinks the dead girl may be the wife of Jeffrey Findlay a man she knows from amateur dramatics. Findlay is into "weird things." (Miss Sarah Lewis)

Used her services. (Anonymous)

An Eastern European Prostitute. (Anonymous)

Thinks the dead girl is the wife of Jeffrey Findlay. They had a bitter row and has not been seen since the girl was found in the river. (Mr. Jack Needham)

One of the girls working at the Percy Arms.

(Anonymous)

Thinks she's a prostitute working in Sunbury. (Anonymous)

After hurting my eyes studying the chart, a cross reference leapt out. A young couple into their amateur dramatics (suspicious I know!) report that fellow am dram member Jeffrey Findlay is into "weird things." Now in itself that's not much, but what got me dropping my Styrofoam cup and reading harder was that his wife was supposed to have attended the last few am dram meetings but had not. When asked where his wife was, he appeared "evasive." Now this is matched by another report on the same Jeffrey Findlay from a neighbour who had not seen Findlay's wife for two weeks – after they had a series of noisy rows. The police apparently had been called on one occasion. I checked out our records and there had indeed been an incident to which our boys had been called. Mrs. Findlay had elected to stay with a friend that night. Before going to see Mr. Findlay, I phoned up one half of the am dram couple. I got the female one, she spoke breathlessly, apparently convinced of this man's guilt in some form.

"So you say he's into weird things. What does that mean?"

"Stuff like the Marquis De Sade."

"Oh yeah – and?"

"Well that's where the word Sadism comes from." "Yes I know that." I didn't really.

Then out gushed this torrent of words – "Jeffrey wrote this play which he was trying to get the company to perform. We usually only perform plays by known playwrights – you know, so we get an audience. He tried to get us on his side and he invited us back to his place for a reading and get us involved. The play was sick, he called it a thriller, but it was ... real woman hating – you know –

misogynist, the woman dies in the end in a horrible way, and then I saw the books on his shelf – apart from all the Marquis De Sade stuff he's got photograph books of women tied up. He kept on mentioning his S&M dungeon in the basement. I don't think he was joking." "Being into S&M doesn't make you a killer."

"I know, I know but his wife. They don't get on. She was there, she was obviously ashamed of him – and after that we never saw her again. She was supposed to have been at the last two meetings, and she looks like the woman with no eyes in the picture."

"She does? A close resemblance?"

"Yeah – quite close," she said with annoying vagueness.

As we drove to see Jeffrey Findlay, I asked Matt what he knew about the Marquis De Sade. The walking Wikipedia of course knew a fair amount. Apparently Mr. De Sade had got himself into a lot of trouble just for writing a story. Just like Versago I mused.

It was midafternoon when we got to Findlay's tree lined neighbourhood just the sort of place where you would find S&M practiced behind the lace curtains.

Findlay was out at work presumably. So I knocked up Mr. Jack Needham his neighbour who had made the call about the row. He was retired and very aggrieved by the shouting scenes that had sullied his neighbourhood. "We don't expect that sort of thing round here!"

I wanted to know about Findlay's wife. Does she look like the E-fit? "Yes!" Said the man emphatically "and I've not seen her for two weeks." He obviously wanted to believe that his neighbour was a murderer. I wanted him to be exact about the last time he had seen her.

"I heard her, it was two weeks ago. She was crying and screaming, another ugly row. Everyone has rows, but this was different. Full hatred and bitterness. The man's a monster."

"Can you do me a massive favor? Can you call me the minute you see Mr. Findlay get home?"

While waiting for the call I looked through our records on Jeffrey Findlay. He is 48, a Marketing Manager in the education sector and commutes to the city every day. No police record except for the domestic incident in April, from which he was not charged or even given a warning. So very commonplace and yet who knows what goes on behind the curtains of respectability?

It had just gone 7p.m. when we got the call that Jeffrey Findlay had got home. I was there fifteen minutes later.

The man who opened the door was wiry framed, with a leathery lined face.

I flashed my ID. "Jeffrey Findlay?"

"Yes?"

"Detective Chief Superintendent Ferdinand of the Surrey Police Force."

"Which police force?"

"Surrey."

"No need to apologise."

That threw me. That's not the first time I'd heard that joke. But it was a first from a suspect in a serious crime. I was about to say – "I tell the jokes" – but instead got straight to the point.

"Where's your wife, Mr. Findlay?"

He gave an exasperated breath – "She's gone away."

"Gone away – where exactly?"

"That's none of your business."

"May I come in?"

"NO, YOU MAY NOT," he said gripping the door and glaring at me. Did he have control issues?

I peered past his shoulder through into his living room. I could see the bookshelf against the far wall, but not the actual titles.

"I wanted to have a look at your bookshelf. I understand you have some ... interesting titles."

"Oh Yes? Who told you that?"

"I hear you like the dark stuff."

"I enjoy a pint of Guinness, yes."

He was strangely cool for someone who was in the frame for a murder.

"So when was the last time you saw your wife?"
"Something like two weeks ago."

"I need an exact time and date."

"Well, I am afraid that's all I can give," he said defiantly, before adding – "Celia and I ... have not been getting on that well. She's having a break, a time away. She'll come back when ... she's ready to come back."

"Well, I suggest you find out where your wife is – and quickly. In the meantime this can be all be resolved very quickly. Just let me come in and take a sample of your wife's DNA and you're in the clear."

"Well, I am not prepared to give you anything. I must ask you to leave."

I walked away fuming. Why would he refuse to let me in and take a sample of his wife's DNA? Because he's guilty? Perhaps. Or perhaps because he knows he is innocent and enjoys being in the police spotlight, and wants to dick me around. The obstructive, pompous, leather-whipping, playwriting ponce. I got straight on the blower to get everything we had on Celia Findlay, her bank account details, her friends and family.

What was interesting was that Mr. Findlay didn't ask why I was asking. As if he knew immediately my questions were linked to the girl found in the river, just a mile from his home.

Tuesday 20th May 2014

While I waited for my Jeffrey Findlay search warrant, I figured I may as well check out my other person of interest – Versago the Vampire. First I wanted to establish that the estranged ex-girlfriend who had received those threats was not the dead girl in the river.

Sophia Etherington was alive and well and moving on with her life, studying journalism at Kingston University. It was round the corner from the nick, so I paid her a visit.

We sat in the designated smoking pen among the other smoking student reprobates. I supplied the fags and she gave me the chat. Sophia is a big-eyed beautiful girl with peroxide platinum white hair, which she raked at as she recalled her tumultuous relationship with Versago. "Roger is an extremely troubled kid," she said in between puffs "I never ever want to see that freak again."

She related a story of teenage obsession with the occult – séances in graveyards, experimenting with drugs and eventual violent first love jealousy.

"Do you think he's capable of committing murder?" I asked.

"Well, judge for yourself."

She got out her phone and scrolled down the menu and pressed play.

The first two tearful messages were more pathetic than menacing. I looked at Sophia, who read my mind – "Now wait for the next message."

The next one began with a screech that did not sound human – then it launched into "You will spend the rest of your miserable life in gut-wrenching pain." He sounded possessed by a ferocious rage as he growled and went on to describe in unpleasantly graphic detail about he was to scrape off all her skin and insert red hot knitting needles in all of her orifices.

I decided I was *not* going to be interviewing this fellow on my jack.

She put the phone away and I was silent for a second,

taking in what I had just heard.

"If you don't mind me saying, Madam, that's a rather strange thing to keep on your phone."

Chapter 4

Haribo Lecter

Tuesday 20th May 2014 – Afternoon

"THAT WAS ALL LIES." Versago the Vampire a/k/a Roger was giving me the Shaggy defense. Apparently he didn't nail that dog to the church door and send the vicar's wife into therapy.

"That was Jeremy. He's the evil one. He's the one who enjoys torturing people. But because he's posh, living in that big posh house, with his posh parents, no one ever points the finger at him. " His bitterness was pouring out by the bucket load.

Versago looked different from his photos in the weirdo file. In there he was gothed up to the max with piercings all over his boat, fringed by a large bird nest of scraggly hair. What else was different? Ah Yes! The makeup. In his weirdo file mug shots he had a black stripe over his eyes and a killer clown smile – painted on with ruby red lipstick.

The Versago of today still had the bird nest hair, but now shorter and tidier, and most of the piercings had been put away, with just a row of studs going all the way up the ear remaining.

"So you're not as black as you're painted then?"

"I was a fucked up teenager, that's all. I know I freaked out some people which I often did on purpose. But I feel really bad about Sophia and those messages. I had a lot of hatred ... back then."

Youngsters. He was talking about last year like it was lifetime away.

"So how come you had this hatred back then, and now it's suddenly gone?"

"All to do with Mum. She abandoned me when I was a baby. I tried to make contact with her when I was twelve and she sent me away. I got worse after that. You can see it on my school records. But the last six months ... well she's back in my life now and it's like ... the anger has lifted."

I had of course read my weirdo file. His mother had been a drug addict and a prostitute which is why she had rejected him at the age of 12. But they had become reunited after she had got herself in recovery and got herself a job as a manageress of a call center. From one form of prostitution to another.

I looked hard at the kid, beyond the hair and his look, his face was heavy set and pudgy, like a lost sheep dog.

"I hear you have a Hannibal Lecter tattoo."

"Close. I have a Haribo Lecter tattoo."

"Haribo Lecter? What the fuck is a Haribo Lecter tattoo?"

He peeled off his shirt to reveal on his lower back a tattoo of the Haribo Bear wearing the Hannibal Lecter mouthguard mask and the text above Haribo Lecter. "I used to be a bit of a Haribo fiend," he explained.

"One last thing Versago."

"Please don't call me that. That was from when ... I was in a dark place. My name is Roger."

"So Roger – where were you on Tuesday the 14th May? I want a full account of your day going into the following morning."

Like a born again mother's boy, Roger had spent all evening watching TV with his mother Veronica. We went to see her and his alibi checked out. Veronica was perfectly charming. She was obviously not thrilled that her son was a suspect in a murder case, but fully understood. She offered

Matt and me tea and a slice of malt loaf cake, which after a hard day pounding the pavements was gratefully received.

Wednesday 21st May 2014

The data had come back on Celia Findlay. There had been no activity on any of her bankcards since May the 9th. Something was definitely amiss. Which reminded me – where the fuck was my search warrant?

"It's still with the magistrate," said the admin staff.

"Well, that's no good. What's he got it for? I am the one who needs it. What about my fast track?"

I sped over to his large home in St. George's Hill, slamming the door on exiting my car. As I loudly crunched my way up his gravel drive, David Montgomery, looking like a debonair cad in his silk dressing gown, came out.

I flashed my ID.

"Yes I know who you are. What are you doing here?"

"I need my search warrant."

"I am deliberating about it – because I wanted to be sure..."

"What? Is he on the level?"

The magistrate gulped and stared. His discomfort told me I had hit a bull's-eye. Both Findlay and the magistrate were free masons.

"I just want to make sure there's a very good reason for you to search his premises."

"Well let me please assure you Mr. Montgomery. His wife is missing and he has not accounted for her whereabouts and I urgently need to search his premises before he destroys any evidence. He may be in your club Sir, but he's also a very suspicious character who made no attempt to help me in my enquiry."

The magistrate invited me in, he offered me a cup of tea, which I politely declined – I'd had my quota for the day. I was there for the warrant and the warrant only, which he signed and handed to me with an apologetic grin.

I took it gratefully – "I keep waiting for you guys to ask me to join," I said as a parting shot.

So Jeffrey Findlay is a Freemason. That could lead this inquiry into all sorts of twists and turns. Wasn't Jack The Ripper a free mason? No he wasn't. Remember the apophenia trap pal!

Let's focus on the case. How much evidence could fuckface Findlay have destroyed in the time between me speaking to him and alerting him of my suspicions, and me finally getting to search his premises?

It was 4 p.m. as good as time as any to go rip the fucker's house from top to bottom. From the house we wanted as many DNA samples as we could get – from towels, hairbrushes, items of clothing. If any of the DNA matched the girl in the river – we could potentially ID Celia Findlay as her.

We were about to charge over there, but then I called a halt. He would be at work in London. If he gets a tip off that we are searching his house while he's away, he may do a runner.

No – we wanted to do the search while he was there. Plus it would be more fun. So we parked an unmarked car at the top of his avenue, instructing our man to give us a call when Findlay walked past.

The call came in at 7.30 p.m. and a fleet of four – a police van and three cars sped over there. Findlay did not look shocked or even surprised when I flashed the search warrant and we marched past him into his home. He was obviously anticipating the search.

I went over to his bookshelf and noted the books by the Marquis de Sade and photography bondage books. I pulled one out, as my boys grabbed the towels.

Presently a PC called out. "We've found the cellar, Sir."

Excellent. My specific instructions were to find that S&M cellar.

I followed the PC through the door down the wooden stairs. With his torch my PC found the light switch to reveal ... a stack of wine bottles, a desk, a computer, a film poster and a vacuum cleaner.

Nothing that the Marquis De Sade could find any use for.

I called out to Findlay, who came down into the cellar scowling like a resentful schoolboy.

"Do you want to explain all this? I was told you had an S&M cellar." "I know for sure who reported me now. That Amy from amateur dramatics – what a silly cow. I joked that I had an S&M cellar downstairs and she obviously believed me. The only S&M I know about is Sales and Marketing." He grinned at his own joke with an air of ugly superiority.

I went back upstairs to get away from the smug git before I throttled him, when my phone rang. It was the desk sergeant.

"I have a woman here to see you. She claims to be Celia Findlay."

At the station, a smartly dressed glamorous woman introduced herself as Celia Findlay saying – "my husband got a message to me to contact you."

But assume nothing, verify everything. I needed to be sure this woman really was Celia Findlay. She gave us a mouth swab for her DNA, and a photograph.

"I've left him – for another man. He's too proud to tell anyone."

She explained that the reason there had been no activity on any of her cards was simply that the man she had left him for was for is very much wealthier and taking care of her. She showed me her passport, her banking card (on a sabbatical), her gym membership. It was looking increasingly certain that this woman was no imposter.

This was a fucker. I so wanted Findlay to be guilty of something. But just because he didn't kill his wife, didn't mean he didn't kill the girl in the river.

"Totally understandable you wanting out," I said to Celia "all that creepy Sadism stuff."

"Oh Jeffrey's not a sadist. He's a masochist."

Thursday 22nd May 2014 – Morning

So armchair detective, I had speculated that because no one directly known to the victim had come forward to identify her, it was highly likely the victim was of the underclass – a homeless drifter or a prostitute. Those of you that had looked over Matt's excellent spreadsheet of the sightings would have spotted four suggesting that she was a prostitute.

Every single one of those tip offs were anonymous. All of the reports were vague, but one had actually claimed to have used her services. I needed to speak to this witness directly and get as much detail as possible. It was time to get sneaky.

Even though the caller withheld his number I was able to get his number from the phone exchange. This is standard, when you withhold your number it is only to the person receiving the call. The police can obtain the number just by contacting the phone company and providing the exact time and date the call was made.

From there I got his address and checked him out first – John Wetherby, IT Manager for a recruitment consultancy. His employer's website had one of those smarmy smiling meet-the-team pages. He looked like a regular guy in his pic. According to his bio he was a fitness fanatic and loved spending time with his two kids. It missed out the bit about the whoring. This was good news for me. He had something to lose and I had something to blackmail him with.

I went round to Wetherby's place of work in Chertsey and told his receptionist that I wanted to meet him outside on the park bench.

A squat sinewy man with a puzzled expression came out looking around. His large bulbous head and a slight body gave him the appearance of a muscular Thunderbird puppet. I had him sized as a welterweight. I greeted him with a big smile and shook his hand vigorously.

"I'm sorry to have to do this Sir. But you left an anonymous tip on Crimestoppers about the dead girl. I need to get more info and I'd really appreciate it if you could help me out. All totally confidential like."

He ungripped my hand. "I said all I've got to say when I called in."

"I need more details to help me ID the girl."

"I can't give any details." He looked around anxiously – "that's all you're getting from me."

"But Sir any detail you tell me, may help me identify this woman."

"I am sorry I can't help you," and with that he began to walk away. I needed some of my best Ferdy diplomacy – I called out to him.

"You know it may only be a matter of time before your wife and your kid find out what a stinking porn addicted whoring low life you are. But how would you like it if they found out today?"

Now I had his attention. "Fancy that? I could get a fast track warrant off my friendly magistrate and go through your computer and phone records – and I bet there's a good chance lots of nasty stuff will come out. I am not asking for much. I just need the facts of your meeting with this girl."

He clenched his fists and his jaws tightened. He looked ready to strike. But instead he sat down next to me on the park bench.

"Tell me as much as you can about her."

"I'm a sex addict. I can't help it." He was now full of self-pity. I nipped this one in the bud.

"Listen. I don't need your life story or any excuses. I'm not judging you. I'm only interested in the girl. When did you first see her?"

"In the car park of a pub."

"Which pub?"

"Can't remember the name – the sign's missing, but they call it the CarPhone Whorehouse. It's round by the Treatment Works. I've been there three times before. You drive into the car park and you flash your lights and they send a girl out. If you like the girl you invite her in and drive off somewhere."

I was taken aback. I didn't know anything like this went on in Sunbury. "How did you hear about this CarPhone Whorehouse operation?"

"A lorry driver gave me a flyer which had written on it 'Turn off Junction1 for a bit fun'. The pub's a short drive from Junction 1 from the Motorway. So I guess that's where they get a lot of their business. "

"Have you still got this flyer?"

"Threw it away."

"Who runs this operation?"

"I don't know – do I? I just see the girls. But the pub itself – it's a right skanky dive but they have erotic dancers."
"Any good?"

"Yeah," he said as if recalling with relish.

"So tell me about the girl. How does she look like the girl in the E-fit?"

"Her jawline, the shape of her face." This was encouraging.

"So she comes out and ... well she looks alright – more than alright. So I open the door for her. She comes in

– she speaks first."

"How does she speak?"

"Eastern European."

"Can you be more specific?"

"No."

"How good was her English?"

"Pretty good, but she could have just rehearsed everything she said."

"So what did she say?"

"She says it is £100 – and you can take me somewhere or £80 if you take me somewhere and bring me back. So I took the discount option and I drove her to the hotel."

"Which hotel?"

"The Jolly Hotel near Kempton Park."

"Hey – that's a nice hotel."

"I like to do things properly."

"What time of day?"

"About three in the afternoon."

"You go whoring in the afternoon? That's pretty hard core."

"I told you I'm an addict."

"I guess when you gotta go – you gotta go. So on the drive to the hotel, what do you talk about?"

"Nothing."

"You must have said something."

"No nothing."

"It was all very basic. I like it rough and she obliged. I was just fulfilling a need. She was stony-faced the whole time. Even when I paid her."

"Whatever happened to service with a smile eh? So you drove her back and that was it?"

"No. I got a text from work and I needed to go. So I told her I couldn't give her a lift back to the CarPhone Whorehouse. So she says – you must pay the twenty pounds extra. Which I did. Then she gets out her phone and calls for a cab. I overheard her ask – 'How much will that be?' And it was ten pounds. So when she hung up I said joking – well done, you've just made another tenner out of me. But she didn't smile."

I showed John the john the photograph parade of the 27 women. John looked at every one with a look of distaste – "they could be all of them, or none of them," he said unhelpfully.

So dear reader, what could I do with John the john's information? Well quite a lot. He told me she had picked up a taxi from the hotel on the afternoon of Wednesday the 7th May. The fare was £10. So with that, the boys got on the phone to every cab firm in the area – they should log every job – asking if they picked up a fare from that hotel for a tenner on that afternoon. Sure enough – that led us to AAA Taxis in Lower Sunbury on Thames.

Thursday 22nd May 2014 – Afternoon

"I don't read the papers, at least not the western ones," Ahmed, proprietor of AAA Taxis said convincingly. I immediately added him to my list of persons of interest. He had bad teeth and was unshaven. He maintained his down at heel motif with the décor of his establishment. We stood in his waiting room, brown vinyl floor riding up at the edges, a worn faded yellow sofa and a wobbly TV with a coat hanger for an aerial.

But this veneer of slovenliness belied that Ahmed ran his business meticulously and kept a log of all his fares. He very openly showed me his book covering Wednesday the 7th May. There was an entry – 4p.m., the Jolly Hotel – the name Daria and a mobile number 077102 91188. Was I getting warmer?

"Daria nice girl. Regular customer."

"Do you know what her occupation is?"

"I do not ask." Indicating that he knew.

"Do you know where she lives?"

"No – she always comes here or gets picked up." "What do you talk to her about?"

"The weather, the traffic. We don't really talk."

"She English?"

"No. Eastern Europe I think. But I do not know."

I flicked through his logbook trying to find the name Daria again. "Was there a regular place she used to go to?" "Yes! The Cat Sanctuary. I would often take her there. Sometimes with other girls."

The Cat Sanctuary – you may have noticed that on the map. It's less than a mile away from where the body was found.

I laid out the photographic parade of the 27 lost girls on his threadbare sofa, and after a minute or so of deliberation Ahmed picked one out. I turned the photo over. Photo K.

I went back to my car and checked Photo K against my list. My heart jumped when I read the name – Daria Lipsinski – a runaway from Poland from the previous year. Clawing at my elbows I called the number that Ahmed gave me. Part of me was hoping she would answer meaning that the girl I had been asking questions about was still alive. But I also hoped that she didn't, meaning that I was getting close to ID'ing my victim.

The call tripped onto a generic phone service 'leave a message'. I felt a shiver as I left one, thinking that she would never hear it and I had identified the dead girl.

I did not need to arrange a court order to seize Ahmed's taxi book. I was given the book to take away and now we could start piecing together Daria's movements.

I gave the 077102 91188 phone number to the boys down the nick to hack for messages, but the factory settings had been changed. We needed the phone company to provide us with the data.

It was a Pay as You Go account – registered under the name *Fanny Adams*. Most likely a false name to conceal her profession, and paid in cash. So Matt gets on the blower to PhonesULike or some such tossy company. They would not play ball, telling him he needed a warrant, and even then it would take three weeks to provide us with our records.

Matt looked vexed and handed the phone to me. I asked the phone company twerp to identify himself. He gave me his name. "Well I am Detective Chief Superintendent Ferdinand and am I leading a murder investigation. It is very important you immediately give us all the phone records relating to this person."

"I am sorry but we have to go through procedures. We need a request in writing and it can take up to three weeks to process."

"I can get you the warrant and all the paperwork immediately, but three weeks is not good enough. We need this data today."

"Well, I am sorry Sir but three weeks is procedure." This needed some more of that Ferdy diplomacy. I launched into this – "Listen you swine – we urgently need this data, it's a matter of life and death. Literally. So how about I call a press conference and tell the whole media that when the murderer strikes again we will all know who to blame – and that's you individually by name – and your company." "Please don't raise your voice to me, Sir."

I knew this tactic. I'd faced it with my mortgage people. They treat you like dirt and get you so riled that when you dare to get angry with them, they use that as an excuse to not listen to you any more, as you've supposedly lost control and got abusive. Actually come to think of it, the Old Bill play that trick as well. Well, I was having none of it. "I WILL FUCKING RAISE MY VOICE – BECAUSE I AM

TRYING TO CATCH A KILLER!"

Everyone in the incident room stopped working and watched me open-mouthed.

I continued – "And the way I see it, by not giving me my phone records, you and your company are an accomplice to that murder. I will publicly tell everyone, the force will publicly tell everyone, and before you know it no one will be able to use your phone company without getting lynched."

By now the whole station was listening.

"So how about you get the information to me by 4 p.m., or else I am calling that press conference?"

"I'll still need a warrant and a written request," bleated the phone guy. "You will have it within the hour," I said, hoping the company wasn't run by free masons.

I put the phone down to an incident room erupting to thunderous applause. Yes to the rest of the world I was a jerk, but to the boys down the nick I was a hero. At 4p.m. the phone records came through.

There was no outgoing activity after the night of Tuesday the 13th, which would indicate that Daria was the victim. The eagle eyed among you will have spotted that she texted four times and called once the 07771 857346 number. Twice she texted that number on the day of the murder – and no one else.

I called the 07771 857346 number – a generic phone service voice – and I left this message. "I need to speak with you about Daria Lipsinski. It is imperative you call me back on this number." It's highly likely this number was the key to opening this case. I could feel the trail getting warmer.

Chapter 5

A Night at Madame Headlock's

Thursday 22nd May 2014 – Afternoon

THOUGH JOHN THE JOHN COULD NOT name the pub, because of its proximity to AAA Cabs I was able to work out that he had visited the Percy Arms in Lower Sunbury. So I went to see the jokers in Vice. "Rumor has it you boys cover Vice in Surrey," I said with my best Ferdy swagger – "know anything about the CarPhone Whorehouse scene around the Percy Arms?"

The vice boys were vague enough. They were aware of it, it was small time, a few girls had been nicked – that was it. I left them to their Angry Birds and Facebook. I found as much useful information from the FancyAPint website:

Percy Arms, Staines Road, Sunbury on Thames, Surrey.

"I have been to this pub and it's a hellhole."

"It's not that bad. I mean a hellhole is not that bad. The girls make up for it – if you get my drift. You do not visit this pub for the beer or the friendly clientele."

If you look on the map it's near the Ashford Common Treatment works, close to the Industrial Estate. This is the part of Sunbury on Thames that no one likes to talk about – why it's virtually Feltham.

Now I was about to go straight into the CarPhone Whorehouse flashing my ID around and a picture of Daria. But I reconsidered. None of the girls had come forward from that scene to report that she had gone. Why not? If someone is killing prostitutes, surely it is in their interest to have him caught?

I needed to get under that wall of silence and find out why. I needed an undercover operation, but I didn't have time to cultivate one. But what I did have was a stalwart veteran warming up on the touchline who needed a game. So I gave the old man a call and introduced him to John the john. After Bremner's acrimonious dismissal from the force there is no way Surrey Police would pay for him to do undercover, and I needed someone I could trust. So I would be paying Bremner a monkey out of my own skyrocket. I got the money out and gave him the cash in an envelope – a half-chimp now and a half-chimp later.

I knew full well that none of the information he would bring me would be admissible in any trial, but I just wanted the lid lifted on that nest for me. "You don't need to ask any questions," I instructed him. "Just hang out there and absorb stuff. It'll be the easiest monkey you'll ever make in your life."

John the Thunderbird puppet john was none too pleased about being roped into this affair. But I had him by the balls. I wasn't going to lean on him too much. All he had to do was go in the pub with Bremner and they would hang out and chat to the dancing girls. Bremner was less than keen to go into a pub after his recent vow, but he agreed. I was giving the post drink Bremner a chance to prove himself and he knew it. He would go undercover and drink Red Bull.

No need for a cover story. He could tell people if anyone asked that he's a disgraced cop and is in-between situations. After planting Bremner in this insalubrious hellhole I left it 24 hours before going in myself.

Friday 23rd May 2014

We drove into the car park on the late Friday afternoon, plain clothes as usual, but not in our suits and in an unmarked car. Matt sat in the back seat, discomfort pasted all over his face.

The architects of the Percy Arms certainly didn't waste any imagination on this square block of concrete. The car park was sparse – just two other cars and a motorcycle parked close to the building. I flashed my lights and sure enough a girl came trotting out. She was boob tubed up revealing a muffin top midriff of milky white flesh. I know I'm hardly slim Jim myself, but at least I don't go around dressed like that. Her fake smile dropped when she opened the car door and saw Matt sat in the back. She slid into the passenger seat and said curtly – "I charge double for a twos up." "We won't be requiring a twos up. I want you to tell me about this girl."

Instead of looking at the picture she shot me a look of spite. "You're cops."

"Nobody's perfect," I shrugged "Now look at the fucking picture. Do you know her?"

"No I don't" and her hand was on the door handle and she was getting up to leave. I pushed her down and planted the picture in her face. "LOOK PROPERLY. Who is she?"

She looked at the picture and I studied her reaction. Was that a look of recognition? I couldn't be sure.

"I told you I don't."

"I want to meet your boss. Introduce me to him."

"I don't have a boss" and with a stunning display of stealth and speed, she had got up and was on her way back to the pub.

So Matt and me strode into the Percy Arms ready to knock a few heads together. We were launching ourselves headfirst into the open jaws of the beast. We had a potential "situation" on our hands. Now a lot of people ask me – how often does your police work get tasty? The answer is not very often. But you have to be ready for it, and when it kicks off you have to end up on top by any means necessary – honest or dishonest. You can't have your reputation destroyed by some lowlife mug.

As you'd expect, the interior of the Percy Arms maintained the exterior's theme of grimness. On the far wall on the left was a small stage and just above it a faded silver disco glitter ball with several squares missing, like missing teeth in a rotting mouth.

The charming girl who had evaded me was now in the corner talking to two more girls. Remembering my training, before striding into the room I did a quick 360 look around to check for anyone who might come a-lunging with a weapon.

Matt headed towards the girls while I made for the bar to talk to the barman. He was a goofy rake of a fellow with long sandy thinning hair in his mid-30s. I showed him the picture of Daria. He said. "She may come in from time to time. I'm not sure though."

"Well, I have reason to believe that she does come down here."

"Well if you say so."

I looked over at Matt and the three girls – his approach is altogether more polite than mine. I could see they were shaking their heads and frowning.

Then I turned to Bremner nursing his Red Bull sitting in the corner with John the john. Bremner looked at me not sure whether to acknowledge me.

"Hullo, hullo. Surrey reject. Surrey reject," I sang to him, to the tune of "Good to Be Back." I turned to Matt on the other side of the room.

"Matt, look who's here. Spending all his pay off money and living the high life." I showed the picture to the two men. John the john looked ready to say something. I saved him the trouble and switched my attention to Bremner.

"Come on – have you seen her?" I waved the photo at him, Bremner spluttered for something to say. "No point talking to you, I can't trust anything you say."

I should have been an actor.

Then I turned to the craggy git by the pay phone on the far wall. He had a drinker's bulbous nose, and a sunken face as if he'd swallowed his false teeth. His greasy receding hair was shaped into something that may have once been a DA. As if he didn't look conspicuous enough he was wearing slippers – and just one leather glove on his left hand. A strange smile danced on his face.

"You! What are you smirking at?"

"I'm not smirking. You have to go outside if you want to do that these days."

Everyone's a fucking joker.

"Seen this girl?" I showed him the photograph and he took a long look.

"Yes I think so. Yes." At last someone helpful.

"Is she a regular?"

"Sort of regular."

"What does that mean?"

"I dunno. I've seen her dance I think. Or did I dream that? I see a lot crazy shit in my dreams."

Flashbacks dude. He went on – "I'm trying to think what her song is."

"Her song?"

"Yes – every girl has a song. You know like darts players." He turned to one of the men sitting nearby. "What's her song?" he asked. They looked back blankly and looked away. He turned to me.

"Shall I tell her to get in touch next time I see her?"

"You can do that, but that's not very likely. I have reason to believe that she is the dead woman found in the river."

The man looked shocked and blurted out an "Oh No."

Matt went to the pillar in the middle of the pub and blu-tacked a poster of Daria – with the legend HAVE YOU SEEN THIS GIRL? And a Crimestoppers number underneath.

After speaking to everyone in the pub we called the shake down to a close and announced our exit with "Okay, we're done here. You can get back to your low life."

Saturday 24th May 2014

I caught up with Bremner the following day at our secret rendezvous – the caff in Addlestone.

"I didn't ask a single question, but I tell you I was bricking it," he said, obviously still dazed from his undercover foray.

"Did you get threatened?"

"No, thank fuck – and no thanks to you telling everyone I'm a Surrey Reject."

"I had to point you out as a disgraced cop to make the undercover operation work."

"A lot of people hate the police and I was terrified some ex-con might have it in for me."

"So what can you tell me?"

"I went to a party afterwards round the corner at Madame's Headlocks."

"Is that the name of a club? Whatever next?"

"No, Madame Headlock was the woman's whose gaff the party was at. A big black lady with bingo wings like cannonballs. I got the impression she was like a head figure among the girls. She may even be running the show. I am not sure because, as you know, I asked no questions."

"So what did you overhear?"

"Snatches of conversations. I heard at least two of the girls say to one another – something like – 'they were showing a picture of Daria.'"

"You heard them say the name? Daria?"

"Yes."

"Did you get talking to that craggy old git who was wearing one glove?"

"Oh him. It's hard not to. He talks to everyone." "What's his story?"

"His name is Andy Mallard. Nice guy."

"That's it? Nice guy?" I was thinking of asking for my chimp back. Nevertheless I made a note to check up the form on Andy Mallard.

"He says he's an artist. He tries to paint the visions he's sent in his dreams and he'd painted the mural over the living room entrance. He's really proud of it, and that's how we got talking."

"Is he a dealer, or a pimp – or both?"

"Dunno. We just talked about his art and what the pictures in his dreams mean."

"So what music were they playing at this party?" Bremner looked at me puzzled – "What the fuck has that got to do with anything?"

"I'm interested that's all."

"Playing all the new stuff – you know...."

"No, I don't know. Like what?"

"All that new stuff that young people like."

"Did they play Mungo Jerry – 'In The Summertime'?"

"Could have done."

"The original version or the remix?"

Suddenly the penny dropped. "I get it – you're checking up on me. You don't believe I was actually at the party."

"I do believe you, but I am just checking you can remember details like the music played."

"Well, trust me, pal, I went to this fuckin' party. With

that fuckin' John the john. He left me on my todd while he went to the cash point to buy some bugle and a girl. I fucked off pretty soon after that because I was standing out like a sore thumb. You get me?"

"How many people at the party?"

"People were coming and going – 30 to 40 people?"
"What sort of people? What age group?"

"Youngish – most were girls. Working girls I reckon. The boys were druggy low life crime types."

"Drugs?"

"Bugle and E."

"What time did you leave?"

"About 1 a.m. Just as they were rounding everyone up to do the song."

"The Song. What sort of song?"

"Dunno – that Mallard and Madame Headlock went around saying – it's time for the song soon. That's when I fucked off."

So I now had two new "persons of interest." I went back to the nick and pulled out Andy Mallard's form. This is how it reads. As you can see he's acquired a taste for porridge:

<u>Andy Mallard (DOB 3.6.1969)</u>

January 1979 – Burglary 12 months – released May 1979
June 1979 – Possession of an illegal substance 6 months suspended
May 1980 – Burglary 2 years released 1981 June 1982 – Sexual Assault 12 months
July 1985 – Burglary 2 years
August 1988 – Selling obscene material 2 years
May 1990 – Selling illegal substances – Heroin 3 years
July 1995 – Selling obscene material 4 years – release July 1997
August 1997 – Burglary 2 years

April 2000 – Selling illegal substances – cocaine 2 years
April 2000 – Soliciting for a prostitute 2 years(concurrent)
January 2005 – Soliciting for a prostitute 2 years –

My search on "*Madame Headlock*" yielded nothing.

Chapter 6

She Sells Cat Sanctuary

Saturday 24th May 2014

THE INCIDENT ROOM BOYS (and girls) had methodically called every number on Daria's phone. By now we had made contact with all of them – but one.

07771 857346 – the last number that Daria had called and texted. This was the big unknown in my investigation, and I was sure it was critical to piecing together Daria's last movements. We pasted the number up on the white board in big black type three inches high.

I called the number once again and left yet another message. Then I got Matt, who had a more friendly voice, to also leave a message. No one picked up – and there was no reply to any of the messages.

The report came back on that number. It was another cash pay as you go, under the name Kelly Grace. The follow up on that name and address came to nothing, so it was almost certainly false.

Next we looked through Ahmed's log of taxi fares. The first trip under the name Daria was seven months ago in October 2014. In all, twenty-three taxi journeys had been logged in her name. Most I suspected were picks up after a job. This way we could identify the regular johns.

What was frequent, about once a month, was a taxi to Kenton Avenue – the street on which the Cat Sanctuary that Ahmed had mentioned was on. So I summonsed Matt over and told him we were paying a visit to the Cat Sanctuary.

In the car Matt was fidgeting anxiously. "I have

something to tell you. I have a phobia of cats."

"Don't be a pussy, Matt. They're only cats."

With no neighbours for a half a mile, the Cat Sanctuary is a solitary building at the foot of a high grassy hill with a reservoir on the other side. It was a simple squat 1960s style bungalow, with a surrounding overgrown garden, fenced in with thick chicken wire. "Isn't this cruel?" I asked Ann MacLean, the batty cat lady proprietor, pointing to the chicken wire – "I thought cats like to roam around and explore."

"Yes they do," she replied in a husky smoker's voice, "but these are cats that were once homeless. So they need to be forced into knowing that this is their home base, because for so long they haven't had one. I'm raising money for a bigger place but for now they are confined to this space."

Fenced up in this garden surrounded by dozens of lazing moggies, Ann MacLean was obviously in feline heaven. Who needs people anyway? Ann's wrinkled smiling face told me that she had seen her sixtieth birthday – and a few more besides. I checked out her attire, an aging hippy chick, wearing a long flowing skirt with a pattern not unlike the stencil graffiti that the BMX Kid had shown me near the murder scene. What does that mean? Almost certainly nothing but a coincidence.

Ann was most forthcoming with my questions – "That girl in your photograph would come down here and just look at the cats through the wire fence. I get a lot of people doing that this time of year as the cats come out to sun themselves in the garden." She distracted herself by a passing cat, talking to it like it was a young child and expecting an answer, to the total indifference of the cat.

She eventually came back to me – "She's usually with a friend or two. Female friends."

"Do you ever get talking to the girls?"

"Yes. They would ask about the cats. What their names are, stuff like that." She then broke off to talk to another equally aloof cat.

"Did you ever talk about them? About their own lives?"

"No. Well, if we did I don't remember. We just talked about the cats."

"Did you get an idea of what they did for a living?" "How do you mean?" "Exactly what I said."

"I formed no impression. I don't judge by appearances." She said a little too self-righteously for my liking.

"What she ever in male company?"

"No, always female."

"Remember any one of these females in particular?" "Usually the same two. A thin girl with very long brown hair and a short dark girl – also with long hair – but black hair, raven black, parted in the middle. All three of them are about the same age. It's hard to be certain though."

"Can you please contact me if you see any of these girls again? I really need to speak with them. Do you have any CCTV around here that might pick up your visitors?" "'Fraid not. I don't have the money for that. Besides I have nothing worth stealing, apart from the cats."

"Well, cat burglary is on the up." Lame joke I know. I looked over at the dozens of cats some lazing in the garden catching the afternoon sun, others clawing vigorously at the wire fence. "Very noble work," I commented. "Taking in lost cats and giving them a better life. It's a shame there was nobody to do that for this girl."

"That's actually also what I'm raising money for. A refuge for abused and battered women."

I wished her luck and returned to the car parked outside where a green and queasy Matt was waiting for me.

I taunted him by singing that Tweety Pie song, "I Thought I saw a Puddy Cat." He was not amused.

Saturday 24th May 2014 (early afternoon)

When we got back to the station car park I noticed a top of the range BMW X5 luxury SUV. The sparkling chrome suggested it was not long off the showroom. It was showing up the rest of the humble marked and unmarked police cars. Did we have a wealthy visitor, or was it a cop unsubtly on the take?

In reception I encountered a man of medium height and build, fair complexion, shed with cropped sun bleached hair.

"I need to speak with you. For reasons you'll soon understand I can't talk here. Will you come to my vehicle?" I was intrigued. I followed him into the car park and he ushered me into his impressive chariot. He sat in the driving seat with me in the passenger. His smile gave off an easy relaxed charm. I took an instant dislike to him.

"I can't tell you my name, but that set up at the Percy Arms is mine. I keep it at arm's length for obvious reasons. I don't run it from day to day."

"Is Andy Mallard your man on the ground?"

He seemed impressed and surprised – "Yes he is, and a lady called Zara. Now Andy told me that you went in there waving your badge about and none of the girls would talk to you. Well you've got to understand that these women have a very deep mistrust of the police, and your approach wasn't going to get them talking to you."

"I've had complaints about my rude method of questioning before, but they don't seem to do any good." "Look," he leaned forward and made a steeple with his fingers, "without wanting to state the obvious, if this Daria girl is the one who's been murdered, it's really bad for business. It gives the whole scene a bad reputation."

"So you do have a missing girl called Daria?"

"I don't know any of the girls. Mallard and Zara do all of that. But Zara tells me, yes – Daria hasn't been seen or heard of for two weeks."

"Why hasn't anyone come forward to report her missing?"

"Because they fear the OB. That's why I am here. To make a deal." He leaned forward again and made another steeple. "If you give me your word that you won't nick the girls for anything – prostitution, drugs – anything that's not connected with the murder. I can get them to open up."

This was a no brainer "Okay."

"But you must give me your word."

"I give you my word. I only want to catch this killer." "Great! I'm like the girls and I also have a natural aversion to the cops, but on this you have my fullest cooperation. So I am going to speak to my girls and get to you as much info as I can for you."

I cut in – "No. You get Chinese Whispers that way. I will need to speak to your girls direct. Taped and on the record."

"But only about the murder. No charges will come from your questioning other than about the murder?" "Listen I really appreciate you doing this. The girls can be completely frank and honest. None of it will get passed onto those lazy sods in Vice. I promise. Believe me, I have even more contempt for that shower than you do."

"Okay, you go it. Tomorrow's the Bank Holiday. I will send the girls over to you then."

"And I will also need to speak to both of your lieutenants – Mallard and this Zara lady."

"Yes, of course."

The man with no name wanted to call the meeting to a close then and there, but I wanted more information about his set up. I expressed my amazement that someone had set up a brothel in sleepy Sunbury.

He explained how Sunbury is actually an excellent location choice for a brothel – just being off Junction 1 of the M3 it's very handy for lorry drivers and travelling salesmen. Remember those flyers "Turn off Junction 1 for a bit of fun!" They also get a lot of business from nearby conference venues like Sandown Park.

Also Sunbury being just outside the border of the Met Police's jurisdiction means they are not dealt with by the Met's large and well-resourced Vice Squad, but instead they fall under Surrey's sedentary Vice Squad which is laughably small and ineffective – allegedly. I pressed him some more about his set up and he told me this. "There are loads of reasons why the girls would work for me and not some other operation. One – they are treated very well. Two they get to keep more of their money – over 60%. Three they get protection. Which is why I am doing this. And that is why – and I don't want to tell you your job you'd be well advised to look at other rival operations. They might have tried to poach this girl or are worried about losing all their girls to us."

I asked for his name and phone number, but he declined. "Sorry. Like I said, I don't trust the police. But I really need you to find whoever is doing this. You have my fullest cooperation. I mean up to a point – you're a copper after all."

We shook hands amicably, I got out and as he drove off I made a note of the number plates and headed straight to my vehicle database.

Nothing. The fucker had been on fake plates. Well that's an offence for a start. He really didn't trust us – did he? But I wasn't going to get beaten.

Since 2008 all motor vehicles sales are required to be registered on a database which the OB has access to. This database gave me a list of just over a thousand Silver BMW

X5 luxury SUVs sold by dealers in the London and South East region in the last two years.

The vehicle looked spanking new so I narrowed the search down to sales in the last six months. This narrowed the list further to several hundred.

From there I narrowed the search again to sales made to male buyers aged 25-40. He did look audaciously young so I took a chance on a search 25-35.

Now I had forty names. Now I have a manageable manually searchable database. Do you think this guy just fell into pimping at entry level? No. The guy's got some previous. So let's take those 40 names to another database and see who has any form.

Hey! Now my short list is down to eleven. Let's take a look at those eleven mug shots.

And so that brought me to Karl King. Managing to look ultra-suave in his mug shot belying the horribleness of his rap sheet: aggravated burglary.

The vehicle sales document had a phone number. I was about to dial when I got an incoming call. Jane Barrow had been constantly calling for updates. Each time I pressed REJECT and this time was no different. I had nothing to say to her until I was certain that Daria Lipsinski was the dead girl.

She sounded indignant and more than a little angry. "I heard you had gone into a pub in Sunbury with a photograph – and it wasn't the E-fit. Have you got a lead? You promised to keep me updated."

I deleted the message and would not be calling her back. It wasn't in anyone's interest – least of all hers to leak out the wrong victim's name. Once I'm sure, she would be the first to know. I like Jane, but right now she's a bloody nuisance.

Now I was going to enjoy this next call.

"Karl King?"

"Who's this?" The voice is aggressive and wary.

"It's Detective Chief Superintendent Ferdy. We spoke earlier today."

Dead Silence.

"I bet you're wondering how I got your name and number."

"Yes I am."

"I'm Ferdy the Fox, the copper with special powers. Just remember that and thank your luck that I'm not working in Vice."

Sunday 25th May 2014

I was at home trying to rest. My fatigue was so deeply ingrained that when I closed my eyes they would quiver, trembling with tiredness. Yet I couldn't sleep, so I went to my desk to go over the case file when I got a call from Ann MacLean the batty cat lady – "the girl with raven black hair is outside, looking at the cats."

"Try and keep her there. Get her talking."

Despite the Sunday drivers doing their best to fuck me up, I was there in ten minutes. As I drove up the lane to the entrance to the sanctuary I could see Ann MacLean talking through the fence to a shorter woman holding a bicycle. As in Ann's description her long black hair was tied back, and parted in the middle.

Before getting closer, I got out my phone and dialed that number of Daria's last contact. 07771 857346. By now I knew I had memorised it. In the distance I saw the girl take out her phone, look at it, and then return it to her jacket.

I marched forward and when I was within twenty feet she broke off her discussion and turned to me. Her stare was steely, glaring. She was obviously smart enough to realise I was a copper. She got on her bike and began pedaling in the opposite direction.

"Excuse me young lady I need to speak with you about your friend Daria Lipsinski," I called out.

By now she was pedaling like the clappers. I dashed after her, but I soon realised I wasn't going to catch up. I breathlessly called back to Matt in the car, but then realised he wasn't with me on this one.

So I ran in the opposite direction to my cycling suspect, got in my car and sped along the lane. By the time I had reached the end of the lane, looking left and right, she was nowhere to be seen.

I drove back to speak to Ann MacLean and in between catching my breath I thanked her for the tip off and asked if she had picked up any info from her conversation. "Very little. She's very cagey. I got that her name is Becky. Very serious girl. I asked if she had cats. She said her landlord wouldn't allow it. I told her to move – and she said that she was planning to do that. She asked if any of the cats were for sale. She especially liked Anubis, that's the Egyptian cat over there."

I went back to the station and on the PC attempted to put together my own DIY E-fit of Becky, trying in vain to capture those piercing eyes. I am sure that the Pros would do better when they came in on Monday. I then called Karl King "Are any of your girls called Becky?"

"As I've told you I don't know any of the girls," was the reply "but I do know of a Becky. I believe she was one of the original girls that set up the operation."

"I need to speak with her."

"Becky will be coming to see you tomorrow, along with all the others."

Chapter 7

Into the Thames Valley of the Dolls

Monday 26th May 2014 (Bank Holiday) – Morning

SO I AM AT THE INCIDENT ROOM at 7.30 a.m. At 8 am I got this text from Karl King "As promised today I am sending over everybody who works for me at half hour intervals beginning at 9 a.m. The first is Zara. Please be nice to her. Please be nice to all the girls"

I texted back "How many girls?"

"7 girls + Zara & Andy."

What do you like to do on your bank holiday? Me – I like to spend it in a windowless room, speed interviewing a parade of hookers. I sprayed on a massive hit of Lynx (the ladies love that) and prepared myself for a heavy day.

Matt showed up wearing his best suit. He had even brushed his hair, spruced up for his day in ladyland.

At 8.50 a.m. I got a call that someone was waiting for me in reception. But instead of my expected Zara, I encountered that BMX Kid wheeling towards me – eyes ablaze.

"Not now BMX Kid," I said. "I've got a big day ahead."

"Have you looked at it yet?" he blurted at me. "Looked at what?"

"I handed in a memory stick of the ritual on Brooklands Park." The memory stick had in fact been tossed into the MISC CRAP file. I was polite. I told him I planned to watch it later. Which I did, leave no stone unturned and all that, and I sent him scuttling out the door.

As the door slid shut behind him, it immediately slid

open again and in walked a toddler. A beautiful mixed-race child with tresses of curly black hair. He looked around our waiting room with a look of wonderment – like the tatty public information posters were works of arts on the ceiling of the Sistine chapel.

He was followed by a woman, early twenties, of eastern European appearance, in jeans and t-shirt and a hairstyle that looked like a large crash helmet. After her came an older black woman – early 30s – her big biceps and thick neck gave her the appearance of a lean shot putter. I sensed that she was Zara and introduced myself.

She was dressed in thick soled jogging trainers, jeans and a hooded London Olympics 2012 sweatshirt with that god-awful jaggedy mess of a logo. How much public money did that logo cost? Now that was a real crime.

"I am here to help, don't nick me," Zara said, her mouth creased into a smile though her eyes showed no warmth. She clearly had a deep aversion to coppers. Her grip was powerful.

I put on my best I-am-one-the-nice-ones smiles.

She introduced herself as Zara Campbell and then introduced me to Maria Grigore and little Cody. The novelty of the waiting room had now worn off for Cody and he stared back at me coldly. Zara asked if little Cody could sit in on the interview. I flatly declined, so the child was looked after by Maria as we went to the interview room.

9:03 a.m. Zara Campbell

Matt and I took her to Interview Room – our very best room. The one with the mirror and the fully working lights that don't flicker and strobe. It resembled a dance studio while Interview Rooms 2 and 3 were well dingy. I got her a coffee. From the kettle not a skanky one from the machine. I pressed record on the tape deck and sat down.

I showed Zara that 07771 857346 phone number

printed on a sheet of A4.

"Recognise this number?"

She got out her phone and scrolled down, eventually she said – "It's Becky's."

"Becky who?"

"Becky Taylor."

I slid over my homemade E-Fit.

"That's a bit like her. But not really."

"Is Becky one of your girls?"

Zara nodded.

"I tried to speak with this woman yesterday. Why would she not want to talk to me?"

"Well that's because she's like me. She don't trust the force."

"Well that is incredibly stupid. I am here to catch a killer. The killer of someone you know, one of *your lot,* who may well strike again."

"Well, it's been my experience that *your lot* don't give a fuck about me or any of us. And if any of us die it's generally seen as good riddance. I used to report violence against working girls to the police and have regretted it every time. I've been beaten up by – *your lot* – I've lost my teeth – got a broken jaw at the hands of *your lot.*"

She had taken my two words "your lot," rolled them in venom and threw it back at me five-fold. All I could do was sit there and take in the tirade.

I decided to change tact. I put on my best solemn and empathetic expression, and went with this: "I am very sorry you feel that way. Ms. Campbell. Let me please try and reassure you. I am only interested in finding this killer. I have strong reason to believe that the dead girl found in the river is Daria, and am going to do everything in my power to stop him killing again. If he is targeting sex workers to me that's no less serious than if he is targeting anyone else. I am not judging you, Ms. Campbell, I must stress – I am not here to attack you or do you harm, I am here to protect. I know you don't trust me and I accept that your past experiences mean that there's a very good reason for that. But I must please ask for your fullest cooperation to help me do my duty."

Damn, I'm good. I glanced over at Matt sat next to me, who looked suitably impressed. But Zara was the one to win over, and her icy stare had not thawed.

"Matt and me are the two good ones in a barrel of rotten apples."

She folded her arms and looked away. "Come on, let's go on with it."

"When did you first hear about the dead girl in the river?"

"About a week ago."

"When and where? Exactly!"

"I don't remember." She stared back defiantly.

"A woman is found dead less than two miles from where you live at around the same time as one of your girls go missing – and you don't think to come forward and report it?"

"No."

"Well why the hell not?"

"For the reasons we talked about. We think you'd use it as an excuse to bust us. But you know what? I honestly had not linked the two. Becky mentioned that Daria was thinking of moving on, finding a change of scenery, so when Daria didn't show up on Wednesday that's what we thought had happened. The dead girl in the river was just something somebody mentioned, like a car crash, or a football result – just something in the news."

"So when was the last time you saw Daria?"

"We have a Sunday get together round mine over a glass of wine. It would have been then."

"Did she seem troubled?"

"Not that I noticed."

"What did she talk about?"

"Her tricks – or something like that."

"Had any of them got violent recently? Any rows? Any incidents?"

"No. None." My exasperation got the better of me and I threw my pad and pen on the table.

"Come on, Zara – help me out here."

Zara rose up in a burst of anger.

"Listen, we run a safe operation. We don't have violent johns; they are all regular guys. Not sickos or perverts."

"Oh really – you must have a pretty unique operation then?" I was bluffing here of course. Vice was a whole new world to me.

I continued: "Tell me about the last violent incident involving a john."

"It was months ago, and it didn't involve Daria. It was some creep who was saying nasty things to Francetta. Francetta is Ghanain and he was a racist. So Andy and me sorted him out."

"What does 'sorting him out' involve?"

"We roughed him up a little and told him never to come back."

I thought that this roughed-up guy could be bent on revenge.

"So is the dead girl in the river definitely Daria?" She asked, for the first time showing any concern. Was it genuine? Or was she asking just because she felt she should?

"No. Not definitely. That's why I need Daria's DNA to match it up. Do you know where I can get a personal item of hers? Do you know where she lives?"

"I don't know where she lives now, but up until a few

months ago she was sleeping round mine's on the couch." "She didn't tell you where she'd gone?"

She shook her head.

"Some landlord somewhere is going to be missing his rent. How long had she been sleeping on your couch?" "About four months. When she first came over from wherever it was she came from"

"Poland. Daria came from Katowice in Poland. So she lived with you for four months and she never once told you why she left Poland?"

"No. She might have told Becky, or one of the others. She might have even told me, but I don't recall."

I pressed her. She replied with "Why does anybody leave home? Abuse at home most probably. Virtually all the girls I work with have left home, so it's no big deal."

"After she moved out, did she leave anything behind – a hairbrush or an item of clothing?" "I'll dig around the flat and see if I can get something for you."

"Like I said I need her DNA to ID her conclusively. Will you excuse me a moment?" I got up and headed straight to admin to arrange a search warrant for her flat. "I want it fast tracked," I ordered and then went back to the interview.

When I later played back the interview tape that I had left running I was able to hear the conversation that Zara had with Matt in my absence. This is how it went.

Zara: He's gone to get a search warrant for my flat? Hasn't he?

Matt: Not necessarily. He often walks out of interviews, sometimes just to stretch his legs.

Zara: I don't mind. He can search the flat and take whatever he thinks will be useful. I just don't want the kids to be freaked out.

Matt: Do you mean your child I saw in reception? Zara: That's him.

The tones were warm and friendly, all ruined by my entering the room. I began my questioning again.

"So why did Daria move out?"

"She raised enough money for a deposit and started renting."

"You had a row. You threw her out."

Zara shook her head with an air of irritation. "Who would have her address?"

"Becky. I guess she was the friendliest with Daria" "Why are you talking about Daria in the past tense?" "Because you are."

"Am I? And just because I am, why would you?"

Zara gave me a fuck-you face.

I continued. "I need to get together a list of her clients. I especially need to find out the last client she was with."

"Well, we don't keep a list. Obviously."

"Why obviously?"

"Because our clients OBVIOUSLY don't give us their real names, addresses and phone numbers."

"Listen I want a lead – a person of interest – do you want to get nicked for obstruction?"

She came back at me angrily, "You listen. I am not on the shop floor; I have a kid at home who I look after. I don't turn tricks any more. I just supervise. I hardly ever get to see or meet the johns. And thank fuck that. I used to be a sex worker. I still work in the business but now I supervise. I'm a minder."

"If Daria is that girl in the river her killer is most likely one of her johns. Come on, if you don't have names at least give me a description of her clients, what sort of car stuff like that."

"I will get the girls to put together a list for you."

"It's very important. The killer may well be on that list. So how did you get working for Karl King?"

"Who's Karl King?"

I snorted with surprise and disbelief. "The guy you work for."

"Oh you mean K. Is that his full name?"

"You fucking serious? You don't know who he is? You only know him as K?"

"That's right – to me he's just K." I didn't believe her. "Who told you to come in today?"

"Andy did. He said that it had been decided we should all come in on the Bank Holiday."

"So how did you get working for K?"

"We don't work for him; we give him a percentage of what we make. "

"So he's your pimp."

"No, he's not."

"Well, why the fuck do you give him money then? Why not keep it all?"

"Because he's the one that promotes the business for us. He gets customers to our door. He does all the marketing. He does the flyers – 'Turn off Junction1 for a bit of fun'. It's because of him the girls don't have to walk the streets or put cards in phone boxes or even run a website. He puts the word about so that only people in the know come to the pub car park and that's how we get decent nonviolent johns."

"Mostly decent nonviolent johns." I corrected her. "One last question, Ms. Campbell. You said you lost your teeth because you were beaten up by the police. Your teeth seem fine to me."

She gave me a smile of unadulterated hatred. "I had to do a lot of overtime to get them fixed."

Next came Maria Grigore, crash helmet head. I resisted the temptation of a cheap gag about what sort of motorcycle she had.

10:15 a.m. Maria Grigore

Maria told me that she lives round the corner from Zara. She sometimes looks after Cody, taking him to school and play groups. Maria's Romanian accent made me think of fortune telling and of course the tarot card angle, which I had totally overlooked when talking to Zara.

Was she into fortune telling? I asked. No. What about Zara? No. Any of the other girls into fortunetelling? No. So much for that line of inquiry.

I then quizzed her about horses and fishing. Nothing doing there either.

I wanted her to list me all the johns that she and her colleagues had been with in the last three months. She put up a loud protest as I handed her a pad and paper.

I pressed her to tell me about anybody at all that was unusual, weird, creepy or intimidating.

Then she suddenly said – "Yes. Slimy Simon. He just likes to talk. He latched onto Danica."

"Daria?"

"No, Danica. She is Slovakian – blonde girl."

"So tell me about this Slimy Simon."

"He wouldn't hurt a fly. Slimy Simon, he never fucked any of us. He would just buy us things. Like bars of chocolate and scarves."

"Last of the big spenders eh?"

"He used to hang out at the Saturday morning parties and just talk. He went out with Danica for a pizza and he asked her out. She turned him down and he stormed out." I looked at Matt - this was dead encouraging.

10:35 a.m. Amanda McNab

Next was the charming muffin top girl who was hostile to me and Matt at the CarPhone Whorehouse. What would the Amanda McNabs of this world be doing if she wasn't a prostitute? I pictured her sour face outside the grey Council

Offices on her fag break, making her "customers" wait and then taking cruel delight in turning down people's parking permit application because they are not "legible."

She barely knew Daria, hardly ever spoke to her, and did not even know that she had not turned up to work.

She knew that Becky was an associate of Daria and they would go and see the cats together.

She had met Slimy Simon at one of the Saturday morning parties at Zara's. He tried to talk to her but Amanda had given him the brush off. "I only talk to weirdoes if I am getting paid for it," she explained, which was fair enough.

10:49 a.m. Francetta Baffour

Francetta Baffour was a very welcome change of pace. Her lilting laughter and bright hoop earrings took me out of the sunless gloom of our interview room.

"Where's the Carnival?" I asked.

"These are my work clothes. I go there straight after this."

Francetta also claimed she had never spoken to Daria. So she did not think to report her missing.

I mentioned the violent incident that Zara had referred to. Francetta played it down "I was not attacked. The man was abusive. Racial insults. I called out to Andy and Zara – and they dealt with him."

She laughed, I thought inappropriately.

"I found out why they call her Madame Headlock," she said. Ah! So Zara Campbell is a/k/a Madame Headlock, and it was her party that Bremner went to on the Friday Night going into Saturday morning.

After the interview I checked on the status of my search warrant. It was on my desk ready to roll, so I would be going over to Madame Headlock's after my round of interviews.

11:19 a.m. Ramona Marks

Next up was Ramona Marks. A slender rake of a girl but with bumps in all the right places. Her ultra long straight brown hair dropping down, contouring around her figure. She was the youngest of all so far, a mere 19, and while all the previous women gave off a hard demeanor, Ramona's eyes revealed a boss eyed vulnerability. She also had the foggy look you see on junkies.

"So Ramona. What drugs are you on?" Her vacant smile dropped. "I'm not. I was. I'm on a script," she said in a bunged up voice.

This of course meant she was on drug treatment. I decided to leave her alone on this subject.

Ramona went on to win the award for the funniest answer of the day. I asked her if she ever saw dodgy people hanging around Daria "Well yes of course. She's a hooker, she spends all her time hanging around dodgy people." Frustratingly, she couldn't think of anyone specific. She had met Slimy Simon a couple of times, but knew nothing about him, except that he was big and soft – and "looked like Bungle the Bear." "He wouldn't hurt anybody...." she offered. Not what I wanted to hear.

"What's it like working for Karl King?"

"Who?"

"He's the guy that runs your operation."

"Is that why they call it the K Ring?"

"Could be." I had not heard the K Ring mentioned before.

She went on: "I've heard them talk about K – but never met him. To me Zara is the big lady boss. Zara's really cool. She's taken me in – given me a place for me and JJ to stay when no one else would."

"JJ is your boyfriend?"

"No JJ is my son – three year old."

"You called your son JJ?"

"What's wrong with that?"

"Nothing. You can call your son whatever you like." "Why thank you." She said with an ironic smile. Showing there was a sharpness within that cloudy haze.

"So don't you want to get away from the K Ring?" "No. No way. The K Ring are cool people to work for. They let me take a whole week off for my sinus operation."

"Wow! That is cool. That sound like brilliant people to work for. Do you think they would hire Matt and Me?" "Hey I know you're being sarcastic, but Zara tells me in all her time working in this game, nobody had ever allowed that before. Listen, I even asked if I could not work Tuesdays and Thursday so I can go to rehearsals for amateur dramatics and then even said yes to that." "Amazing. Where can we see you perform?" "You can't. I forgot to turn up to the rehearsals." She said it like it was the sort of thing that kept happening with her.

"Hopefully I can get it together for the next production, because I really want to get into acting." Towards the end of the interview she asked me "You don't think Daria's is dead, do you?"

"I don't know yet."

"I refuse to believe it."

"Why?"

"Just don't. Until it's proven. We're the three musketeers. Me, Becky and Daria. The three cat ladies. We often go and see the cats together. I can't believe Daria's gone. She'll come back, I know it."

I was left feeling that Ramona was a blind optimist. Believing against all beliefs that her friend would come back, and even more naively thinking that amateur dramatics was a route into a career in acting.

12:00 p.m. Danica Brezanik

With Danica we were back to the hard-boiled ladies of the night. She was a blonde of the Aryan variety. If Nazi Germany ever did a Playboy magazine, she is the sort of girl who would be on the cover.

I dived straight into talking about Slimy Simon. "Do you have his phone number?" She got out her phone and showed me his number. She even had a surname for me. Slimy Simon was Slimy Simon Todd.

Matt wrote down the number and 'whoosh' the man was out the door. He did not have to tell me that he was off to get a warrant. We are like the telepathetic (sic) twins us two.

"But he is harmless," Danica went on.

"Well they said that about a lot of people who weren't harmless at all."

She asked me for some examples but I couldn't think of any.

She told me that Slimy Simon Todd had been showing up to the Friday night stroke Saturday morning parties at Madame Headlock's and got talking to the girls but never ever about sex. He bought them drinks but seemed especially keen on giving them chocolates. Most of the girls were off with him, but Danica had started chatting to him. He eventually asked her out for a pizza and her attitude was – "Free pizza? Why not?" Slimy Simon Todd obviously wanted to make an impression as he had arranged to meet Danica at the Pizza Express in Walton on Thames.

It was there, over the flickering candlelit and soft background '80s music that Simon asked Danica out – and offered to save her from the life of sin. Danica started laughing and Simon ran out into the night, leaving her to pick up the bill. She had not heard from or seen him since. This was looking ultra-hopeful. A weak and pathetic man, laughed at by women and prostitutes in particular, the women he set out to save, who takes out his puny rage on one of those women. He couldn't get to Danica – for whatever reason – so he went for another Eastern European with a similar name.

12:45 p.m. Polly Webster

Polly was the girl with the long eyelashes and straight blond hair that Matt tried to speak to in the pub. Polly was consistently frosty in the police interview room; I guess she's just that type of girl.

"I couldn't stand her. She nicked my cigarettes. She nicked everyone's cigarettes."

"That's not a reason for killing her," I said. She didn't laugh.

It was clear that Polly was angling herself to go up a league. She only wanted to do the top jobs – the big businessmen with real money. I wished her luck.

And so the last of the seven working girls was waiting in reception, Becky Taylor. Remember her? The dark haired girl who did a Bradley Wiggins the evening before and the last person that Daria contacted on her phone. I felt a warm tingle, but don't worry, readers, I often get that when I sense a big break through coming in a case.

13:10 p.m. Becky Taylor

As soon as I walked into the room, Becky launched in with – "Is Daria is dead?"

Before I answered I looked at her hard. To study her. Her lips were quivering with worry. I owed her the truth.

"I have reason to believe that the woman found dead in the river is Daria. But we are not certain yet. That is why you are here," I pressed on. "Why did you not answer any of our messages? Why did you run away from me yesterday?"

"Because you're police."

"Daria was phoning and texting you in the days

leading up to her disappearance. Is this your number?" She nodded. "I have a warrant here to search you and your phone."

"No need for that," she said and without hesitation she whipped out her phone. I scanned the phone and found this text correspondence.

3:30 p.m. Sorry if I was a bit of a bitch.
3:33 p.m. I am sorry too.
4:12 p.m. Fancy going to see the cats Tues eve?
4:36 p.m. Yes. Let's do that. Don't you work Tuesday?
5:33 p.m. I can switch shifts. It's cool.
8:47 p.m. OK. That is surprising – but good.
2:14p.m. Still on 4 the cats? Meet 7?
2:17 p.m. Yes. See you then.
6:30 p.m. Running late. Leaving now.
6:55 p.m. SOZ it's a blowout 2nite. Something cum up.
7:12 p.m. Whatever.
9:03 a.m. Morning. Try again this evening?
11:23 a.m.?
2:11 p.m. ???
4:17 p.m. Suit yourself ☹

"So you were supposed to meet her at the Cat Sanctuary and she then canceled. So why did you not report her missing?"

"I didn't automatically think that something was wrong, she had told me she was thinking about leaving. Moving on. Not going back to Poland though. She was going to stay in this country. She even talked about saving up and leaving the life."

Then she thought some more. "Plus I didn't think you lot would care."

"A girl matching her description was found dead less than a mile from the Cat Sanctuary. Don't you read the papers?"

"No I don't read the papers."

"And you don't talk to people who read the papers?" Matt was now looking at the text. He noted that the very last text from Daria is in a different vernacular. "SOZ it's a blowout 2nite. Something cum up." All of Daria's previous texts were not abbreviated and looked as though a spell checker had been used, as you might expect from someone who was not texting in their first language and not familiar with English slang and abbreviations.

Becky went on "As you can see I texted her again on the Wednesday morning. And then texted her and phoned her every couple of days till now. There's never been any reply."

"On the Sunday before ... we had a bit of a row. Not a big one. She was talking about moving on again and I got a bit narked and said to her – don't talk about it, just do it. It's like me – I'm studying psychology at the Open University on my days off Sunday and Monday. I'm actually doing something about it. But she just moans all the time."
"So where did Daria move to after she moved out of Zara's"
"I don't know."

"Of course you do."

"I don't. She was renting a bedsit in ... I don't know where. I never went round there. She didn't want to give her neighbours a bad impression. She told her landlord she was a student."

A landlord! Now I had something to go on. Pretty soon a tenancy that started in that area around February time is going to be defaulting on their rent.

As I called the interview to a close, Becky asked how the girl in the river was killed.

I gave her a basic description without embellishments. I didn't want to upset her. She shook her head in horrified disbelief. "No one deserves that, not Daria, not anyone. Please find the guy who did this." I gave her my word that I would, which seemed to comfort her. I looked down at my notes and when I looked up again, she had gone.

During the interview with Becky Taylor I had been given word that Slimy Simon Todd had been taken to Interview Room 3.

13:57 p.m. Slimy Simon Todd

For the Slimy Simon Todd interview I put on the videotape as well as audio. This could be the big one. I even did a little practice of the "you-have-the-right-to-remain-silent" bit when I went to the kharzi.

Simon had been at home; he lived alone, watching the football playoff on TV, when two uniforms called telling him he was urgently needed at the station to help us with our inquiries.

I walked in to meet a bulbous face of total bemusement. Hc was a large man, over six foot but unimposing just as Ramona described him. Like a large man in a cuddly bear suit at a children's party.

"What's this about?" He asked immediately.

"What do you think this is about?"

"I don't know."

"Take a wild guess."

Simon stared down at the desk, and then offered: "Is it to do with my friendship with the girls?"

"I don't think they particularly want to be friends with you."

"Why do you say that?"

"Because they call you Slimy Simon."

"They don't call me that."

"They do."

"They don't all call me that."

"They all call you that. Especially Danica. I can play you the tapes if you like." His big soft eyes started welling up. I slid over the big box of tissues.

"Don't take it like that son. There's plenty more prostitutes to save."

This man was obviously an emotional car wreck but I didn't want tears. I wanted the rage of a man who would strap a woman up and stone her to death.

"So Simon if you were looking out for the girls so much, why did you not come forward when we found out about the dead girl in the river?"

"Well, I did come forward." "Well, you didn't." "Oh yes I did." "No, you didn't" "Well, I think you'll find I did" "Well, we can cut this pantomime short and provide the proof.

Matt here has put together an impressive Excel spreadsheet of all our reported leads." Matt came back with the print out and I scoured the list.

"I reported it on the Saturday after your appeal. I gave my name as Simon but withheld my surname."

Sure enough there it was. Entry: Simon (Surname Withheld) *Have you checked out whether the victim is a local working girl? Please try all the nearby places.*

I asked for Slimy Simon's whereabouts on the Tuesday of the murder. Turns out he worked for a confectionery supplier, which is why he was so handy with all the chocolate gifts, and he was at a trade show at the Birmingham NEC all of that week. His alibi checked out and his colleagues were with him all of that day setting up the stand, and they all went for a curry afterwards. Damn those cast iron alibis.

Before my final interview of the day I called Karl King to thank him for his help in making today possible. I also wanted his assistance in putting together a list of CarPhone Whorehouse clients – realizing of course this list would mainly consist of descriptions and hardly any names. Karl King's reply was "I promote the operation, but I do not know any of the clients personally. The networks used are strip joints, conference centers, the clientele are mainly lorry drivers and travelling salesmen."

Next was Andy Mallard, the one that Bremner had described as a "good bloke." He was still wearing the one glove, but at least the slippers had been replaced by cowboy boots.

15:03 p.m. Andy Mallard

Before he sat down he asked, "So how did you get on with Becky Taylor? Did she tell you the one about her being the illegitimate daughter of a famous actor?"

I shook my head.

"She says she can't tell you who it is at first, and then when she tells you, it changes each time. Did she tell you she was studying psychology at the Open University?"

"Yes, she did," I replied flatly.

"Lies all lies. Don't believe a word she says. She would tell a lie even if the truth was more interesting."

"Well, you're hardly a paragon of truth and virtue yourself. I've been reading your previous. You're a right slime ball aren't you?" After a long day of interviews, my diplomacy chip had eroded.

"Slime ball? Me? Well, I've been called a lot worse."

"I don't doubt it. So how did you get into whoring?"

"If you're going to be like that I'm off." He stood up from his chair, I grabbed his shoulders and slammed him back down. I proceeded with my questioning.

"You still dealing drugs?"

"I thought you were only interested in Daria."

"Yes. So why did you pretend not to know her when we spoke in the pub on Friday?"

"I offered to help – didn't I? I just didn't want to incriminate myself."

"You lied."

"I didn't want to get her, or me, into trouble."

"Why didn't you report her missing when she didn't show up on Wednesday?"

"These girls come and go. Becky said she was thinking of moving on."

"I thought you didn't believe anything she says."

"I don't."

He tried to give me a beseeching look. He looked like a pathetic wounded dog that should be put out of his misery – "I don't know why you are being so mean to me. I am being 100% up front. When you came over on Friday with your picture of Daria it really got all of us worried that she might have been murdered. So I got on the phone to the K Man. Normally we don't talk to the filth for obvious reasons, but in this case we both agreed that we should come and see you and give you as much information as possible to help you find this guy."

"Why do you wear the one glove?"

"Dunno."

"You must know. Where's the other glove?"

"I think I lost it."

"Yes I think you have. So what do you do when you're not whoring?"

"I'm a painter."

"Have you a studio?" I was thinking of a murder location.

"Just my house."

"And what do you paint?"

"Visions. Stuff the angels send me."

"The what?"

"The Angels. They show me things. I have a talent for clairvoyance, I get it from my aunt...."

"Was she a craggy old git like you?"

"You really hate me, don't you?"

"No, it's not hate. Just contempt."

"Well, I feel the same about you."

"I wouldn't have it any other way. So where does Daria live?"

"She was staying with Zara and Ramona for a bit. Then she moved out. But I don't know where."

"I thought you had a gift for clairvoyance."

"I have no control over what they show me. It's more of a curse than a gift. The things they show me sometimes." And he appeared to relive some horrible vision.

"So what have they told you about all of this?" "Nothing. I'll let you know if I get anything."

"Who was Daria's last trick?"

"Some guy in a Fiat Uno. I didn't see the trick – just the car."

"You are not leaving this room until you give me a full list of your johns. And don't mention Slimy Simon."

As the man on the shop floor, I got him to list as many of these johns (or at least their vehicles) as possible. As he was writing, I pressed him "Any one creepy? Anybody who looks a bit weird?"

Mallard thought hard for several seconds and then reacted with sudden decisiveness.

"Sure! He's not a client, but he's been to the parties. There is one guy that sticks out a mile – Dazza – that's what we called Daria was talking to him at Zara's a week or two ago. That vampire guy with the Haribo Lecter tattoo."

Chapter 8

Tossing Madame Headlock's Flat

Monday 26th May 2014 (Bank Holiday) – Late Afternoon

WITH THE SUN LOW IN THE SKY and taking shelter behind the clouds, the bank holiday was winding down, and the people of Surrey were bracing themselves for a return to work the following day.

But for Matt and me there had been no rest or recreation, and now the investigation was going up a gear. Roger Farrady, the local weirdo most likely, had shoot back in with a bullet to the top of our persons of interest hit parade. We will be doubly scrutinizing that alibi of his, but in the meantime we were off to toss Zara Campbell's a/k/a Madame Headlock's flat.

It was a short walk around the back from the Percy Arms pub. An alcove of post war council style three-storey high flats with walls of pimpled cracking concrete the colour of egg boxes. Zara's was right at the top and at the back under the balcony shadow.

To get to the top floor you had to step into the black hole entrance of the stairwell. Parked by was a Vauxhall Astra. I walked up to it and rapped on the windscreen. Inside were two of my CS boys. In the driver seat was the older one with the shock of silver grey hair. He rolled down the window, and I apologised for cutting his bank holiday short. I explained that it was vitally important to ID the girl in the river and we had to do it today for fear of anybody destroying vital evidence. The younger CS in the passenger seat next to him smiled a 'no problem', while the silver fox just scowled. He was clearly not a member of the Ferdy Fan

Club.

The CS boys got out of the car decked out in their de rigueur canary-yellow jumpsuits. I explained that this wasn't a crime scene – that we were just collecting evidence, but the wise looking grey one said that they preferred to wear their colours.

So Matt, me, and the two very conspicuous-looking canary boys marched up to the flat and rapped on the door. On the inside I could hear the sound of children merrily chanting. The door opened and a blast of icy wind hit me in the face, it was the arctic reception from an unsmiling Zara. I pulled out my warrant.

She rolled her eyes. "You didn't need to bother with a search warrant. Come In." The place was basic, cheap functional furniture. Untidy, brought about by the inevitable chaos that comes from having two young children living with you. I could smell fresh paint, a recent job.

Cody who I had seen at the police station was playing on the rug in front of the TV, with a smaller, younger child who I presumed was Ramona's JJ as Ramona was on the floor with them.

I made straight for the threadbare couch in the center of the room and turned to Zara.

"Is this the couch Daria used to sleep on?"

She nodded. So I gestured to the two CS men to get all over it. Young JJ was staring.

"Mummy – what are these men doing?"

"It's okay, JJ. There are here to help. Help find a friend," said Zara.

"Mummy why are those men dressed in yellow?" "They're trying to start a new fashion," I quipped.

JJ stared at me for a bit and then declared, "Mum, I don't like him."

"Your son is a good judge of character," I said

keeping the unappreciated wisecracks going. Ramona took both the boys into the bedroom and away from me.

I said to Zara, “We do not want to be here long; we just want to take away some items that may have Daria’s DNA. Do you entertain johns here?”

Zara was appalled at this suggestion. “Of course not. We have two children growing up in this flat. Mine and Ramona’s.”

“We do have parties though,” chipped in Ramona, coming out of the bedroom.

“Yes – but nothing dodgy goes on. Just a bit of drinking and dancing,” said Zara. As she said this, the younger CS guy pulled out some interesting costumes from the other bedroom – a nurses uniform, a school uniform, a French maid, a horny devil.

“It’s the role play collection,” explained Zara. “Anything like a toothbrush – or underwear. Something like she and only shc would use?” Asked Matt.

“She had been wearing my Mad Cat Lady t-shirt. I’ll go find it,” offered Ramona as she went to the bedroom. Zara gave me a hairbrush, “loads of girls have used it, but Daria definitely did.”

Eventually Ramona came out of the bedroom. “I can’t find it – she must still have it.” Ramona suddenly slumped down on the chair, tearing up. “It’s just starting to sink in that we probably won’t be seeing Daria again.”

We said our goodbyes and walked out onto the balcony. I was about to go over a few things with Matt when out walked a roly-poly round-faced woman with thick pebble glasses wearing what looked like a knitted tea cozy on her head.

“Are they in trouble?”

“Actually no.”

“Well, I’m not being funny but they should be.”

“Oh yeah? What about?”

"Them parties. Them noisy parties. Three times I've called you lot."

"You Lot? What do you mean?"

"The Environmental Health," she said nodding over at my colleagues in yellow. I was indignant. "We are not Environmental Health! We are the filth. We are the Old Bill."

"Old Bill. I'm not being funny you lot are even worse – all mouth and no trousers. I stopped complaining after a while. It did no good. The police turn up. The girls have a laugh and a joke. The police go and it starts up again. But I don't like to complain."

"I can tell."

"No. I don't. I'm not being funny but it turns you into a something you don't want to be. Just my luck to be housed next to them though. Cos them parties, they're like magnets to every weirdo from miles around." The word weirdo triggered off the bells. Matt fired up his tablet and he showed Miss Tea Cozy Head the mug shot of Roger Farrady a/k/a Versago.

"Stone me. I'm not being the funny. He was having a fag on that there balcony just over there a few weeks ago."
"You sure it was him?"

"Yes, I was watching through the letterbox."

After the ID from the long-suffering neighbour I went back and flashed the Versago pic to Zara and Ramona. Zara had definitely seen him, but Ramona was not so sure. We were closing in a red-hot suspect, and yet we had a problem. His alibi. Matt and me headed back to the nick to work out our next move.

I was about to phone my wife to tell her my investigation was keeping me away from home, but I knew she'd only be unpleasant to me, so I didn't bother.

Matt hit the PC and immediately got onto Facebook. As I said before, while Matt and me are not exactly best pals we do have a telepathetic (sic) understanding, so I knew exactly what he was up to. Meanwhile Gaffney and a bunch of the uniform gang dropped by the incident room. I just about manage to hide my contempt for my colleague DC Gaffney. He's got a face like a chewed up piece of gum and always talking as if he's about to say something amusing, but never does. A deeply unfunny man always trying to be funny. No one takes him seriously.

Gaffers and his crew had all been on an adrenaline rush dealing with some bovver down the Cowey Sale fayre. They were off down the boozer to go over some replays and asked me to join them. With my head swimming all day with the case I thought – why not?

They didn't ask Matt. They never do. They left him alone in the dark of the incident room and one of them made a crack about him spending time with his Facebook friends. Matt stared harder at the screen, his face getting redder, while I tried to stick up for him, telling them he was actually working the case.

"Bloody looks like it 'an all." They sniggered like a gang of school bullies.

Going for a couple with the boys was a mistake. I got home at just after 11p.m. with my breath reeking of ales, so the T&F didn't believe that I had spent all bank holiday weekend working this very important case.

I slept like a log – woke up in the fireplace. No I actually I woke up on the couch. The wife started slagging me off as usual as I was trying to sleep, so I had to get away to get some peace. This is was the first chance I had to get some decent kip since I first landed this case. I was hoping the excess beer would really help send me to sleep, and I wasn't going to let the wife's low opinion of me ruin it.

It was Matt what ruined it. My mobile rang at 4:30am. While the ringing tones pierced into my resting brain like knives, I got the sense that this was going to be good.

"Veronica Farrady accepted Jez Taylor's Facebook friend request."

My brain scrambled. Yes! Jez Taylor was one of the twenty or so fake Facebook Ids (they call them sock puppets) we had created to ensnare and get under the skin of fraudsters. Jez Taylor is 28 with rippling muscles, a brickie and an aspiring actor who loves to go clubbing. Only we made him up.

"So Veronica had a girl's night out on Tuesday the 14thth May. They went to see a boy band at the O2. I have pictures of the whole night – including the after show at the Indigo until 2 a.m."

Bang! And with that the legendary Matt the Stat had rumbled Roger Farrady a/k/a Versago's alibi.

Tuesday 27th May 2014 – *Morning*

So we got ourselves a fast track warrant and a dawn raid scheduled for 7.30 am. Not too early like, we're the Surrey Police, we like to keep things civilised.

I was going to enjoy my opening line to Roger, I had been practicing it in the car. Soft under my breath so no one else can hear. I didn't want to ruin the impact.

Now let's not get carried away. We have a fake alibi and a prime suspect lying to the police. It doesn't mean we have our killer, there was still lots of prove. Apart from him knowing the victim, I still had nothing to link him directly to the murder and I was certainly not going to announce yet that we had found our man, or was even close. I called Bremner to tell him that a prime suspect had come straight out of his Weirdo file. He got all excited, obviously hoping to get some credit for this collar. I told him to back the fuck off – all jokily like.

So the arrest warrant was for the fake alibi – and for both Roger and Veronica. The murder was hopefully going to come later from the search of the flat. Hinty got word from his magistrate friend that we were going to arrest someone so he came along for the ride.

One police van and a police car carrying me, driving, Matt and Hinty pulled up outside Veronica's house. I wanted to ram the door in, but Hinty said we needed to save the budget and we had to give them the chance to let us in first.

So I knocked on the door and Veronica opened up – she was dressed up smart and obviously about to go to work. I flashed the warrant and barged through into the living room, where Roger sat in his pajamas with a bowl of cornflakes watching *Good Morning Britain*.

His head snapped back at me and his cornflakes hit the deck.

"Schoolboy error," I said savoring the moment to deliver my line "If you're going to get your Mum to give you a fake alibi – make sure she's not out at a boy band concert. You're nicked!"

And with that a uniform took him out the door. I was expecting a look of panic, a shriek of anguish, a howled proclamation of innocence. But instead he was a rabbit in the headlights, not fully conscious and in a trance. I turned to Veronica. "And you're nicked as well. Take her away!" The word had got around fast. Jane must have spoken to Hinty because she was outside the station as I marched in to do my interviews.

She ran after me, pulling at my jacket. "I hear you've arrested Roger Farrady in the case."

"I can't talk about it right now Jane." I continued walking.

"Why have you arrested his mother as well?"

"We found out she'd been to a Take That concert." We gave Roger Farrady Interview Room 1. Before I went in I studied him in the see through mirror. He was the picture of worry, rubbing his face and fidgeting.

I was fully expecting him to go silent at any point in the interview and call a solicitor. Well let him. CS was scouring his and Veronica's place – they may well uncover the smoking gun evidence before it's time to go for lunch. CS was instructed to look out for horse snaffles bits, decks of tarot cards (preferably with the Devil missing) and Wellington boots.

As Matt and me walked in, he got up.

I kept this line in gags going with my opening: "You told me you were into the dark side Roger – but we have found out that your mother is into something much more evil. She has been to a Take That concert!" (Don't worry readers – that is the very last boy band/Take That joke.) Roger was immediately pleading, desperate: "This is not my Mum's fault. It was me who got her to fake the alibi. She didn't want to, but I put it onto her. So please – please don't charge her with anything."

"A killer who loves his Mum. How very moving."

"Do what you want with me. Just don't charge her."

"Let's make a deal, Rodge. We have the tape running all recorded. We won't charge your Mum, if you make this easy for us."

"If you want to fit me up for this. Then so be it. But please, let my Mum alone. She's rebuilding her life."

"So you killed Daria Lipsinksi?"

"No. I haven't killed anyone."

"Look I should I tell you – I am going to start asking you questions about a murder that took place on or around Tuesday the 15th May – you do not have to say anything but it will harm your defense...."

He interrupted me, "I don't want a lawyer. Let me tell you why I faked my alibi."

"I know why you faked your alibi. Because you're guilty."

"Somebody is trying to frame me. Look. On that Tuesday afternoon I was walking home from college like I do every afternoon. A vehicle pulled up and I could sense someone coming up behind me. Before I could turn around and see the person, I felt a cloth over my mouth. I smelt this smell – and I passed out."

"You were chloroformed? What did the cloth smell of?"

"Like a chemical."

"Like a chemical? That's very good, son. Very descriptive."

"It smelt ... sweet."

"Got a description of this 'person'? Did you see the vehicle?"

"No, nothing. My eye sight's not too good."

"So why don't you wear glasses then?"

"They'd make me look geeky."

"Vanity is for mugs, mate. So what can you tell me? Anything at all?"

"I remember his laugh. Horrible laugh"

"An evil laugh, eh? Stroll on – Matt and me are a bit old for Jackanory."

"This is why I lied. You wouldn't believe me. But it's true. I passed out and I didn't see who did it. Just it was a large figure – probably a man but I'm not even sure of that."

"So what happened when you woke up?"

"I was in this large cell. Just a big square room. No light, no nothing. In the corner they'd left a bottle of Jim Bean – and packets of Cat Food."

"Cat Food?"

"Yes, Whiskas – Tuna in Gravy. I also found a box of matches so I could at least see something. I was fucking terrified. I had no idea how long I was going to be there. I screamed and screamed and screamed."

"How long were you there?"

"I lost track of time. But eventually I heard this sound of unlocking and this stone door slide back slightly. Then the sound of running. I got up and slid the big stone door back some more and saw that I was in the tunnels down by Brooklands. You know the evacuation tunnels. I ran through the maze of tunnels and finally found the exit. I looked at my phone and the time was 9.30 a.m."

"Well, why didn't you call for help before?"

"I couldn't get a signal down there."

"Got any proof to back up this steaming horse manure of a story?"

We took Roger over to the tunnels in Brooklands Park and with a torch flashing, walked deep into the bowels of the tunnel. Now this vast network of tunnels were originally used as World War Two air raid shelters and built to take up to 5,000 people. Roger was shadowed by two uniforms all the way. He was looking more and more like murderer material, and maybe Veronica was in on it. An ex-prostitute who had it in now for prostitutes.

The reason I didn't buy this new alibi was simply the lack of detail. He couldn't give even an approximation of the vehicle or the people who did it. Or how many. Or what they said.

Roger eventually was given a torch of his own to hold as, with two uniforms stuck by him on either side, he went charging around among the stone tunnels trying to find the room where he had supposedly been locked in.

"I remember I turned left to get out," he said, sounding increasingly desperate. I left him to it to go outside to call Roy, that's the name of the senior grey haired Crime Scene fellow. Have they found my smoking gun? The answer was, after a thorough search of Roger and Veronica's, no they fucking hadn't.

When I went back into the tunnel I eventually found Matt, Roger and the two uniforms in one of the square cells deep in the bowels of the tunnels.

There was a sliding door that could be padlocked, and Roger was claiming he had been kept prisoner here. "Look, I pissed against this wall," he offered hopefully. "What does that prove?" I said.

"That I pissed against this wall. That I was here, a prisoner. Get your CSI people to test that wall. You'll find my piss on there."

"Roger, I want to believe you. But that will only prove that you pissed against this wall. It doesn't prove that you did it when you said you did it, nor that you were a prisoner here."

Matt was on call here with one his fascinating facts – "Urine itself does not contain DNA, but it may contain epithelial cells, which *do* contain DNA. However, most healthy individuals do not have epithelial cells in their urine."

"There you go. Matt the Stat is the font of all knowledge. Especially when it comes to piss and DNA. Listen, Roger. This is looking bleak for you, son. You have nothing to back up your story."

While I was saying this, I had something foul smelling waved in my face. The last time I smelt it was round Ann MacLean's. The smell of stale cat food. Matt the Stat was holding with a pair of tweezers a wrap of cat food. He put the torch on it and it read, "Whiskas Tuna in Gravy." Back at the nick I was still trying to disprove this alibi. Like for instance in all that darkness – how the fuck could he identify that specific brand of cat food? But of course there was the box of matches. Plus in the hours before nightfall some daylight had seeped through the gaps in between the metal door.

Then forensics came back with the results on the cat wrapper. It had Roger's fingerprints and his saliva from opening it with his teeth. Of course, this alone does not prove his story. It just proves that Roger had been down there eating cat food. I mean the kid's into weird things. Right?

But Matt and I had a long chat about our person of interest and we decided that it was time to move on and look at other people.

I called Bremner to talk about the case. I explained that we were now ruling out Roger Farrady. First – after 12 hours of searching, CS had found nothing to pin him to the girl in the river. Bremner hated our second reason, which had clinched it for us. Roger was so protective over his mother, insistent that we didn't charge her. He was so adamant that she should not be implicated, even going as far as to take more punishment for himself than see her be punished. We were hunting a sociopath and most likely a misogynistic one, and Roger displayed that he was the opposite. Bremner blew up here – "What the fuck does that prove? The Krays loved their Mum."

"Yes and the Krays never committed a murder like this."

"Don't get into this psychological profile bullshit."
"Bremner – he didn't do it. He's a mixed up kid, he loves his Mum. I like him – but not for this murder."

I put the phone down and went back to Matt for a proper adult conversation about the case. We had reached an important conclusion. If Roger is innocent, and his alibi is true, then the man or men that abducted him were trying to frame him and are behind this killing.

Thursday 29th May 2014

I came into the station this morning to find a telephone message that had been left overnight. Here's the transcript:

"(Eastern European accent) *Ello, I am calling you about Daria. I must tell you that her boyfriend from Poland had tracked her down. He met her once and got angry when he found out what she had become. He started stalking her and Daria was very scared. Her boyfriend is a very bad guy. It is must be him who killed Daria."*

Once again this message was rather unhelpfully an anonymous one. I played it back to the Polish girl in accounts. She started listening intently, and after a few seconds began to laugh – "That is not a Polish accent – that is a cartoon made-up accent." It confirmed my thoughts. The call was traced back to a petrol station payphone just before the M3 starts and a walking distance from the CarPhone Whorehouse.

So we played back every interview tape of the CarPhone Whorehouse girls. We played them a few times, and it became clear that am dram hopeful Ramona Marks was the one with the cartoon Polish accent.

What the fuck was this dappy girl playing at? We were going to bring her in and find out. We picked her up as she turned up to work at the CarPhone Whorehouse pub and brought her back to the nick.

In Interview Room 1, I played back the message and she owned up immediately. "I didn't mention it at the time because I'm scared. Listen, I know what you said to Zara, but who's going to protect me? If that guy can do that to Daria, he can do it to me, right? I only saw him once. When Daria was staying with us, I left one day and he was hanging around outside by the balcony. When I got back someone told me it was her ex-boyfriend and he was angry because of what Daria was doing for money. All the other stuff I said was just stuff that other people said to me."

"Who said this to you? Daria herself?"

"I can't remember. I'm an addict, I have trouble remembering things, places, faces. I'm sorry," she said pathetically.

"You saw this guy once, right?"

"Just once. He had a very mean face."

I passed her over to the E-fit woman. I was not convinced and Matt even less so. He had spoken at length, through a costly interpreter, with Daria's parents, relatives, carers and friends – and not heard anything about a boyfriend who might follow her to England.

I took the liberty of grabbing Ramona's phone. Who had she been contacting? Was she really friends with Daria? I scanned her photographs. There were many pictures of her son JJ or her with an assortment of female friends. I recognised one location as being Zara a/k/a Madame Headlock's flat. I whizzed through the pictures and then whizzed through them again, and a picture stopped me dead in my tracks. It was of three girls – smiling – I recognised Ramona's goofy look, raven haired Becky and Daria – but it was the backdrop that grabbed me. They were standing at the entrance to the living room at Zara's place and above them in the background was a black spray-painted mural. A pentacle in front of a horned figure with large spiked wings spanning the whole width of the entrance and spread over the three girls as if about to swoop on them. This mural was not seen in Zara Campbell's flat when we tossed it earlier in the week. That must have been why I smelt fresh paint.

I sent the picture to my phone. Zara Campbell had some explaining to do. Meanwhile the E-fit woman came back with this. Have you seen this fellow walking around? Does he even exist at all?

Part 2

Chapter 9

Worst Day Replay

Saturday 31st May 2014

SATURDAY MORNING OFFERED a rare chance to spend some meaningful time with the offspring. Luis is ten years old and a rapidly growing missile of free flowing joy and energy. The trouble and strife hasn't totally poisoned him against me yet – but give it time. But for now, Luis and me are getting on brilliant. He's football crazy and started supporting Chelsea, I didn't manage to knock that out of him. What he has developed with my instigation is a fascination for Brazilian football, and one day I will take him to a game at the Maracanã, the big stadium in Rio. Luis had his Borough Sports Football Final coming up in the week and so was in full-on football crazy mode today.

We had taken a break from the Xbox to sit down and work out our best formations, now that we had qualified for the quarterfinals of the Champions League. Luis was emphatic that we went with a 5-3-2, using his beloved touchline hugging wingbacks, his favorite players being Ashley Cole and the mighty Brazilian Cafu.

I am a 4-4-2 man. I like my two solid banks of four, so I was unconvinced. Of course, I was going to let him have his way. I mean, he's my son. But I was going to at least make him put his case to me – clearly and logically. And he did an excellent job. He has the makings of an excellent lawyer. Which is good because that's where the real money is – not being a copper that's for fucking certain. So with our strategy finalised, we fired up the Xbox to put our wingback strategy into practice against the mighty

Barcelona.

It was then that my phone rang.

A Saturday afternoon jogger found a dead woman as the tide pulled out by the waters near Walton Bridge. This woman had been fixed to the riverbed with horse bit snaffles. They were ligatures marks around the wrists. Her eyes had been removed. Because of the similarity to the MO of the previous killing, CS looked inside the woman's mouth and found a Tarot Card – once again it was Fifteen the Devil.

"We have a serial killer," announced the CS guy with a relish I found distasteful.

Driving to the scene, I phoned Matt who was already there. He had arranged what he had done previously – the sandbagging around the body so the footprints could be made out, and the filming of the onlookers. "There are a lot more of them this time because it's Saturday," he commented.

He sounded as shell-shocked as I felt.

I screeched my car to a stop just by Walton Bridge and as I stepped over the crime scene tape, a question burned into my brain – "Why dump the body on my patch again?" From the bridge I walked down the sharp decline towards the shallow waters. At first glance it looked as though someone had pitched up a tent. But in fact CS had erected a square of high canvas screens around the body, so the bastard onlookers could see nothing of the corpse.

I took in these bastard onlookers a general collection of shoppers – all ages and shapes and sizes, craning their necks trying to see over on and in between the canvas screens, chattering excitedly. I wanted to grab them one by one by the shoulders and shake them out of their vile curiosity.

I walked over and peered over the canvas screen to once again see a hideously disfigured face, discoloured green and puffy, severed nerve ends sprouting out of empty eye sockets. I immediately looked away and at the crowd. Wednesday the 14th May 2014 had been the single worst day of my life – and today I was getting a replay.

Walking away and with nausea still in my lungs I got out my phone out and called Mallard – but got nothing, not even a 'leave-a-message'. I then called Zara.

"Any of your girls missing?"

"Ramona's here. I'll check on the rest and call you back." She sounded panicked.

I hung up to face a uniform tugging at my sleeve. A nearby houseboat resident had heard loud splashing around 2am. He was standing some distance away from the crowd waiting to talk to me - a fussy looking man with frizzy hair and bushy pointed eyebrows.

"I was woken up at 2am, by a loud splash," he told me.

"Did you look outside?"

"No."

"Did you hear anything else?"

"I heard laughter – like snickering. It made me think that there was more than one person doing the splashing."
"Anything else?"

"No, that's it."

"You heard a splash and some laughter. That's it. Thank you you've been most helpful." That last sentence was soaked through with sarcasm.

As I walked away the man shouted out at me. Something about my attitude. I should have gone back and apologised, but it would have just made me look worse. The cracks were starting to show.

My phone rang; it was Zara calling back. "All the other girls are okay," she said with a huge huff of relief.

"Has there been another murder?" she then asked.
"Yes. But I can't talk about it now. I've got to go."

After hanging up I remembered that I needed to speak with her about the painted over satanic mural I'd seen in Ramona's photograph.

Next Matt was waiting to speak with me; he had filled in his victim list:

Age – 18-25,
Height – 5 foot 7,
Weight – 119 lbs.,
Hair Colour Natural – Reddish Brown,
Ethnicity – White Caucasian

He went on: "A local girl matching this description was reported missing in the early hours. The parents are at the station. I'm worried that if they hear we've found a body, they will come here and cause a horrible scene in public." Not long after that, the body was released from the snaffle bits and put into an ambulance. The sandbags could not contain the rapid incoming tide and pretty soon the crime scene with all the footprints would be washed away.

I drove back to the station and as soon as I walked through the sliding doors a middle-aged man and woman approached me.

"You have found a dead body in the river. It may be our daughter, we want to see it." There was desperation in their eyes and terror in their voices.

"The body has been heavily disfigured by the water," I told them.

"We will recognise her, if it's her."

I hesitated, not knowing the correct procedure.

"WE DEMAND TO SEE THE BODY!"

The tension was killing them. I had to let them see the body.

I stood outside in the corridor as a medical officer took them into the room holding the body.

The two sets of loud and bitter crying told me

everything. I now had the task of having to get as much information as I could from these two distraught people. They told me that the dead girl's name is Angela Ashdown. "Why Angela? Why our little girl?"

I could not comfort them. There was no comfort for them. They had lost their beloved daughter and life for them would never be the same again.

Nevertheless I needed to get from them as much information as possible. I discovered that Angela was 19 and a Media Studies student at the University of Westminster. She lived at home with her parents. I needed to ask them whether she had been working as prostitute on the side, but I just could not bring myself to frame the question.

But the parents were able to immediately provide me with her mobile telephone number, email address, bank account details, list of friends, ex-boyfriends. From here I would be able to get her actual phone records from her phone provider, access to her email and bank activities. I would find out that way if she were leading a double life. The last time the parents had seen their daughter was the morning of the previous day at their home as she was setting off for University. Nothing was unusual except for her telling them that after college that day she was going to see an old school teacher from primary school who was sick – they couldn't remember the teacher's name.

But when the mother next spoke to their daughter on the phone at around 5.30 p.m., Angela was having a drink at the Student Union bar and she told the mother that she had put off going to see the sick schoolteacher until the following week. Instead she was going to her friend's house in the evening to watch DVDs and to expect her home at midnight. That was to be the last time the mother spoke to her daughter.

When Angela had not returned home at half

midnight – they assumed she had decided to sleep over at her friends'. But when they phoned to check they were alarmed to discover that Angela had not shown up – and had cancelled via text.

The parents were now very worried. The mother called their daughter again and again, and then starting calling as many of her friends that they knew. The father got in the car and drove around – going to the train station to pick up the last train from Waterloo. He even drove up to the student union bar in London, which by the time he reached it, had shut down many hours before.

So at 4 a.m. they finally called the police to report Angela missing. In the UK you don't need to wait for 24 hours to report a person missing, so the report was filed then and there.

Saturday 31st May 2014 – Afternoon

Matt and I walked into a buzzing incident room. The whole team had cancelled their Saturday and so we had a full house, chattering on the phone, occasionally shouting out at each other and bashing at their keyboards.

One of the team had drawn up a map of the crime scene, and another had created a map illustrating the proximity to the previous murder scene. Perhaps from looking at the two locations we could work out the kill location.

The two murder scenes were just less than two miles apart. Was the kill location somewhere between these two points? Or is that too easy and logical? Then, of course, there was the new tide chart that Matt had put together: What good looking at the tide chart would do, I don't know. It certainly hadn't helped any with the previous murder. But maybe there was a significance we hadn't seen yet. Maybe the killers are keen fishermen who study the tide.

It did at least give us an approximation of when the

body was fixed to the riverbed. We also had my mate, the houseboat resident who heard a splash and a laugh at 2 a.m. We would look at any nearby CCTV just before and after that time.

After looking at the tide chart, Matt found Angela's Ashdown Facebook page – her last posting had been at 10.34 Friday morning: *"A very unexpected blast from the past going to a mysterious reunion with Penny Dreadful"* Two friends had posted requesting a fuller explanation – which were not replied to.

I needed to speak with the two friends that Angela had blown out the previous evening. I needed the key facts immediately, so for expediency I phoned them first and the formal statements could come later.

The parents had given me both their numbers. I called Emily or "M" first. A well-spoken girl answered the phone. She was clearly in a shock and spoke slowly. She did not go to Angela's primary school and so had no idca who the sick schoolteacher might be. She also could not tell me who Angela was with at the SU Bar. "Talk to the Vix," she said. "Angela tells her absolutely everything."

Vix or Vicky was the other friend. She did not answer her mobile. I called her parents landline and she was sobbing when she got to the phone. I offered to go over there but she said she preferred to answer my questions then and there.

She told me that the teacher's daughter had called Angela out of the blue telling her that her mother was very sick and expressed a wish to see Angela as she had something very important to say to her. Angela had agreed to meet with the sick teacher the following day, but she later told Vix on the phone that after agreeing, she was going to cancel because she would rather spend her Friday night with her two friends.

Then Vix had seen the Facebook posting on the

Friday morning and had called Angela about it. Angela had told her that she had called the teacher's daughter to reschedule for the following week and the daughter was very insistent that she see her mother that Friday as she was critically ill. Angela had got the impression that the teacher was at death's door and would quite possibly not see the following week.

Her next contact with Angela was at 5 p.m. Friday. Angela texted: "I am going to the SU bar for a drink with Jack!!"

The SU Bar being the student union bar and Jack – a boy on her course she had an interest in. Jack was now a person of interest to me too.

Angela called from the bar to tell Vix that she was going to have another go at cancelling the meeting with the schoolteacher and daughter. She was going to have one more drink at the bar and she would be joining her two friends at around 8 p.m. She sounded perfectly sober and untroubled.

When Angela was a no show – Vix called Angela and got her voicemail. She left a message and a few minutes later got a text from Angela's phone that read. *"Not coming over now. C U soon."*

In the meantime Matt had obtained data from Angela's Oyster Card and Banking Switch card.

The Oyster Card on Friday 30th May logged a tube journey from Waterloo to Oxford Circus in the morning, as per her journey to University, and one going back to Waterloo at 18:14. We got this activity on her Switchcard:

5:31 p.m. £9 – Well Street Bar, University of Westminster

6:35 p.m. £17 – Waterloo Florists.

The Switchcard activity showed a purchase at the SU bar of £9 – two large glasses of wine perhaps. Then at 18:24

there was £17 spent at the Waterloo Florist. Maybe she was going to see the sick teacher after all.

We now had an excellent understanding with the phone companies. After my big shouting match over Daria, they would now provide us with everything we needed as quickly as possible, as long as they did not have to have any contact with me. So later that afternoon Matt received this report from the phone company:

What we can give you is a transcript of every text sent from Angela Ashdown's phone. Also because the voicemail messages to her are stored in the Cloud we can also get those for you. Her address book is also stored in the Cloud so you will also get her full set of contacts. However because her actual phone is missing we can't give you the full transcript of messages. We can't give you incoming calls, and incoming texts.

Now as you'd expect from studying the phone activity of a popular young lady there was tons of activity to sift through and I felt quite dirty doing it. From her texts and emails there was much talk about boys – but no boyfriend – secret or otherwise. This "Jack" is mentioned on three occasions. I discover that Angela likes him but she thinks he wears rather too much hair gel.

Angela's parents had told me she had a boyfriend with whom she had split up with just before she went to university. This was backed up in my trawl of her emails. There were a number of pathetic pleading emails trying to win her back. I would obviously be talking to this jilted ex. But there was no evidence or even hint of an "other" life – and certainly no evidence of any work as a prostitute. Instead she gave every impression of being a bright articulate young woman with excellent prospects.

My afternoon's work was interrupted by Hinton coming to see me alongside a thin tall bespectacled bird-like woman. It took me a good while to recognise her as Surrey

Police's Head of PR. She aggressively clucked at me, insisting I call a press conference first thing Monday because, most inconveniently for her, she was being inundated with phone calls from the press. This was ruining her weekend and she was talking to me like the murder was my doing. With light but detectable sarcasm I apologised and agreed to the press conference. She flashed her teeth in a grin of pure insincerity and dashed off.

I gave Hinty a rushed and slightly garbled overview of the case and the lines of enquiry thus far. He then told me "This is high profile now. You may well be taken off the case, and it will be given to someone more senior and experienced. I am sure you understand. But for now just keep running with the case until you get the nod."

That suited me just fine. Let someone else shoulder this awful responsibility. Let someone else be sick with worry. I wanted to be back on fraud anyway.

So I went back to sifting through Angela's phone records. She was frequently phoning and texting her two closest friends M and Vix – and all her other contacts were from the other friends in her address book. Apart from one. A three-minute outgoing call to this number 0771 354212 on Thursday 29th May at 8p.m.

I called the number and got a generic voicemail. Another pay-as-you-go. Pay-as-you-go are always suspicious. This phone had been registered to a Sadie Marks earlier in the week. Maybe this phone was set up purely for this murder.

Now this was clearly the person Angela was meeting on the Friday as we found these outgoing texts to the same number.

Friday 5:30 p.m. *Sorry about this had to study late may not be able to make it this evening.*

Friday 6.30 p.m. *On train due at 7.02*

Friday 6.55 p.m. *Pulling into station now.*

Okay, amateur sleuths where can I go with this info? Her first text was an attempt to cancel for the second time. We know she had received an incoming call after that which we can assume was from the "teacher's daughter" to persuade her to stick with the appointment. In her second text Angela was very precise about the train's arrival time – so she may have got this from the timetable or from customer information to arrange being picked up at the station. What we needed to do was look at the timetable for all trains leaving Waterloo at around 6.30 p.m. and due to arrive somewhere at the precise time of 7.02 p.m.

We spent half an hour in train timetable land (hog's heaven for Matt!) and this gave us a shortlist of three train stations – Hinchley Wood, Weybridge, and Woking. Now I had something to the appeal to the public about in my press conference.

Chapter 10

Surrey on Serial Killer Alert

Sunday 1st June 2014

I GOT HOME AT MIDNIGHT with the wife and son sound asleep. I did my best not to disturb them and curled myself down into the couch. I was up again at 6 a.m. Sunday morning. I didn't shave or shower and, throwing on whatever clothes were around, drove straight to the incident room.

I was alone in the incident room for a couple of hours, until around 9 a.m. when the incident room boys (and girls) came in, bringing in, along with their take-away coffees and pastries, a selection of the Sunday Papers. This killing had made one national tabloid front page: SURREY ON SERIAL KILLER ALERT. On page 5 of one of the "serious" broadsheets there was this: RIVER KILLER STRIKES AGAIN.

I instantly felt the itching rise around my elbows and right thigh. But I didn't need to read this salacious nonsense to find out what was going in the case – and neither do you. You've got the lead instigator to tell you what's going on, and something big is about to happen this morning.

I get a call from Angela's father. There was something unusual he had just remembered. Earlier in the week he had got a call from a cheerful upbeat young woman claiming to be from Angela's university. She wanted Angela's mobile number to tell her that a lecture was being cancelled. The father had offered to pass on her message but the lady, still very cheerfully, insisted on taking her mobile number to tell her directly.

He got suspicious when he spoke to Angela later that day. She had received no call from the university, and no lecture had been cancelled. In any case, the university already had her mobile number. With the approximate time and date of that call we could now trace that incoming number. That would indicate that Angela had been chosen, selected in the week before **and a woman was involved.** Next came a call to the incident room to report a sighting of a vehicle with no lights on, coming out of the bridge end of Walton Lane at just after midnight. You will notice from the map that Walton Lane is the road that runs parallel to the river. The reporting driver hooted at the vehicle which drove away. In the darkness he was unable to identify what sort of vehicle it was. The incident room scoured the CCTV around Walton On Bridge and they too saw a vehicle driving away from that vicinity with their lights switched off. But all they could make out was a moving black shadow, they were unable to get a read of the number plate or even take a guess at the vehicle type.

Throughout the day in dribs and drabs forensics came through with the following data on Angela Ashdown. As it came in, Matt put each piece of info on the board.

- She was not on the pill.
- She had not had sex in the last 24 hours.
- She did not smoke.
- No traces of any drug in the bloodstream.
- Traces of alcohol.
- Time of death assessed at between 10 p.m. and midnight.
- She was moved there – not killed in the river.
- Her hands had been tied and hung up.
- Her head caved in with a rock. Cause of death was blood loss from Hemorrhaging of the brain.
- The heavy metal staples are snaffle bits that are used on horses. *(Exactly as before.)*

- The snaffle bits were nailed in with a hammer. The nails were generic, can be obtained from any hardware shop.
- The photographs taken from above had once again revealed footprints consistent with size 9 Wellington boots.

Just after 10 p.m. I was about to turn in when my good friend, the clucking PR lady, called to remind me about the press conference. She wanted to see what I had prepared. I told her I hadn't written anything yet and that I would busk it on the day. She said that was not good enough and insisted I write something and email it to her for approval. So that would take care of the next couple of hours.

Monday 2nd June 2014 – Morning

I was in no mood for a press conference and to make matters worse an outraged Jane Barrow was there to harangue me outside the building. "I've been trying to contact you all weekend. I thought I was getting an exclusive!" "Jane, you must understand, I can't tell you things until ..." I struggled for words as I kept walking on with her snapping at my heels "... till I can tell you them." "What the fuck does that mean?" she hollered after me, as I pushed past a uniform, acting as security, and got into the incident room to look over my prepared statement one last time.

This second press conference was a sold out show, packed to the rafters with a frenzy of media holding cameras, lights and microphones all pushed in my direction. The dynamic was totally different from the previous time. At the first press conference it was me speaking to a handful of media (three to be precise) to make an appeal to the public for information. Now the media was out there in force to hassle me for sensational details about their serial killer. But I wasn't going to give that to them. It was really important to me that Angela's parents' suffering was not aggravated by the press. My prepared statement was glib and matter-of-fact. Here is how it goes:

"On Saturday the 1st June just after 2 p.m. the dead body of a young woman was found attached to the riverbed of the Thames just by Walton bridge. The young woman has been identified as Angela Ashdown, nineteen years of age, resident of Walton-on-Thames and a student at the University of Westminster…."

The constant cameras flashing were distracting, but I proceeded.

"We know that Angela was at Waterloo Station buying flowers at 6.30 p.m. And we believe that Angela was at one of these three train stations at around 7 p.m. Hinchley Wood, Weybrdige, Woking. Now she would have very likely been carrying those flowers that she bought."

"So my appeal to the public is this …" I pointed up at the large portrait of Angela behind me: "DID YOU SEE THIS WOMAN? We also need to speak with whoever was with her or saw her at the Student Union Bar at Wells Street."

You get the picture – a typical non-committal stick-to-the-facts police statement with an appeal for information.

As before, I did not mention the tarot card, and I did not mention the meeting with someone posing as the daughter of an old school teacher. The final part of my prepared statement was a load of huff about our determination to find the killer before he kills again. But before I got to the end, some rude fucker interrupted.

"Have you looked at previous murders with a similar MO?" The male voice was so loud I could not just brush it away and move on. I looked out at the sea of faces, camera lenses, and lights. "Well of course we have," I said.

"Well, what about the River Tyne murder of '94?

Could that be the work of this killer?"

I had a huge file on previous killings, but could not remember that specific one. I fumbled for something to say, something reassuring and meaningful, but instead my mouth opened and closed like a goldfish thrown out of its bowl. Matt the Stat came to the rescue "The River Tyne murder has only a passing resemblance to these two killings." He went on – "We are looking at murders in the UK, but also internationally, because this serial killer could be someone who recently moved to the country." Our serial killer could be an immigrant. *The Daily Mail* would love that, I thought.

But Matt was not finished "We have the very best database resources at our disposal and if there is a pattern from previous killings we will find it. But at the same time we must urge the public to play their part."

And so with a twist of his neck and a straightening of his shoulders Matt took over my press conference. "These women have been stoned to death. So the murders must have taken place somewhere secluded, even sound proofed. Anybody know any place like that where they have seen strange coming and goings? Anybody you know unaccounted for on Friday night and the night of Tuesday the 14th May? Anybody see any out of place vehicles along the river in the early hours of the nights in question? Please come forward with whatever information you have. Lastly – there is a killer out there – be vigilant. It is very likely he will choose the river again as his dumping ground. So you must keep an eye out on the rivers, especially at low tide at night."

I got the impression Matt had rehearsed all of this. After the press conference, Hinty came to see me to tell me that Top Brass had not yet allocated a senior detective to take over the case yet, so in the meantime it's "business as usual." He then introduced me to some bearded jerk who called himself a profiler from the Met. He ran through his findings, a misogynist – a power thing – wanting to put on a spectacle – quite possibly more than one involved. All mind numbingly obvious and nothing that got me anywhere closer to finding the people who did it. This was bullshit - we had some solid leads to follow up so I quickly scurried back to the safety hole of my incident room, before more time wasters like Hinge and Bracket showed up.

Meanwhile back at the incident room, Matt had put up this handy chart of the investigation:

Monday 2nd June 2014 – Afternoon

Matt drove to Angela's old primary school in Sunbury on Thames to get a list of Angela's teachers and class mates, while I headed to the West End to the Student Union Bar. I needed to find this "Jack."

The head barman remembered serving Angela and Jack. Jack is a regular who comes in most lunch times. I hung around and within fifteen minutes in walked a troubled looking slim young man with an explosion of hair gel. The barman gave me the nod, so I closed in on him.

"Am I suspect?" Jack asked wide-eyed as I introduced myself.

"At this stage everyone is a suspect. But if you don't answer my questions clearly and fully you will make top of list."

Jack gulped and proceeded to offer me as much information as he could. He'd been waiting all term to ask Angela out for a drink, and realizing that term was finishing very soon, he finally plucked up the courage to ask her that Friday. They walked to the SU Bar, talking about the course and making fun of the lecturers.

He bought her a glass of wine but was disappointed when she told him that she would have to leave very soon as she had to see a school teacher who was very sick and about to die. At first he thought this was just an excuse to get out of spending any more time with him, but it seemed like such an especially elaborate and odd excuse to make up, when she could have just said "I am seeing a friend."

They talked some more, they seemed to be getting on and as she talked she whizzed out a text. Apparently it was to the teacher's daughter. It was to tell her that her lectures were running very late and she will probably not be able to make it this evening. Jack then heard Angela call a friend and though she went outside for most of the call, he did hear her say that she had just had "another go at cancelling." When she came back from the call, she was smiling and she said to Jack – "I owe you a drink." She put two large white wines on her card and after two sips she got a call that she went outside for. When she came back she announced that she was going to have to drink up and go. She commented that the teacher's daughter really knew how to pull the heart- strings. Apparently she had laid it on thick that Angela must see the sick teacher before she died.

"I suppose I'd better get her some flowers," she had said. Jack tried to make her stay for one more, but she left him with her half full glass.

"Do you think that if she had accepted my drink, she would have lived?" Jack asked. "She may have lived longer," I said. "But it appears she was targeted. They would have got her eventually." This made it an untypical serial killing. On the way back to the station I called Matt to get an update on his progress at the primary school. He was checking up all the female teachers from ten years ago, but of those who were still alive – he had so far found none that were ill.

As I was stuck in traffic, edging my way inch by inch towards the nick only around the corner, I got call from the incident room boys. A nurse had called in after seeing our appeal for information, or should I call it the Matt the Stat show. On Friday evening the nurse had just finished her shift and was still in her nurses uniform as she grabbed a coffee from Puccino's the kiosk on the platform of Weybridge Station. A woman looking like Angela carrying flowers approached her and asked "Excuse Me. Are you Mrs. Warren's nurse?" Or at least the surname sounded like Warren.

I immediately called Matt still at the school and asked if any of the teachers at the school were called Warren. He said No. So what about any with a name beginning with W that could sound a bit like Warren? Yes a Mrs. Welham – now retired. Is she called Penny – as in Penny Dreadful from Angela's Facebook posting? Yes she is. Bingo! We had found our teacher. Penny Welham had in fact been Angela Ashdown's form teacher in her last year at the school. Her only daughter Martina was also at the school but in a different form in an earlier year.

Mrs. Welham is retired and was living in Norfolk but was not ill – terminally or otherwise. Matt phoned her again and she told him that her daughter Martina was now living in Staines. Matt got the impression they were estranged and when he asked about this, she replied with "I don't have much to do with her these days."

So next stop, Martina Welham – Staines.

Monday 2nd June 2014 – Evening

We traced an address for a Martina Welham in Staines. Matt and I drove over there, saying nothing on the way. Hoping for a speedy conclusion to this nightmare, knowing that for now, until the case got reassigned, it was all down to us.

Martina was living in a shared house in the drab part of Staines. She was holed up in her bedroom with her boyfriend playing video games. The room reeked of stale spunk masked by Lynx. She appeared listless, dull and an unlikely daughter of a school mistress. Martina claimed that she had spent the entire weekend in that room watching her boyfriend playing Call of Duty. "We can't afford to go out," explained the boy. Martina expressed complete surprise at the suggestion that she had met Angela Ashdown on Friday night. She claimed not to even know an Angela Ashdown until I reminded her that they went to Springfield primary school together.

Then recollection finally reached this girl's dreary sensibility. Although Martina recalled very little of Angela, she remembered that she was in the year above - Angela was a girl that everybody liked and was good at sports, good at classes and got good parts in the school plays. She had not seen Angela for ten years or more.

I took down Martina's phone number and unsurprisingly, it did not match the number that Angela had been texting. Though we had drawn a blank with Martina Welham herself, we had ourselves a very significant breakthrough - a chink of daylight in the darkness. Penny Welham and her daughter just had to be the cover to lure Angela. This meant that the killers must have knowledge of Angela's primary school and of the people who taught there.

When we got back to the incident room we found the back room boys hovering excitedly around a video monitor. Were they skiving? Not a bit of it. Now that we know from the nurse that Angela was at Weybridge Station at 7 p.m. on the Friday they were scouring the British Rail CCTV footage from that station.

As I watched with them, reception buzzed to tell me Jane Barrow was waiting to see me. Since the second murder she had been hovering all over this like a fly over an elephant's behind. I was about to go out there and talk to her – but then thought fuck it, I'm too busy. So I sent out two uniforms to get her thrown out. I needed to watch this CCTV.

On the platform camera we see a woman – looking like Angela carrying flowers leaving the train. She talks briefly to a woman in a nurse's uniform by the kiosk with the sign Puccino's and then moves away from the platform. Switch to the next camera showing the length of the covered bridge. It picks up the woman who might be Angela carrying the flowers. In among the procession of glum faced commuters, is anybody following her? Watching her? Not that we can see. Switch to the screen outside by the taxi rank, she is now with a woman in a different nurses uniform – she wears a nurses cap and glasses. This uniform appears to be light blue in colour with white collar and sleeves. She is of medium height but slightly shorter than the woman carrying the flowers, whom we are presuming to be Angela. The "nurse" walks slightly ahead, as if leading the way.

They walk past to the taxi rank. Switch to a camera that provides an exterior wide shot of the station. They appear to be getting into a vehicle that is just out of shot. It was if they knew that by parking their vehicle right there it would be just outside the CCTV camera's field of vision.

The lad at the controls rewound the video and freeze framed on the second woman in the nurse's uniform. Now in those Yankee TV shows, you'd get a hi-def zoom and all those rough pixels would transform into a crystal clear picture using the latest facial recognition software. Well if any of that technical wizardry exists at all, it has certainly not reached the Surrey Police yet.

So we were left staring at the video monitor, at a woman we couldn't make out going into a car we couldn't see.

They had told Angela to meet a nurse at the station, because if she had met the person claiming to be Martina Welham, Angela would have realised it wasn't her and smelt a rat. It was looking increasingly clear we were looking at an entrapment and abduction, involving this woman posing as a nurse.

I got someone to call Jane Barrow because we needed her for a specific appeal for information. Were you at Weybridge Station at 7 p.m.? Did you see this woman carrying flowers? Did you see the vehicle she went into? Did you see this woman with glasses in a nurses' uniform? Nurses' uniform. Hang about. When did a nurse's uniform crop up earlier in this investigation? Do you remembers readers? Wrack those little grey cells. I'll give you a moment or two.

It was when we searched Zara's Campbell flat. I dashed round there and rapped on the door. "Open up! Police!"

Zara opened up, with bags under her eyes the colour of coal.

"I've come to borrow your nurses' uniform," I said. She gave me a puffy eyed blank stare.

"Seriously. Where is it?" She let me in and I marched into the bedroom.

"I remember seeing it in here, along with the devil's outfit and the school uniform. Your role play collection" Zara rifled through the racks, then looked in the draws then in another cupboard. The school uniform, the French maid, and the horny devil were all present and correct but no nurse's uniform.

"I can't find it," she said eventually.

"Well that makes things interesting because a nurses uniform was used to entrap and abduct Angela Ashdown." Zara stared blankly at me with an "Oh!"

"Is that all you've got to say? Oh! Who's taken it? Where is it now?"

"I have no idea. I have all sorts of people come here. I can't keep a track of everyone."

"Well, you're going to have to give me a list of everyone, and I mean everyone, who has been here in the last two weeks."

Had Zara herself used the uniform and disposed of it? Possibly. But Zara is definitely not the fake nurse on the CCTV. Zara is noticeably taller, with a more muscular build with a thicker neck. Oh and she's black.

I then remembered I needed to quiz her about the Satanic mural and why she had it painted over. She was totally unfazed by the question – "It was weirding me out. Mallard painted it. I never liked it. Mallard went mental when he saw what I'd done. But fuck him. I have to live here."

I walked over to the living room entrance and looked at where the mural had been – over their heads. Now masked by several hastily daubed coats of Dulux.

"But why paint it over on the day you knew we were coming over for a search?" "I know you lot. You'd jump to conclusions. It's just a mural – that's all. Doesn't mean anything."

Nevertheless I was going to go back to the nick and get another search warrant and get CS to do an ultra-thorough toss of Madame Headlock's flat. Maybe they would find Angela Ashdown's DNA.

But I wasn't going to leave it there. I will also be ordering a phone tap on her landline and mobile number – and get my man Bremner to put a tail on her.

Chapter 11

What the BMX Kid Saw

Tuesday 3rd June 2014 – Morning

AT JUST BEFORE 10 a.m. I had a visitor – "It's that kid on the bicycle," reported the desk sergeant. The BMX Kid had a barney with the sergeant about bringing his bike into the station, so I found the BMX Kid waiting for me outside in the car park.

I wasn't in a position to entertain time wasters, so I gave it to him straight – "Look here, I'm not interested in any satanic conspiracy theory nonsense. Unless you've got something concrete for me, by that I mean proper information, then get on your bike and bother some other copper."

The BMX Kid eyed me impassively for a sec and then said: "I see you're having a bad day. So I'll keep this to the point. I am not saying I have found your killer. But this is definitely worth investigating." Now you will remember from this book's opening paragraph that The BMX Kid held some intrigue for me. So I said - "I'm listening."

"I went by Walton Bridge this morning. I had a look round."

"That's nice."

"I saw that same graffiti like the other murder scene."

"What graffiti is that then?"

"You remember. That stenciled swirling globe." He did a swirl with his hands. I did of course remember, but I had deemed it unimportant. He showed me the pictures on his camera phone.

"I mean is that just a coincidence?"

"Yes. Probably."

"Thing is. That same graffiti is near where those satanic rituals are held in Brooklands Park."

"Really?" I said flatly.

"Yes, really. In amongst loads of other Satanic stuff. You should go and take a look." So we headed over to Brooklands Park. He challenged me to a bet that he could get there before me. I declined; I don't gamble. Which is good because I would have lost. We set off. Me in my car and him in his two-wheeled chariot. I got caught up in the morning traffic, while he raced ahead, as ever the master of the highway.

As I eventually drove into the car park of Brooklands Park, The BMX Kid was beaming at me, straddling his prized vehicle. Still on his bike the BMX Kid led me through the undergrowth. As I followed, it got progressively deeper and overgrown. Where the hell is he taking me? Maybe it's an ambush. He led me towards an eighteen-foot high crumbling brick wall that cut across the park. Inside the wall about four foot up was a large round viaduct hole six foot in diameter – the BMX Kid placed his bike into the viaduct and pulled himself up and into it. He turned to me and gestured an offer to pull me up. I'm too proud, so I turned him down and attempted to pull myself up. It was quite a struggle but I got there after three tries. We walked through the dark viaduct, water dripping to create a pool on one side. We walked around it and jumped through to the other side.

Here were more trees, but about 30 foot in and away from the wall, four trees had been knocked down, sawn off or somehow removed, and a large slab of marble, seven foot by four foot, placed over the four stumps.

"This is where they've been doing it," pronounced the BMX Kid.

"Doing what?"

"The ritual of course. This is their altar. The last time they had a girl on there, she was blonde, I think they were about to do ... something to her."

I inspected the marble and the symbols scratched upon them. What were they? Pentacles, swirls, runes? I don't know what they were – see what you can make of them:

"I threw a rock at one of them," said the BMX Kid. "What did you do that for?"

"For a laugh. So they'd chase me. And they did. They came tearing after me like mad muthafuckers, shouting at me. I burned rubber through the tunnel. But my wheels were too fast for them." He tapped them fizzing with pride. He continued, "They kept after me. I rode to the top of the hill, looked back at them still chasing me and shouted out 'FUCK YOU SATANISTS!' and I bolted home." I congratulated him and he puffed out his chest.

"Exactly – 'Fuck You Satanists!' – who do they think they are? Performing them rituals – doing all that chanting...."

"This is all on that memory stick I gave you. I take it you haven't seen it then."

"I will be sure to dig it out when I get back to the nick to relive your glory." I asked, "Have you seen the pictures of Angela Ashdown, the last girl to be killed? Was it her on the altar?"

"Nah! This girl was blonde." The BMX Kid thought a bit – "Hey maybe I saved the girl. After I rumbled them – they thought we've been seen and canceled their killing for the night."

"Can you give me the date of this incident?" "Wednesday the 21st of May," he said with absolute certainty.

"Any idea of the identity of the people doing this ...

ritual?"

"No clue, I'm afraid. Unfortunately if you look at that memory stick I gave you, you can't make out any of the faces or nothing. You really had to be here."

I went back and examined the marble slab, taking another look at those scratched in symbols. I then did a 360 look around from the viewpoint of the altar. I saw trees, bushes, decaying concrete, and spray paint graffiti on various trees and stonewalls. I saw more symbols. Then directly to the left on the brick wall I saw that stencil globe that had been seen at both of the murder sites.

"Have you seen it?" asked the BMX Kid, pointing at the black swirling globe graffiti reaching out to me. As I looked at it I felt a tingle, a buzzing sense of discovery that everything was falling into place. Like the sun appearing in between the stones of Stonehenge and lighting up a path of discovery. Yet what this discovery actually was, I had no idea.

I took photographs of the swirling stencil globe graffiti and emailed them to the Enviro Crime unit. So we had ourselves a potential murder site. I called CS to search the altar and the surrounding area around for blood, and the DNA of any of the two victims.

Ten minutes later Enviro Crime emailed back. They know the kid behind the swirling globe graffiti. He goes by the tag of OzMan and they had served an ASBO on him six weeks ago. Further information on OzMan came through while I was in the car stuck in the usual traffic. OzMan's real name is Keith Reynolds. He is just 17 years old and he lives in Walton on Thames.

Tuesday 3rd June 2014 – Afternoon

If you want to get on the right side of a copper always offer them a cup of tea. We often don't accept but it's a nice welcoming gesture. Stats from the Met show that you're

30% less likely to be charged if you offer a policeman a cup of tea when he comes through your door. Keith a/k/a OzMan offered me tea and even threw in some Garibaldi biscuits. He was tall, thin, with razor sharp cheekbones. He readily admitted to his stencil work at both the murder scenes and at Brooklands Park. In fact, you could tell he was very proud of his "tag."

He spoke in that rolling deep barely intelligible West Indian "urban" tone – "Thing is right. That tag can be found all over the shop. Drive from here you'll find it near Sainsbury, near the station, near the library. It's my tag, innit? That's why I got my ASBO."

"So when did you tag the locations I mentioned?"

"'Bout two months ago. My court case was a month ago. They haven't got around to painting over them yet. I guess they'll get me to do it myself with my community service."

"So you've had to give up your art now?"

"No way." He took me to his garage, which in fact was his Mum's garage, now turned into a studio for his stencil art. He showed me a book of artwork symbols similar to the one we were talking about – "This guy is where I get my inspiration. Austin Osman Spare. He's the don." And he showed the page of similar looking symbols. I would get the incident room boys to thoroughly check him out and his alibis, but my instinct told me that this kid was an artist, whose only weapon was a spray can. Just one thing made me suspicious of this young man, so I had one final question.

"So, OzMan, I looked at your file. You were born in Surrey, went to school in Surrey, lived all your life in Surrey."

"Yeah?"

"So why do you speak in that accent?"

He struggled to answer that one: "It's just the way I talk."

On the way back to the station I observed his stencil graffiti near the train station and the wall of Waitrose, one by where the town hall used to be, and along the shopping center car park wall. His tags are at places close to the murder scenes and rituals only because his tags are everywhere in the area.

Chapter 12

Welcome to Slaughter on Thames

Wednesday 4th June 2014 – Morning

AT 10:30 a.m. I had CS on the line. They had spent the last two hours thoroughly scouring the altar at Brooklands Park where the rituals had taken place. They found nothing of interest. No blood, not even any bleach or any other cleaning agents.

Roy the silver fox head canary boy was emphatic: “No bloodshed, no violence, and no murders have taken place at this location.”

The next call was Jane Barrow, I immediately pressed REJECT. When I played back the message a few minutes later, I was expecting another hounding message about her illusive exclusive. Instead she was palpitating with excitement.

“Ferdy – we’ve had a letter ...” pause, as she gathered her breath “... from the killer. Come over immediately.”

I sprinted over there and was led to Jane and her male editor in his office. Wearing bright yellow Marigolds, Jane handed me with a pair of tweezers, a sheet of folded A4, laser printed on one side in black on a Times font.

Welcome to Slaughter On Thames
(twinned with Dangereusement In Seine)

This is from the deepest waters of the river, where you will find much worse things than the foul stench of rotting fish and plankton.

This is from the darkest bowels of the underwater streams where pure evil thrives.

The water keeps rolling, it knows too much, seen too much and now it's payback time.

Be warned, stray too close to the river you will be sucked in and it will spit you out.

Just ask Daria and Angela. No you can't they're dead. Their souls were offered to me and I presented them back to you by the tide.

The parents of Angela took their daughter to the slaughter. While Daria's heart was made of Brass.

I won't stop and I cannot be stopped. I gouge out their eyes, put death in their mouths, and strap them to the riverbed.

Everything will come out on in the wash.

Who's Next?

The Slaughter on Thames Killer

~ ~ ~

"Do you think it's actually from the killer?" asked Jane. "Probably not. Nevertheless, I am going to need to take this in for fingerprints and DNA. Do you have the envelope it came in?"

Jane gave me the white envelope holding it with tweezers. I took over the tweezers and looked at the postmark ESHER.

"It's going in Friday's edition," said the editor, "and we are going to put it up on the website later today."

I took photographs for my own records and would transcribe the letter. Maybe the choice of words might reveal something about the killer. Or at least the person who wrote it. I arranged for CS to come over and pick up the evidence and for a junior to take statements from Jane and the editor.

Walking back to the nick, my head twitched with niggling thoughts. Both bodies were dumped on my patch. Who knows my patch? How about the man who covered that patch before me? Bremner.

Then I thought back about Roger Farrady. It would seem that "they" had attempted to frame him for the first killing. Who pushed me to him as a suspect? Bremner, with his weirdo file. And he was especially narked when I told him that Matt and me had ruled him out. Yes – he was majorly annoyed by that.

Both bodies were revealed by the tide at times that were most inconvenient for me. The first ruined my meal coming off my 7-day egg diet. The second ruined my day with my son. Who knew that revealing the body at those times would do that? Bremner possibly. I had told him about my 7-day egg diet. Or was I getting paranoid?

I callcd up Bremner and we met at our usual place the caff in Addlestone. I wanted to observe him. He reported back to say it appeared to be 'Business As Usual' at the CarPhone Whorehouse. A new girl recently joined the firm to replace Daria an erotic dancer poached from the Molesey scene. Bremner describes her as blonde, with straight hair, long eyelashes – and "very doable."

At the Percy Arms Bremner had got chatty with the sandy haired landlord who told him that he had been struggling for years to make his pub work. He'd done all the social media and even arranged events like a pub Olympics. All to no avail and that mountain of debt kept growing. So when the CarPhone Whorehouse opportunity came up, he grabbed it with both hands. He gave them a back room in the basement behind the pumps – where Mallard counts up all the money and updates his records.

Talking of that one-glove-wearing scroat Andy Mallard, Bremner had also got on friendly terms with him.

"He's completely weird, but once you get to know him, he's actually a good bloke!"-I asked if he'd overheard anybody talking about the Angela Ashdown case. "Not that I heard," was Bremner's reply. "They just seem to be going on as normal."

I then told him to do his best to get invited to Madame Headlock's parties and keep an eye out on her. "This is important," I told him. "Go to the Percy Arms Friday night and ask if Madame Headlock is having a party and just go straight over there, and stay right till the end and observe. I badly need intel on what's going in that flat." I then gave Bremner an overview of recent developments – the entrapment of Angela, the tantalizing CCTV footage, the nurses uniform and the Slaughter On Thames letter sent to the *Surrey Star*.

Bremner then offered some more of those priceless pearls of advice – "You should go back to the weirdo file," he said with dogged self-assurance. "It's now clear you are dealing with a local fellow, with a local history. How about that letter post marked from Esher? That's a specific MO – a nutter in the Esher area who likes to write taunting letters."

Wednesday 4th June 2014 – Afternoon

Bremner and his weirdo file. Ha! I didn't go back there, but with Monday's press conference grilling still smarting I decided to take a deeper look for other murders with a similar modus operandi. Scrutinizing the list and re-scrutinizing it, I narrowed the search down to murders along the river and it threw up this unsolved case in Maidenhead in 2003.

Escort girl Andrea Perry's murder bore only a passing resemblance to our two killings, the body was found in the shallow waters of the river Thames, heavy trauma to the head from objects that could have been rocks. But that was it. There were none of the specific trappings, no eye removal, no affixing the body to the riverbed, no ligatures and no tarot card.

There was a court case but the man was acquitted – insufficient evidence against him and DNA evidence pointing towards another unknown perpetrator. I checked out the acquitted man. He looked the part in his mug shots – an unshaven mountain of a man with a face of cold malevolence that would bring a squeak to the pants of the hardest of men. But Nick Shoosmith committed suicide in 2007 by leaping off a bridge.

I next looked at solved killings with a passing similar MO. Maybe the law had got the wrong collar, or he had got out, or had an accomplice that was not caught. This kept me occupied for the rest of the day, and as I sat there the knot in my stomach tightened. The 48 hours on the second killing was up and I was terrified of going off on a time wasting tangent that would derail and eventually destroy my investigation. I felt like I was running through a tunnel with no light at the end. When the fuck was Hinty going to give me the tap and take me off this case?

I got home to find that Luis had turned in for an early night. He had his big day tomorrow, the borough sports cup final, and I of course would put everything on hold to be there.

I stayed up to watch TV alone. The news came on, showing videos of Angela. Playing musical instruments, performing in a play. Then they played back her voice – a voicemail message to her parents. Her voice was lilting, joyous. Even in my downtime I felt the pressure increasing.

Thursday 5th June 2014 – Morning

Believe it or not, I gave myself a lie in this morning, and got to the incident room at a most decadent time of 9.30 am.

This time the boys and girls were having a riot. They were quite literally dancing around with excitement. This is because Angela's smart phone was not a mere pay-as-you-go and so this meant the phone company were able to give us a lot more intelligence on her phone data. The company had provided us with some detailed Cell Site Analysis. Now with this data we could run a triangulation of masts exercise and get a very good approximation of Angela's location when she received her last phone call and where the phone was when the last text was sent back. Now for the incoming call. She was 600 meters distance from Mast A, 1200 meters distance from Mast B, and 800 meters from Mast C. Time to get your dividers out people.

And the location it gave us was somewhere around Kenton Avenue. Do you recognise where that is? It's the neighbourhood of the Cat Sanctuary, close to where we believe Daria was abducted.

Angela's friends had called her at 20:06 – the text back had come back 4 minutes later. So we now had an almost definite location for Angela's phone at this time. I immediately ordered an exhaustive search of the area. The team was to knock on every door of every house and every business. On the drive there I called Ann MacLean the lady who sells Cat Sanctuary. Had she seen anyone around the place on the Friday evening at around 8p.m.? Unfortunately she was not able to help, she had been out on a date, and not got back until just gone 1 a.m.

When I got there I very apologetically told Ann MacLean that for the next 6 hours we would be sealing off the entrance to her street as it was now believed to be a crime scene. I offered to send someone to the supermarket for her and get some supplies.

But after six hours of exhaustive door to door, pushing people to comment on anything unusual on Friday evening we got nothing. Maybe the killers were just passing through. Then I looked at my watch, it was 4 p.m., and I had missed Luis's football match. I called Cassie to find out the score. Disaster! They had lost 4 nil and with Luis playing in the back four, he had to shoulder some of the responsibility. When I got home Luis was in his room. He had declared that he did not want to have anything to do with the sport of football ever again, and was the very picture of glumness. I tried my best to cheer him up with examples of teams that got thrashed and came back stronger than ever, but he wasn't having any of it. I wanted to tell him to get a grip and snap out of it, that losing the borough sports football final was meaningless compared to the misery and suffering I was dealing with, but I left it.

Cassie turned in to watch TV on the portable in the bedroom, leaving me in the living room alone. The TV was showing even more images of Angela. The big pile of flowers left at her resting ground by the Bridge. More happy home videos. This news item even extended to mentioning the Slaughter On Thames letter. They had hired some gravelly voiced moody actor to do the voice. "I gouge out their eyes, and put death in their mouths...." They then reported that the Surrey police "were scrambling around for clues." Miss Aviary the PR lady would love that.

Friday 6th June 2014 – Morning

So the cover story on that Mickey Mouse rag of a local paper the *Surrey Star* was the Letter from the Slaughter on Thames killer. They reprinted the text of the letter in full, with a photo of it. Just what I needed to ramp up a bit of extra pressure.

As a result, there was a flotilla of press outside the station, all of them specifically waiting to speak to me, the poor sod in charge of the case, expecting any day now to be relieved of his duties. Hinge and Bracket had left a telephone message for me, wanting to talk. The letter had apparently validated their satanic theory and they wanted to tell me about the revealing clues in the text.

At my desk I read and reread the Slaughter On Thames letter. But when the Forensics team came in all excited to tell me they had found a partial fingerprint on the letter, I did not share their excitement. Instead I went over to the *Surrey Star* offices and demanded to see Jane Barrow alone.

With just us two in her editor's office, I held up her paper and told her flat that I knew who had written it.

She looked confused. I then told her that she had written it.

Jane put on an I-can't-believe-you'd-say-that face. But, of course, the proof was the "I put death in their mouths" line. I had told only Jane about the death Tarot card.

"Not necessarily," came back Jane. "Somebody on your investigation – or the killer would know about it."

"I told you – and only you – it was the death card. The card in their mouths was actually 15 – The Devil."

She tried to wriggle out of it. But she had nowhere to hide and she eventually broke down and confessed.

She tried to explain why she did it – something about needing a big story. She wanted a scoop before the nationals took over the coverage. She needed a circulation boost for the *Surrey Star* because she was offered shares in the paper as they couldn't afford to give her a wage rise. She even indirectly blamed me for not having given her any exclusive information.

She blabbered on.

But I wasn't interested in any of that, instead I was now thinking about how I could use this to my advantage. "I could report this, and it would destroy you and your career," I put in a long dramatic pause, I could see it was agonizing for her, "but I won't."

She looked up at me beseechingly. Yes, I am a softhearted old Hector. The truth is, I like this woman and I did not want to destroy her life and career even though she had brought it on herself. But I also smelt the whiff of opportunity, and had a cunning plan up my sleeve. This is what I said next: "Instead, I will be calling in a series of favors. The first is a little one and it involves my son who played in a football match yesterday."

Chapter 13

Too much of a coincidence

Friday 6th June 2014 – Afternoon

"TOO MUCH OF A CONCIDENCE," Matt said to me for the fifth time in as many minutes. I had just told him that I had rumbled the Slaughter On Thames letter as a hoax, which he shrugged off with a "I knew that already." Instead Matt had a bee buzzing away in his bonnet over a series of "coincidences."

It was all about the Cat Sanctuary. This refuge for lost moggies that was frequented by Daria, and had just cropped up again in the investigation as the approximate location of Angela's phone at 8 p.m.

If you forgive the word play I thought he was barking up the wrong tree on this one. "Matt, mate, I went into the woman's cottage." I reasoned with him. "It's smaller than many people's shed. You literally couldn't swing a cat in there. It's certainly not a venue for ritualistic killings."

But the coincidences were piling on for Matt, as he pulled out a book called *"The Evil Church."* It looked suspiciously like the sort of trash Hinge and Brackett would have written.

"Have you heard of the TCT – the Transcendental Church of the Transformation?" Matt asked.

"Is that anything to do with John Travolta's lot?"
"They had connections to the Church of Scientology but they broke away in the 1960s. A man and a woman founded the Transcendental Church in San Francisco. They believed that you should worship Satan as much as you worship God, because they are two sides of the same coin."

"Have you been talking to Hinge and Bracket?"

"No. I've been doing my own research." Matt continued "The church's symbol is two T's – like the horse snaffle bits that pin down the victim's hands and feet to the riverbed." He placed this graphic on the board.

"There's also loads of stuff in their scriptures about water, transformation and becoming." I wasn't used to the normally sensible Matt getting all feverish like this. "Matt, do you need to lie down?" I offered.

He declined and went on – "This is the church that has suspected links to Charles Manson, the Zodiac and the Son of Sam Killings."

"And you think that batty old cat lady is behind all of that as well? Listen Matt, she doesn't come across like the satanic killer type."

"I think there's more there if we dig deeper. The Transcendental Church of Transformation was founded by a young couple." He opened up *The Evil Church* and showed me a grainy black and white photo of a man and a woman in their twenties. The text read – *Joshua and Anna De Ren returning to London 1962*. Matt pointed at Anna De Ren – "Could that not be Ann MacLean? Their names are similar."

"Ann and Anna yes similar names are not the same names though."

"Ren means Clean in Swedish. MacLean. De Ren Coincidence?" He pushed the photo in my face. "Look closely at the photograph. It could be her."

"Well, it's such a bad photograph it could be her, but it could just as easily be Gaffney."

"How about if Ann MacLean is Anna De Ren under an assumed name?"

"Yeah? Well how about if John Gaffney is Anna De Ren under an assumed name?"

"I have another coincidence for you."

"I'm listening." I said, though I wished I wasn't.

"The Transcendental Church dissolved in 1984 when Joshua De Ren died and became ... wait for it...."

"Yes Matt I am waiting."

"The Heart of Gold Animal Shelter. All the leading people went underground and the only public face of what was left of the church became this animal shelter."

I remained unconvinced as he showed me the passage in the book.

"Look! We know for a fact that a woman is behind these killings because a woman entrapped Angela. A woman met Angela at Weybridge dressed as a nurse. Could that woman not be Anna MacLean? She was supposedly out that night. Have you checked her alibi?"

I thought about this for a second. Still not convinced. "Has this got anything to do with your phobia of cats?" "Nothing to do with it whatsoever."

"So. What do you want to do about it?"

"I want to go over and ask that woman some hard questions."

"You are going to conquer your fear of cats to talk to this woman? I admire your pluck!"

So we went to see this Ann MacLean woman. When we got there, Matt got out and purposefully rang the bell, staring straight ahead and avoiding the stare of the dreaded cats. When Ann MacLean opened, he said. "I am Detective Inspector Wolgrove. I must speak with you alone. In a room without cats. "She took us to the living room and shut the doors and windows, leaving the cats to form a posse outside.

"What is your real name?"

"Ann MacLean."

"Have you ever gone by the name of Anna De Ren?" "Not that I recall."

"Ah! So you have."

"No I haven't. I've only ever been Ann MacLean – apart from when I was married...."

"Yes married to Robert De Ren."

"No – a Trevor Simpson."

Matt pulled out the book with the photograph.

"Why are you showing me this photograph?" She asked.

"Are you not the woman in that photograph?"

Ann looked at the photograph and smiled. "That woman is flat chested. I don't like to boast, but I have an ample bosom. Plus I'm old – but I'm not THAT OLD. I was 14 in 1962. That woman is obviously older." But Matt was unrelenting.

"Have you ever been a member of the Transcendental Church of Transformation?"

"No – never been a member of any church."

"Have you ever been a member of any cult?"

"I was in the girl guides. Does that count?" And with that Ann began laughing. It was so infectious I cracked up as well.

I was still drying my eyes when we got back to the car. Matt said to me "I would appreciate if you told nobody about this ... episode."

I gave him my word. Poor old Matt had fallen victim to Bremner's apophenia, demonstrating that it can happen to the best of us.

On the drive back he was silent and still in obvious and very understandable deep embarrassment. Eventually I said to him, "Matt, listen, the last month has been very rough. If you want to take a couple of days off..."

Matt looked at me insulted. "No way. I am going to bounce back from this." So with a massive tail swinging between his legs Matt went back to the incident room to hit Holmes2 and to start sifting through Angela's records.

At around 8 p.m. the incident room cleared as

everyone went to the pub. I left at 10 p.m. to go straight home to my unloving wife and deeply despondent son, leaving poor old Matt all alone in the incident room.

Saturday 7th June 2014 – Morning

So with my son Luis still being the Incredible Sulk over the Borough Sports and Cassie being her usual sour faced self, my pleasant Saturday morning at home was disturbed by a phone call from Matt. "I have found something REALLY important this time."

Just like a stopped clock tells the right time every 12 hours, sometimes the most solid and reliable timepiece can go a bit silly once in a while. So even after yesterday's debacle, I was going to give Matt the benefit of the doubt on this. "I went through a list of Angela Ashdown's class mates – not just her last year, but her second to last."

Okay, sleuths. Here's your chance to prove how eagle eyed you are. Have a gander yourself at this list of her female classmates and tell me what jumps out:

ADAMS, Janice
ASHDOWN, Angela
BATHENAY, Francine
BELLCHAMBERS, Sarah
GREEN, Theresa
JARMAN-BROWN, Christine
PATEL, Priti
PETERS, Beverley
SMITH, Jane
TAYLOR, Rebecca
TELADIA, Hawa
UNSWORTH, Helen
WADEY, Kirsti
ZACHARY, Mandy

~ ~ ~

Rebecca Taylor – could that be Becky Taylor? Becky of course being the commonly used abbreviation of Rebecca. Becky is nineteen the same age as Angela Ashdown. Matt went on – "I looked at the class photo from 2002 and I am definitely not getting apophenia this time. It's the same girl. I can tell by her eyes. She has a very distinctive piercing glare. It was all there. We just had to look properly." He declared. I was silent – processing, as he went on. "I called the headmistress from that time. Rebecca Taylor was a problem child and she attacked Angela after school. Angela reported the attack, and Rebecca then got sent to another school. Which is why she wasn't on the register for Angela's final year." I was silent – still processing.

"I've just called Angela's parents. They remembered the name Rebecca Taylor and the incident from primary school. This is what happened - Rebecca got nicknamed the Goblin by the other girls at school, because she was short and impish. Angela had written a Harry Potter type play and had a Goblin character in it, which Rebecca took as being a dig at her, and that's why Becky attacked her."

I was silent – impressed.

Now the fact that Becky a/k/a Rebecca knew Angela and had a "beef" with her does not necessarily mean she is behind her killing. But why has she not come forward to say anything? I left my happy home and got in my car. As soon as I got to the office, I got a warrant raised to search the premises and phone of Rebecca a/k/a Becky Taylor. Now I was going to play it smart and crafty on this one. So I got Becky's address and drove over there. She lived in Feltham, in a scuzzy block of flats that was just over a mile away from the CarPhone Whorehouse set up.

Outside the flats I called her. I did not expect her to pick up, so I left this message.

"Hullo, Becky? Inspector Ferdy of Surrey Police. I need you to answer some questions. I am especially keen to locate the nurses uniform that went missing from Zara's flat. Would it be okay to come over in a couple of hours – say about 3p.m.?"

And with that I watched her front door. Within ten minutes she was out the door and walking away at great speed. I dashed out of my car and stopped her at the lift. She was carrying something in a black dustbin bag and a look of panic flashed across her face when she saw me. "Hello Becky – thought I'd come over early. What's in the bag?"

Can you guess what it was? A NURSES UNIFORM! I instantly called the Incident room to get them to send a screen grab of the fake nurse at Weybridge station. I don't like to blow my own trumpet, but who else is going to do it? I was especially clever on this one. I had a search warrant on Becky's place, but had I dived straight over there, we would have found the nurse's uniform and her lawyer would have just said 'coincidence!' and most likely got away with it. But by catching her leaving the flat with the nurse's uniform an hour before she knew the police were coming around would strongly indicate that she was disposing of the uniform because she knew it was evidence against her. Pretty smart eh?

With my full name being Colin Ferdinand, as you'd expect the boys down the nick call me Ferdy. I've tried to get them to nickname me Ferdy the Fox, on account of my excellent track record in solving fraud. I've tried subtly, and then not so subtly (as in 'why don't you fuckers call me Ferdy the Fox'). I've even resorted to bribery, but like Diana Ross, I'm still waiting. Now if this coup isn't worth calling me 'Ferdy the Fox' I don't know what is.

I had another go of getting this prized nickname when talking to Matt in the car. But Matt was having none of it "you have been called many things in your time – but no one will ever call you Ferdy the Fox." He was beaming.

Our exchange was light hearted and humorous. We had ourselves a major breakthrough in the case and we both knew it.

Becky was taken back to the nick for some very hard questioning, while I let the boys rip open her front door with their big banger. They get upset if they don't get a chance to use it at least one a month. WOSH! The door crumbled in like cardboard and we waded in.

The interior was all Ikea – neat and tidy. The pictures on the walls were abstract representations of flowers –nothing to reveal an obsession with sadism or the satanic. It had all the appearance of a rented place, where the person who lived there was never fully at home.

I looked at her shelves, some books on cats, some DVDs on cats. But no cat. I opened a few draws to find a load of notes messily stashed, and a few wraps of powder, while the search parties opened every other set of drawers. We found lots of books and papers on psychology. Turns out she really was studying for a degree at the Open University.

We moved on to the bedroom, soft feminine colours, underwear and socks on the floor. Once again nothing to jump out as proof positive to her being a ritualistic killer. So I let the lads continue the search while I went back to speak to my top suspect.

Her phone was taken away from her and she was thoroughly searched. In her wallet they found a folded Tarot Card – number 15, The Devil – the same illustration as the ones found in the mouths of Daria and Angela. Like the nurses uniform this was linking her to the murders but not quite the case closed evidence I needed to put the lid on this case.

So we sat Becky down in the interview room. She was looking down, staring at the table. I turned the video on and I began.

"So Becky. Tell me about your row with Angela Ashdown in primary school. "

"I want a lawyer."

That to me immediately rang the guilty bell.

"That's your right. But don't you want to explain any of this?"

"I want a lawyer."

"Where were you on the night of Friday the 31st?"

"I want a FUCKING lawyer." She growled.

I called the interview, such that it was, to a close and Becky was given her phone call. To quote Matt from the previous day, the tarot card and the nurse uniform were just "too much of a coincidence" for her not to be involved in these murders. She had almost definitely posed as Martina Welham but there must also be an accomplice, someone with a vehicle, with a secluded premises.

With Becky doing a Tommy (that's police slang for someone doing a deaf, dumb and blind act) we had to hope that the search would throw up something else incriminating beyond the nurses uniform and the tarot card. With Becky meeting with her lawyer, I met up with Hinton and our briefs Chapman & Hendy – who I used to very un-amusingly refer to as Chapman & Bendy. This meeting was very much on the serious side, so I kept my playground humor to a minimum. The suited posh lady from Chapman & Bendy (sorry Chapman & Hendy) told me categorically that we needed more evidence and without it we could not take her to trial. The heat was well and truly on.

Late in the afternoon I had my second interview with Becky Taylor, this time with her lawyer present, but I knew how this would play out.

"I have a video footage of you wearing that nurses uniform leading Angela Ashdown to her death." (This, of course, dear reader, is a bluff. We couldn't identify anybody from that poxy CCTV.)

"No comment."

"Where were you on the night of Friday the 31th May?"

"No comment."

I even threw a bit of light relief.

"Matt looks good in that jumper – don't you think?" "No comment."

Becky did not look at me or Matt once. She either stared down at the table or towards the door. I tried another angle. I was thinking of those size 9 Wellington Boots, the fact that Becky apparently did not drive or have access to a vehicle. She must have an accomplice, most probably a male. If only I could get her to grass up that accomplice. "Look. I know that your silence is most probably out of fear. Fear of the person who committed these murders with you. We can turn this around. Tell me who your accomplice is and I can offer you witness protection. Who else is involved?"

"No comment."

I stared hard at her; she continued to avoid my gaze. "Did you throw the stones? Did you gouge the eyes out? How much of it did you do?" I showed her the forensic pictures from the first crime scene. "This is your friend Daria."

"No Comment."

On top of the pile I added some more forensic pictures of the second murder "This is Angela – you went to school with her."

"No Comment."

"Did you really hate her that much?" "No Comment." Eventually I said: "Now if you are innocent you would want to try and explain away all this. But if you don't, I can only assume the worst."

"My client is exercising her right to silence." Said her

lawyer.

"Ah! Somebody speaks."

"My client is also demanding damages for her front door." "Well, she won't be needing her front door. That's because I am charging her with the murder of Angela Ashdown. Her front door from now on will be a big heavy metal cell door. Take her away."

I needed more evidence, and fast, or else I was going to look sillier than Humpty Dumpty after his fall and with more egg on my face.

Sunday 8th June 2014 – Morning

I got to the incident room this morning to discover that those lazy fuckers in Surrey Vice had actually dragged themselves away from their desks and raided the Percy Arms, nicking all the girls from the CarPhone Whorehouse. I was fuming. I needed to continue observing this set up to find out exactly what was going on, and this had ruined all of that. But something very curious had come out of the searches – each and every girl was found with a Tarot Card of the Devil on them.

When asked about it, most had said nothing. But one girl – Polly Webster (remember her, the gold digger) had said, "It's our membership card." One woman not arrested from the scene was Zara Campbell. So I went over there for a friendly visit. I knocked on the door and got no answer. All the lights were out, as I walked away I remembered the long suffering neighbour – who kept on saying 'I'm not being funny." I knocked on her door.

She was in, still wearing the hat tea cozy, and I asked her some more about the parties she had complained about. "What sort of music do they play at these parties?" "It's not the music that bothers me. I can stick the music. It's when they start all that chanting."

"Chanting? Chanting what? Like football chants?"

"No like a monks' chant. THE DEVIL WILL HAVE HIS TOLL – they kept saying over and over. I'm not being funny but it been making me go all batty. I even find myself going round the shops saying it – THE DEVIL WILL HAVE HIS TOLL, THE DEVIL WILL HAVE HIS TOLL, THE DEVIL WILL HAVE HIS TOLL – like a proper mad woman."

Chapter 14

Mallard – I Have a Dream

Monday 9th June 2014

ALL OF MONDAY WAS GOING to be devoted to gathering evidence on Becky, by interviewing all of her associates, from primary school right through to the CarPhone Whorehouse. But my plans changed when I encountered a pair of wild staring eyes waiting for me at the station reception. They belonged to Andy Mallard Space Cadet, still wearing that one leather glove.

"You know it's not a good idea to come and see the cops when you've been on a drug binge." I said.

"Who's been on a drug binge? I've come to tell you about this dream I had. I saw how Daria and the other girl were killed. It may help you catch the killer." I looked at him through narrowed suspicious eyes.

"Go on then. But I should warn you – wasting a police officer's time is a criminal offence."

I sat him down in the interview room and he appears totally serious. Completely insane mind, but nevertheless totally serious. "I saw it all last night. It was awful, the gruesome detail they showed me. My two angels carried me over to where the body was found."

"Your two what?"

"My two angels. They come to me in my dreams and they show me stuff."

"And last night they showed you the murder of Daria." He nodded. I motioned to Matt to turn on the video recorder and I gave a quick formal intro.

"Okay, Mr. Mallard – so what did you see?"

"I saw Daria being killed. It was horrible because I couldn't stop it. I could only watch. She was blinded, screaming. They strung her up and used a woodwork chisel to gouge her eyes out."

"They? Who are they?"

"I couldn't see clearly. I just know there were two of them."

"A man and a woman? Or two men?"

"I told you. I couldn't see clearly. But I could hear it. The screaming. The screaming was blood curdling. They then stepped back about twelve feet away and started throwing rocks at her head. Throwing rock after rock after rock. Every time a rock hit, her head would jolt – and they would cheer. After a while she stopped screaming."

"Where was this?"

"In the woods."

"Which woods?"

"I think it was Brooklands Park. It would be useful if we went there, it would help me remember what they showed me."

So we switched off the video camera, and set off for the woods in two cars. Me, the dreaming nutter and Matt holding the video camera in one car, followed by two uniforms in the second. Mallard led us deep into the woods – and reaching a clearing looked around. He stared at a tree as if he was listening to it tell him something. Eventually he declared: "I sense it happened here."

"This spot? You sure?"

"No. But it's a place like this, surrounded by trees. Far away from any houses so no one could hear the screams."

"So it wasn't here. It was a place like here."

"Yes, but it could be here."

"Good. Well, I'm glad you're not being at all vague about this." He then ran towards a pile of rocks beside a tree.

"I sense the murder weapons were in this pile. The rocks came from here. One of these rocks may well have been one the murder weapons." He picked one rock up and shook it slowly up and down as if trying to guess its weight. "No – it wasn't that one." He put it down again.

"So did your angels show you anything at all about who committed the murders?"

"No. They did not show me any faces. I sensed that one of them knew Daria. Like an old boyfriend – from far away and long ago. Maybe a previous life. The other girl did not know him."

"The angels showed you both murders?" I felt a right div asking this.

"Yes and where they dumped them. He wanted to punish Daria, make her suffer. He liked it so much, he selected another girl – at random – and he put the devil in their mouths."

"How about you show us how he dumped the body?" So we got in our cars and went back to the spot by the river where it all began. He got out and walked straight to the point where Daria's body was dumped, all caught on camera by Matt. He then showed us the precise position the body was strapped to the riverbed. "This is where the body was dumped."

"Where was the head?"

"Right here," and pointed to the exact spot she was found.

"She was strapped down by her arms and legs like this." Again the exact position, the exact pose.

"She was lifeless, her suffering was over, but the killers wanted to make a show of her." I made sure this was on camera as I asked this.

"And you say the devil was in her mouth?"
"Yes."

"What do you mean?"

"A picture. It was a picture of the devil."

"Andrew Mallard I am arresting you for the murder of Daria Lispsinski. You do not have to say anything but it may harm your defense if you do not say anything now that will later rely on in court."

And with that, two uniforms swooped either side of him and attempted to drag him to the police car. He pulled himself away and launched himself head first in my direction.

"But I am trying to help!" He bawled at me – his face contorted in an ugly savage rage just inches away from mine. Thankfully the two uniforms had pulled him back before he could spray any more angry spittle over me.

He continued shouting at me all the way to the police car.

Monday 9th June 2014 – Afternoon

With Mallard howling to himself in the cell and his lawyer on the way, we set about searching Mallard's flat. No breaking down the door this time, we just took his front door keys.

So Mallard lived in Hanworth just by the busy dual carriageway road at the two up two down he'd inherited off his dead mother. We opened the door to encounter mountains upon mountains of junk, newspapers, clothes, toys and obsolete electrical appliances. It was as if he'd been to every car boot sale in Surrey, bought the lot and thrown everything into his house.

Sprawling chaos ruled in every room but one. His mother's bedroom. This appeared to be preserved just as it was, since her death. The room had been dusted and the surfaces polished. The make-up box open on the dresser, with the mirror aimed in the direction of the person who would have sat in the empty chair. A half full cup of tea also on the dresser, the contents had long gone moldy. As the lads peeled away the junk from the wall of the living room, a large mural of black painted satanic imagery was revealed in similar style to the painted mural in Zara's flat.

It was in the garage that they found the stash of sadistic pornography. They also found a stack of photographs of Mallard with a fuller head of hair with a young girl that looked like Becky. We also found two pairs of size 9 Wellington Boots. CS reported that they had been thoroughly bleached. Now why would you bleach a pair of Wellington boots? In the driveway there was a decades old battered white van. Just the sort of the thing to carry bodies in.

In the interview room my first question at Mallard was not flippant and came out of genuine curiosity.

"Why are you living in your dead mothers house? Doesn't pimping pay better than that?"

Mallard stared and said "No Comment."

"Where were you on the night of Friday the 31st May?"

Another – "No Comment."

"Okay then. You can fuck off back to the cells."

I now needed to gather as much info from his associates to build this conviction. So I hurled that playboy pimp Karl King in for some hard questioning. This smartly dressed, normally cool person was obviously quite agitated by this development.

"I never thought it was him. I mean, I knew he was weird and into odd things, but never thought ... I trusted him...."

"I want to know about how you got to be working with this guy. Don't hold out on me, or I'll nick you for obstruction. When did you first met him?"

"Becky Taylor introduced me. She had been working for me and she said she knew a guy who had an in with a pub where we could operate. That guy was Mallard and the pub was the Percy Arms. That was about a year ago."

He sat back and looked at the glass wall – his shocked expression eventually gave way to one of annoyance.

"I had a nice quiet operation going, a good little earner, and he's gone and fucked it up."

"What a pisser eh? Any clue that he was capable of something like this?"

Karl thought about this.

"The only thing, looking back, that was a bit sinister, was he used to say – 'I've got my own special way of keeping my women in line'."

"What do you think he meant by that?"

"He'd make the girls do all the black magic chanting and calling up Satan. I was never there, but Zara told me and I think that was his way of making them think he was all-powerful and that they couldn't lie to him. But as far as I know, it was all just a bit of a laugh and no girls did it if they didn't want to."

Later I decided to call Jane and be true to my word. "Okay, Jane, are you ready for this? I can only tell you so much. But I can tell you this – I have made two charges for the murders of Daria Lipsinski and Angela Ashdown – they are wait for it – Andy Mallard and Becky Taylor. Yes a man and a woman. These charges are still warm and I cannot tell you any more at this stage."

Jane hit me with question after question. None of which I could answer for fear of ruining my prosecution. She would have loved the black magic ritual angle, but I needed that under wraps for now.

Tuesday 10th June 2014 – Morning

In the morning Becky Taylor's solicitor came into my incident room to tell me that her client was ready to make a statement. I hollered over to Matt and we raced to Interview Room 1 and got the video rolling.

We sat at the table – me and Matt on one side, and Becky and her brief on the other. The solicitor started talking as Becky looked away. "I am going to read you a statement from my client. I have helped her with the wording just for the purposes of clarity, but the intentions and meaning of these words are purely from my client." The brief then read from a sheet a paper:

"I, Becky Taylor, am now in a position to make a full statement about the murders. I apologise for not doing so earlier, but my silence was out of fear. For over seven years I have lived in terror of the man Andy Mallard. Now that I know that Andy Mallard has been charged with the murders and is in custody I feel a little bit safer now to tell the horrible truth of what happened.

I must stress that I feel safer but I still do not feel safe. This man has a terrifying hold over me. Let me explain the history.

I first met Andy Mallard when I was 13. He started talking to me at a bus stop and invited me to his home to listen to records. He was in his mid-30s and I became his girlfriend. So you can see right away there was something very wrong.

I was a very unhappy girl with no friends. You already know about my time at primary school. My history of trouble continued at secondary school and I had become an outcast. As such I was easy prey for a controlling person like Mallard.

Within three months of my first meeting with him he manipulated me into sleeping with other men for money. I knew it was wrong but I was given no choice.

I gave him everything I earned, I felt so dirty I didn't want the money. He made me dress up in a way that was not suitable for a young girl and he made me walk the streets. He also made me sell and take drugs.

Mallard would make me chant and perform satanic rituals with him. I would think that we had really summonsed the devil and he was inside Mallard and he was all-powerful. I felt that I could not escape him, I could not lie to him and I had to give him whatever money I had. I hated Andy Mallard for what he had done to me, but he had a hold of fear over me. A hold of fear I felt compelled to obey or else I would be punished. He used these mind controls techniques on the other girls at the Percy Arms, they too felt as though he was watching over them at all times with a supernatural power.

I realise I will have to tell you about the murders. I hate to relive these horrible and traumatic experiences, but I know I will have to give you the full details in due course. For now I want it known that I did not actually kill the girls – but I did help to lure them away to where Mallard would kill them. For that I feel sick and guilty. On both killings I was in Mallard's van. I stayed there playing the radio as loud as possible to drown out the sounds of the screams.

I have done terrible things and I fully expect to go to prison for them, but you must understand that I did them under fear and duress. I offer this in mitigation and so expect a reduced charge of manslaughter instead of murder.

Signed Becky Taylor
Tuesday 10th June.

I had a few questions. My first was this: "Andy Mallard said to me you were a born liar...."

The solicitor cut in "My client..."

I interrupted back "Fuck off. I want to hear her speak, in her own voice and in her own words. In the courtroom she can hide behind you as much as the law allows, but in my interview room I want to hear the woman speak for herself." So I began again, "Andy Mallard said to me you were a born liar. His exact words were that 'you would tell a lie even if the truth is more interesting.' So why should I believe you?"

Becky replied, "He said that because of the awful truth I know about him. Right back to what he did to me as a child. He told everybody I was a liar so that people would just ignore what I said. "

I continued: "I would like to refer you to the way you behaved a few days ago when you were questioned about Angela. You were far from helpful, and not acting like someone who was concerned or feeling guilty. Do you want me to play back the interview tape?"

"I was scared. I wasn't showing it. But I was terrified. At the time Mallard was free and he would have killed me to silence me. Even though he's behind bars I am still scared. Scared he'll manage to escape and do to me what he did to those poor girls." She was tearful, she sounded panicked, full of terror and remorse.

She sounded genuine. But was she?

Tuesday 10th June 2014 – Evening

I got a call from Bremner. Like a good snout, he had gone down the Percy Arms on the Monday night and soaked up the conversation. He learnt that Zara a/k/a Madame Headlock had called an Emergency Meeting round hers. Some of the girls had come back later – and he overheard them saying "it's business as usual" and laughing like it was some in-joke.

"So this bloke Mallard, the one I've charged for the two murders, who had details of the case that only the perpetrators could have known...."

"What about him?"

"I seem to remember you telling me he was a good

bloke."

"Are you having a dig Pal?"

"Just a little."

I thanked Bremner and promised to get him his half monkey. "Don't spend it all on booze – sorry I mean cappuccinos and croissant."

Wednesday 11th June 2014 – Morning

So I had my collar but I wasn't fully happy. I needed more evidence against Mallard. Not just the shaky testimony of Becky Taylor. And I did not want her to play the passive accessory card. She had chosen and entrapped Angela. She must have known full well that it was going to lead to her death. That's conspiracy to murder and not manslaughter.

What I needed was evidence from the Car Phone Whorehouse girls, so I would kick things off with the woman they call Madame Headlock.

This time she was in. Zara was in her dressing gown by the kitchen table, guzzling black coffee, while making us no offers of tea or biscuits. Behind a shut door, two kids were shouting out, perhaps playing – maybe fighting.

"You think you know someone." She said as she poured out more coffee for herself. Matt and I looked at each other feeling excluded. "But I always thought there was something odd about Mallard."

"Really like what?"

"Just a nasty side to him. He's into the occult – dark stuff. But that doesn't make you a murderer."

"Did you suspect him for this?"

"I thought about it."

"Well why the fuck didn't you say something at the time? We could have saved Angela Ashdown's life."

She looked at me affronted – "Because I had nothing definite. I just knew that him and Becky went way back. He had a hold over her. But I am so shocked they killed Daria. I can't believe it."

I showed her a photograph of the nurses' uniform taken off Becky.

"Is that the nurse uniform that was taken from you?"

"It could be."

"Well I am telling you it is. So how did she get it?"

"I don't know."

"Did you give to her?"

"No."

"Did she steal it then?"

"She must have done."

"If I discover something that you know about, which you haven't told me, I am going to have to nick you – and you know what that means don't you?" I didn't want to spell out my threat, that imprisonment would mean losing custody of Cody.

"You don't need to threaten me with anything. I've told you everything I know."

"Have you spoken to the K man?"

"Yes – and he's as shocked as I am."

"What's going to happen to the K Ring?"

"He said it's business as usual. We just hope we don't lose any business."

"Does that mean you've got some more of them chanting parties coming up?" Zara looked thrown by this.

"What do you mean?"

"The Devil Will Have His Toll. The Devil Will Have His Toll." I chanted at her.

"Well, now that Mallard's behind bars we won't need to be doing that anymore."

"Your neighbour will be delighted. So what about the membership card?"

Zara poured some more coffee and said nothing.

"I am talking about the Devil Tarot Card."

"That was all Mallard. Mallard made them do all of that."

"So where were you on the night Friday the 31st May? That's two Fridays ago." "I was here. I had my usual get together with the girls and their friends, till the early hours. And ... Mallard is normally here. But he wasn't, neither was Becky."

"Okay, can you clarify? In the early hours of Saturday morning you have your weekly party and you are saying categorically that on the day of the 1st June, Mallard and Taylor who are usually here – were not." She was decisive. "Yes. I remember that neither were there."

"Will you make a statement?"

She thought a bit before saying "Yes."

Get in! We were in business. "Thank you. This will help them to not go free and go on and kill more women." I tried not to sound sarcastic, but as I went to walk out, clocked Matt looking at me with disapproval.

I could hear the kids continue to shout behind the door. The younger child was shouting, "I want my Mummy. I want my Mummy." Over and over. It was heart wrenching. Zara went to quiet them down and when she came back guzzled down some more coffee. She then looked at us and said, "I'm really sorry. Can I get you guys a coffee or a tea?"

In the car back to the nick, Matt took me by surprise. He said to me "I don't think you should be so antagonistic to Zara Campbell. We need her on our side."

I seldom get criticism from my partner, but when I do – I listen. So I agreed to be more diplomatic with my dealings with her from now on.

Over the next 24 hours we dragged in all the girls from the CarPhone Whorehouse and none of them had seen either Andy Mallard or Becky Taylor on the night of Friday the 31st May or the early hours of the following morning. The first time either had been seen was at the Percy Arms late Saturday evening. I also talked to the landlord of the Percy Arms who also did not see Mallard on Friday night. Mallard had come in the pub early afternoon – got a text and he left.

I crossed off my list of girls and we still had to talk to Ramona Marks. Now Ramona could be crucial. She was one of the crazy cat lady trio – the other two being Daria, the victim and Becky, the accused. She would surely shed some light on what was going on between the other two.

You will also remember she was the girl that threw us that apparently bogus story of the angry Polish ex-boyfriend. Had Mallard and Taylor put her up to it? Very possibly. I called Ramona's phone time and again and got nothing. I recalled that Ramona lived with Zara Campbell so we headed back to hers.

Thursday 12nd June 2014 – Morning

I encountered Zara with the usual two children running riot, this time they had the freedom of the living room. I noticed that the eldest child Cody had a scar on his cheek that I had not registered before.

"What happened to your son's cheek?" I asked straight to point.

"He had an accident playing with some other kids. And it's none of your business." Was Zara's hostile reply. "Where's Ramona?" I asked.

"She's gone away."

"Where to?"

"I don't know. She left a note, saying that she had to go away and she'll back when she gets her head together." "Can I see the note?" It was handed to me. It was laser printed in a Times New Roman font with her named signed in biro.

Dear Zara

I need to get away from it all for a bit of head time. I hope you understand. Things getting on top. Please be a sweetheart and Look after JJ. Will square up with you when I get back.

Luv

Ramona

"So she's left you to look after JJ?"

Zara nodded.

"That's disgusting. Any idea at all where she may have gone?"

"She may have gone to stay with her grandparents."

"And where can I find them?"

"Don't know. I just remembered Ramona telling me that she had made contact with them."

We went back to trace both sets of grandparents. One lived in Wales and had no contact with Ramona. The second lot lived in Oatlands. We sent a uniform over there and got no reply, and according to their neighbours they had gone away on a cruise. Maybe Ramona had thought that with the evil power mad Mallard behind bars, this was her chance to escape the life. But leaving her child behind was as low as you can get.

Back at the nick, Matt and me sat down with Andy Mallard and his brief to question him some more, now taking into account Taylor's testimony.

Predictably, the brief had advised Mallard on the stonewalling "No Comment" line. Lawyers are so fucking clever aren't they? Normally I find this highly annoying and so would use up the interview time to insult and bait the suspect. But this time I was actually delighted. Because on giving him the chance to provide an alibi for Tuesday 13th May and Friday the 31st May – he came back with 'No Comment.' His silence spoke volumes. He couldn't even make up a lie.

Out of the interview room I went over my case notes over and over. I was meeting Hinty with the solicitors the following day and they would tell me whether we had a sufficient case to take Mallard and Taylor all the way. I was confident they were both killers, but admittedly there were gaps in my evidence. For instance I had no definite location for the murder – just "somewhere in woods" – and there was no DNA and fingerprint to link the two accused just yet. Were these gaps glaring enough to undermine a conviction? I would find out in the meeting tomorrow morning.

Before turning in, I called Jane Barrow – "Look no hard feelings about you trying to distort and wreck my investigation. You're still my favorite journalist. Listen I've got a meeting with our solicitors tomorrow. We are going to go through our case and how good it is, I will give you a call after that and give you as much as I am able to. This is my Exclusive to you!" She sounded thrilled and delighted. I would of coursc bc calling in some more favors, but for now I just needed to check on my first little one.

Chapter 15

Where is Ramona?

Friday 13th June 2014 – Morning

THE SURREY STAR HITS the newsstand every Friday morning. This is an important fixture in the weekly calendar for virtually nobody in Surrey. But it was to me today. I grabbed my copy and found that the review of the Borough Sports Final had made the back pages. I called my wife Cassie to make sure that she got a copy and put it under the nose of my son Luis. The important part of the review was this paragraph tagged on at the end:

"Young Luis Ferdinand showed great promise at right back, with some great runs on the wing reminiscent of the great Brazilian Cafu. He has potential to make it to the very top of football, but he must take great care that he does not to neglect his studies." I called Cassie half an hour later to get a reaction. She told me that Luis had punched the air in jubilation on reading the word Cafu! My work was done. I dropped heavy hints to Cassie that I had pulled the strings for that article to happen. She didn't believe me, so I had to spell it out – "Cassie, I blackmailed someone at the *Surrey Star* to write that article."

She still didn't believe it and dismissed me with a – "Colin, if you really can pull those kind of strings, why don't you do it to earn some proper money?"

Colin. She calls me Colin. That really hurts. I mean, I know that's my actual name, but it never ceases to cut me to the quick when she calls me that.

Nevertheless the first bit of the day had gone well, now for the tricky one. You may well have noticed that my narrative had become a lot less jovial since the second murder. Normally I would rip the piss out the people around me – but that all stopped on the second murder. That's not because Daria's death was any less important. But Angela's was especially distressing because I witnessed at first hand the grief and shock of Angela's parents. From that moment on, the sense of responsibility had become crushing.

I knew I would have to come over well in this meeting with the solicitors with no silly Chapman Bendy jokes. I started getting those stomach butterflies that flapped more furiously the closer I got to the meeting. Neither Hinty nor the Chapman Bendy – sorry Chapmen Hendy – woman smiled as we sat down to our meeting. I felt sick. Had I blown the case?

But the more the lawyer spoke, the more of her frumpiness dissolved. She was now positively glowing as she went through my checklist of evidence:

Mallard's knowledge of the facts of the case that only the killer or people close to the case would know:

The devil was in their mouths
The death by a series of rocks
Hands tied up and held up
The exact position where Daria was found

The size 9 Wellington Boots – bleached. (Who bleaches Wellington Boots?)
His refusal to give an alibi
Zara Campbell certainty that he was not around the CPW on the Friday night
Becky Taylor's testimony

We played back Mallard's video taking us to the woods and the line "the devil was in their mouths," then how he showed the exact spot and position Daria had been found.

Our video evidence showed that he was not one of the onlookers on the day. Then him repeating again the devil in their mouths, meaning a picture, without me prompting him. I reiterated that the only people who knew about the Devil tarot card was me, Matt, Hinton and Roy the silver-maned CS person.

With Mallard continuing to refuse to give any alibi or explanation other than he saw it in a dream, he really had no defense at all. The bastard was going down.

My misgivings were melting away, and there was even a hint of a smile on the lawyer's lips as she presented a psychiatric report backing up that Andy Mallard is the type of person who would commit these crimes and then out of attention seeking narcissism would try to help us with our enquiries. "It's text book," she said. When Mallard learnt that Taylor had been caught, he knew he would be implicated and so decided to come forward under his own terms.

Hinton gave me his firm congratulatory handshake "Well done, Ferdy. You've cleared this whole business up within four weeks of the first murder." I felt as though my invitation to join the Freemasons was in the post.

As I took up my seat back at the incident room, while I felt relieved, I also started to feel hollow. I am such a miserable fucker me. As soon as something gets sorted out, I start trying to find something else to worry about. Matt had done a great job in spotting Becky's name in Angela's class records, but without Mallard's stupid dream story I would have been stumped and that just fell in our lap.

Now I was happy to give my exclusive to Jane Barrow. She loved the satanic angle and the S&M stuff. She lapped it up like a thirsty cat given a saucer of milk. Though I still had to hold back some of the evidence until the trial. The two prisoners were taken from the station cells to a remand prison. And two weeks later the police incident room was taken down. It felt premature – not something I am used to experiencing you understand. The investigation, or more precisely the gathering of evidence against the two accused, would continue right up to the trial. But it would continue from the familiar location of the King Edward Suite and overseen by the constant grin of Ferdy, the stuffed toy fox office mascot, who was still sat on top of the filing cabinet just as I'd left him.

Tuesday 1st July 2014

Today I received in the post a Manila envelope marked Brixton Remand. What was inside was most irregular, a page ripped from the bible and scrawled all over with messy writing in red biro:

My nackers (sic) are on fire and it's all because of you. I need to empty the sack, to ejaculate clean, everyone knows where to find Beaver in Slaughter On Thames. How do you make Cherry wine? You kick her in the throat – she's not laughing now. Only the clowns laugh behind painted faces. What you see is not the full picture. You've been spending all your time talking to horses. Nay! You think you're clever but the Boatman is laughing at you.

This was followed by a drawing of what looked like a beaver smoking a cigarette and this nonsense text was coming out of the smoke.

The letter was registered from a Mr. Andrew Mallard.

He was obviously playing the write-a-letter-of-looney-gibberish-to-the-officer-in-charge-in-the-hope-of-coping-an-insanity-plea-card. I was not impressed. I threw his letter into the "miscellaneous crap" file.

Monday 7th July 2014

Six days passed, and we had been working on other, less traumatic cases. But on this morning I got thrown back into the case by a phone call from an elderly woman who identified herself as Mrs. Isobel Marks. Her voice was anguished "We have reported our granddaughter Ramona Marks missing. We came back from holiday this morning and she has disappeared."

I was silent momentarily.

"Hullo? Do you know who Ramona is?"

"Yes of course. She had been living with Zara Campbell, she left a note...."

"We don't believe that note. Ramona would never ever leave without her JJ. Something terrible has happened."

My mind began racing with all sorts of horrible scenarios. I felt instantly guilty about not investigating the note further.

I asked, "When was the last time you heard from Ramona?"

"She left a message on our ansafone while we were on holiday. She said she was going to accept our offer of her bringing JJ to come and live with us. So the first thing we did when we got back was to try and contact her."

Matt and I drove over to the grandparents' house, now considering the terrible prospect that Ramona had been the third victim of Mallard and Taylor, precisely because of what she knew.

The grandparents lived in Oatlands in a large two-story house set back from the main road. The child JJ was now there, liberated from Zara's house. Isobel was keeping him occupied while out of earshot Matt and I spoke with Ken the grandfather. Ken explained that Ramona's parents disowned her when she was 15. They would now have nothing to do with her, which greatly hurt Ramona especially as she had attempted to make contact when JJ was born. She had written to Isobel and Ken six months ago, asking if they wanted to meet their great grandson. They wrote back, and since then have been in regular contact. "She couldn't conceal what she had become and we obviously hated it, but we saw the good in her. So we offered her the chance to escape the life she was in and come and live with us – rent-free with JJ. At first she was scared, saying that they would never allow it. But we kept on at her." He explained.

"We were delighted to get the message that she had decided to live with us. But now we can't find her."

"May I listen to her voicemail message?" They played it back - Ramona sounded as though she was out in the street, constant moving traffic behind. Her bunged up giddy voice was instantly recognizable. *"Hello Gran and Gran Pa. Hey! When you first said you were going cruising I thought you meant you were going around gay bars to pick up men (Laugh). Of course that's not what you're doing at all. Listen. I've decided that I am probably need to get more decisive.*

I've thought about it long and hard. Your proposal I mean – and I've decided. Definitely. I've made my mind up I want to bring JJ and move in with you – if you'll still have me. If you haven't changed your mind like. I so appreciate this. ... Mum and Dad won't have anything to do with me ... I am going to get away from these people, and start again. You won't regret it – I promise ... and JJ will be so happy. He loves you both very much you know. So I think you may have gone on your cruise. Or maybe you're listening to this and pretending you're not home .... But I'll call again. You won't get rid of me that easy. Thank you once again."

From there we headed straight to Brixton Prison to talk to Mallard, waiting several hours for his crappy solicitor to be present. I wasn't going to allow a No Comment smoke screen over this. It was far too urgent.

In the interview, Mallard talked to me directly. He looked helpless, downtrodden, jaundiced – he said with a roll of his manic eyes "the angels did not show me anything on Ramona. I hope she's okay."

"Did you get my letter?" He asked. I wanted to grab him by the throat and beat an answer out of him. Instead I got up and walked out.

From Brixton we went over the river to North London – Holloway Prison, where Becky had been staying. Becky seemed distressed at the suggestion that Ramona might be dead. "No – not Ramona. Not Ramona." She said over and over.

"If Andy Mallard killed her, he didn't use me to entrap her." She said, looking me straight in the eye. She had claimed that the last time she had seen Ramona was the day before she was arrested. Everything seemed fine then. She had not mentioned that she needed to get away.

We then went to Zara's flat. A third time in two weeks. This time we took away the note, which she had kept, under a pile of bills and other papers. This was now evidence in a missing person investigation that may become a murder. I took a statement off Zara and grilled her about being party to Ramona's disappearance.

She told me that the note had been left on a Friday. Mallard had come in on the Monday with his dream story, so the timeline fitted to collar Mallard for this.

Friday 11th July 2014

The last few editions of the *Surrey Star* had been milking the Slaughter On Thames case. The Slaughter On Thames moniker from the spurious letter stuck, which only the privileged few, including you dear readers, know to be a certain fake.

The letter itself was never mentioned again by the *Surrey Star*, instead Jane Barrow had latched onto the Ramona Marks story, interviewing her grandparents and so had begun a HAVE YOU SEEN RAMONA? Campaign.

I was all set to toss this morning's rag in the bin but instead I flicked through it and found tucked away on page 5 a picture of the BMX Kid posing next to his pride and joy. It was the headline next to it that pushed my heart into my throat.

TEENAGE CYCLIST KILLED IN HIT AND RUN

It had happened on the dual carriageway of the Byfleet Road (A245) on the 9th July – two days before. I was outraged. Why wasn't I told? Don't I do homicide? But this one had taken place just outside of my patch. Matt and I ran to the officer who had taken the report.

It was sketchy. No CCTV coverage and no clue of what the offending vehicle might be. I went over with Matt to the accident spot. It was an ugly wide stretch of tarmac blighting the countryside. We got out and looked around. If the hit and run had wanted to avoid killing the BMX Kid, he would have been breaking – and breaking hard. So we were looking for the tire marks – and there weren't any.

I remembered the BMX Kid telling me about the rituals he had filmed, and he had handed over his memory stick. Where was that memory stick now? We went back to the station to discover that it had been filed away – and was now "lost in the system." The incident room had been taken down and it was perhaps lost with that. So I commissioned a search for the memory stick in the archive room deep in the bowels of the station's basement. But could it be that the BMX Kid's death was just a random accident after all?

Monday 14th July 2014

The weekend had been spent preparing for my Monday morning meeting with the solicitors. Everything else was blotted out as I gathered as much relevant evidence as possible to put the finger on Mallard & Taylor.

Yet other things were tugging at me that I felt needed to be further investigated - the disappearance of Ramona and the death of the BMX Kid.

Chapman Hendy announced that the trial was set for Monday the 7th October. Mallard had entered a Not Guilty plea, though they expected this to be converted into an insanity plea at the actual trial. Becky Taylor was going to enter a plea of Not Guilty to murder but Guilty to accessory to murder citing mitigating circumstances. She had given a very detailed blow by-blow statement of how the murders were committed which they hoped would lay waste to Mallard's defense.

Mallard sent me another of his red biro rambling bollocks. Another page torn from the bible, and more fucking nonsense. I cursory read it for any standout clues or admissions of guilt, and then threw it into the MISCELLANEOUS CRAP folder. Here's the opening sentence of one of them:

You're still looking for the Beaver in the river. Gone underwater. The Boatman and the Chutney Ferret know. Much cleaner work after Andrea P.

I called Brixton Prison to tell them that one of their prisoners was defacing their bibles, and they should sort him out.

Chapter 16

Together In Murder

Monday 6th October 2014

FAST FORWARD TO three months later – the nights draw in, the days get cloudier, the wind chillier and all the shops are warning us of the immanency of Christmas.

But before the festive insanity, my mind was focused on something rather major standing in the way – the crown court trial of Mallard & Taylor. In the week before the start of the trial, the *Surrey Star* cover page was a portrait of Mallard and one of Taylor split down the middle and facing each other. The headline read "Together in Murder," which played its part in whipping up the dozens of haters to wait outside the courthouse. With the arrival of the police van each morning, this rabble were on cue to loudly boo and jeer at the heavily protected focus of their hatred – trembling but unseen under tightly held blankets. The haters were split into two camps – those who hated Mallard and those who, after reading about her trick to lure Angela Ashdown, had taken a particular dislike to Taylor.

Matt and me were suited and booted and I was as nervous as a turkey watching the Christmas decorations go up. Matt seemed to share my anxiety but neither of us articulated it. We both knew that our reputations as coppers would hang heavily on the outcome of this case.

Now as everybody knows, trials are one big bore fest. The only time they get a little bit interesting is when we hear a bit of crucial testimony. Zara Campbell, Karl King, The Percy Arms landlord, some of the other CarPhone Whorehouse girls all took the stand with nothing especially revelatory to say. Mallard was into S&M – he liked the dark stuff and I'm not talking about a pint of Guinness.

Becky Taylor needed to take the stand in order to get her reduced charge. It was her testimony and her testimony alone that was going to shed light on these terrible events. She was in the stand over two days. I had read her prepared statement but that was not read out in court, instead both prosecution and defense had a go at questioning her in the dock. Here are the selected highlights from the court transcript. Here she is being asked questions from her own counsel:

Q: Who chose Daria Lipsinski to be killed?
A: Andy Mallard.
Q: Why her?
A: Andy *suspected that Daria was planning to run away from the Percy Arms set up. Also someone told him that Daria had been disrespecting him, you know like impersonating him, to the other girls.*
Q: And who told him about this?
A: I don't know. One of the other girls.
Q: Did you tell him?
A: No it was definitely not me because if I did, I knew she would be ... in ...
Q: ... in what?
A: Trouble. That Mallard would punish her. Like he would punish me.
Q: So what happened?
A: He asked me to arrange to meet Daria. He didn't tell me why and I didn't ask. I knew it would be bad but I thought she would just get roughed up.
Q: So when and where did you arrange to meet?
A: We would often go for a walk and look at the cats.
Q: The cats?
A: Yes there's this place that keeps loads of cats and we would go there just to have a look at them. We arranged to

meet in the road leading up to the Cat Sanctuary. Mallard drove me up there in his van.
Q: And you waited for Daria to appear?
A: Yes.
Q: And what happened when Daria showed up?
A: I told her that Mallard was here and I led her into the van. Inside the vehicle he ...
Q: What?
A: Chloroformed her.
Q: How did he do this?
A: With a handkerchief ... over her nose and throat.
Q: So what happened after that?
A: Mallard tied her up ...
Q: Did you help tie her up?
A: No.
Q: So what were you doing when he was tying her up?
A: Just staring ahead. I did not watch.
Q: So what happened next?
A: Mallard drove the van deep into the woods.
Q: Where was Daria?
A: In the back of the van.
Q: And was Daria struggling in the back of the van?
A: Not at first – she was out. But as we got deeper she ... woke up. She tried to scream but ... her mouth was covered end up.
Q: With what?
A: Tape. Gaffer tape.
Q: So what happened next?
A: Andy stopped the ignition, turned off the lights and took her out the van. He then ripped off the tape and she starting screaming – running. I didn't look.
Q: So what were you doing?
A: I shut my eyes. I turned on the radio as loud as I could to block out the screams.
Q: What did you think Mallard was doing?

A: I still did not know what Mallard had planned. In the dark I saw him string Daria up from a tree. Daria kept on screaming.
Q: String her up? How did he string her up?
A: By the hands. But I looked away. I could not bear to look or listen. So I still had the radio on full blast. I lost track of time – but eventually Mallard came back with Daria's body put inside plastic coating.
Q: Did you say anything to him?
A: Nothing ... I was too scared.
Q: Did he say anything to you?
A: He said – 'this is what happens to disrespecting bitches. The Devil will have his toll.'

Now this is part of her testimony covering the selection of Angela as the next victim.

Q: Why was Angela selected as the next victim?
A: Andy came to speak with me. He said – "You need to arrange to meet another girl. Any girl. But she cannot be connected to this scene in any way."
Q: And by "scene" you mean the prostitution set up at the Percy Arms?
A: Yes.
Q: Where did this conversation take place?
A: It was at the pub. In between shifts. He took me to one side. Away from the other girls.
Q: And why did he do that?
A: He didn't tell me. But ...
Q: But what?
A: But I think he wanted to select another girl not connected to us, so if she was killed in the exact same way, it would take the police attention away from the Percy Arms scene.
Q: Why was Angela Ashdown chosen?

A: (Crying.) I had to choose someone.
Q: But why her?
A: (Still crying.) I just had to choose someone.
Q: So you chose Angela Ashdown?
A: (Breaking down) I knew she would be killed. But I felt powerless. Andy would kill me I know and I was just so controlled by him. I felt sick that I chose a girl that I had a row with. I had to choose someone to be killed and I thought I might as well choose someone that hated me and had destroyed my life in getting me expelled. But I know it was wrong.

At this point Becky looked directly at Angela's parents who were sat in the second row. "I know you can never forgive me. I am so so sorry I chose your daughter. I did a terrible thing I know it. But..." and she burst into tears again.

Angela's parents stared back and then looked away. The mother then broke down sobbing and the father escorted her out. They did not return for the rest of the trial. It was harrowing, heart wrenching. Jane Barrow and her lot were enthralled. Our prosecution team chose not to cross-examine her. I thought this was a strange tactic. In her testimony Becky was trying to pass herself off as an unwilling accomplice, but she effectively condemned both these two women to their deaths. She could have warned off Daria and she actually selected Angela to settle a juvenile grievance. But because her testimony was the single biggest wedge to slide into Mallard, our counsel did not want to pick holes in it. So her claim that each time of the killings she was in the van, playing the radio at full blast to drown out the sound of the screaming, went unchallenged.

But to me it was clear that Becky, of her own volition, had devised the 'my mother the primary school teacher is sick you must come and see her' ruse. Prosecution should have really been all over this and not allowed her a mitigation of diminished responsibility.

Becky in the dock was emotional but lucid. She must have thoroughly rehearsed it. Her testimony was detailed, but still somehow sketchy. She had been the star of the show playing to a packed courthouse. The normally disengaged jury members, journalists and court staff were all looking up with pricked up ears and hanging on every word. Becky was a hard act to follow, and guess who had to do it? Normally I am quite the shining star in the dock, but I was feeling especially jittery about this one and I realised that the Ferdy humor, which was my favorite way of winning over the jurors, was not going to be appropriate in this case. My evidence was focusing on how Mallard had knowledge of facts that only the killer knew about. I worked that Devil Tarot Card very hard.

In cross-examining, Mallard's brief doubted that Mallard had specifically mentioned a devil tarot card. But his exact words were "the devil was in their mouths," "a picture of the devil." Which to me was enough. But it was what the jury thought that mattered.

After the Ferdy show our Chapman Hendy brief showed the jury the video of Mallard talking to me about the dreams. The brief then did a great job in underlining over and over what I had said in the stand. It's a courtroom strategy that works – repetition, repetition, repetition.

So after all this what did the defense have? I could see Mallard talking animatedly at his lawyer, tugging at his arm, rolling those manic eyes. I think he wanted to take the stand and show off, but the lawyer obviously thought he would blow it. This has never felt like justice to me. If you have to decide if someone is guilty or innocent, you really should get to see and hear that person proclaim their innocence in their own words.

Instead, Mallard hid behind his drab-ball brief who droned on about burden of proof, and how we did not have enough of it. With Mallard not taking the stand and a lame closing defense speech, I sensed victory in the home stretch.

Friday 17th October 2014

The ten-day trial ended on Friday with Hinty promising a grand piss up in our favorite pub by the river if we got the two counts of guilty. I think the head jury member was a big X Factor fan because he left a gap you could drive a lorry through before announcing Mallard guilty on both counts. Taylor got two counts of accessory to murder. Sentencing would take place next week. As Mallard was taken away he shouted across at his brief – "You should have let me speak!" The brief didn't care – he was already thinking about the next case.

Outside the court, as I dodged the occasional reporter, Isobel and Ken Marks found me and asked whether I thought Ramona had also been killed by Mallard and Taylor. I said I thought it was likely, and I swore I would continue to try and get to the truth, and with that I was scooped away to the pub.

Have you ever been in a pub full of coopers and lawyers on the piss? No? You don't want to either. All the other coopers were there to share my glory. There was so much backslapping going on you'd think there was an epidemic of hiccups. Gaffney the rubber masked old sod had hogged the jukebox and with a pile of coins was dictating the soundtrack of our afternoon.

But it wasn't the same without Bremner. I kept looking over to the corners of the pub, hoping to see him there ready to slay me with a funny story. I sent a text telling him of the collar and thanking him for his help. He didn't reply. When I saw Gaffney gyrating to some track from the '80s, I decided I needed to go outside and get some fresh air.

I walked along the river towpath, looking out onto the riverboats bobbing up and down in the breeze. Ahead of me I saw Matt sitting on the dock of the bay. I walked up to him and sat beside him, looking out at the fishermen on the other side of the river.

"Well done, Matt."

Matt said nothing. He just stared ahead. Just the sound of the rolling Thames and the muted music and chatter from inside the pub.

Eventually Matt spoke. "Mallard's van is an old transit; it was built in 1984."

"Yes and –?"

"You can't have the radio playing without the key being in the ignition. If you take the ignition key out to unlock the boot – you lose the radio."

Part 3

Chapter 17

The One That Got Away

IN THE MONTHS THAT PASSED Matt and I got on with other cases. There was enough to keep me off the streets and out of the off license, and much of it involved fraud. My crime of choice, my comfort zone. But In my moments alone, when I'm shaving or taking out the rubbish, I would suddenly seize up in terror. Terror at the thought of another Slaughter On Thames killing happening with the exact same MO and proving to the world that we had not caught everyone behind it. I wouldn't dream of telling Cassie. It would just reinforce her opinion of me that I'm a loser. That would never change. The thing is, though, I was starting to agree with her.

Oh Gawd! I am going all deep and personal on you and I really wanted to avoid any of that. Every so often I pick up a crime novel, just to see what crap those writers make up about us. They always have the main cop being a sickeningly decent sort – wrestling with his demons and baring his soul to the reader. There's even a page or two given over to his sex life describing in cringy detail how he makes love and in so doing relating the intimate vulnerable thoughts of the central character. Well you can rest easy, readers, you won't be getting any of that crap from me. All I am telling you is that I make love like an Olympic athlete. Once every four years.

Cassie may think I'm a loser, but it's not because of that. Believe me. And I keep fit and healthy. I've got a body of a man half of my age. I really should get rid of it – it's starting to smell.

So that's the private life dealt with. What was going on down the nick? So we finally relocated out of the King Edward Suite and got to experience a bit of daylight – from a fifth floor vantage point which gave us a grand view of the rolling River Thames. I think Ferdy the office mascot appreciated the change, but you never know with him. He just grins away regardless, whatever the progress of our cases, whatever the weather. He and the Matt are the only constants in my life – solid, dependable.

And Mallard continued to send me his letters from the other side of sanity. All scrawls in red biro, all written on pages torn from the bible, and all given a cursory read before being tossed into the MISC CRAP case file. I got seven letters in all - approximately a monthly occurrence. But I missed my April 2015 letter, and page 7 of one the nationals newspapers revealed why. "Slaughter On Thames Killer Dies In Prison" was the prosaic headline for the story on how Mallard's life sentence was reduced to a mere six months courtesy of the Grim Reaper.

I contacted the coroner for the autopsy report and read it in detail. He died of renal failure, a condition that was pre-existing to him going inside and the coroner found no reason to believe the death was suspicious. That, of course, is not to say that the death was not suspicious.

So the closed Slaughter On Thames case continued to gnaw away at me. It began with Becky's testimony. Here's a recap:

Becky: Andy stopped the ignition, turned off the lights and took her out the van. He then ripped off the tape and she starting screaming – running. I didn't look.

Solicitor: So what were you doing?

Becky: I shut my eyes. I turned on the radio as loud as I could to block out the screams.

And Matt pointing out that she could not have drowned out the sound of screams in Mallard's vehicle if Mallard had turned off his van's ignition. Meaning either that another vehicle had been used to transport the bodies, or that her testimony was pure fiction.

I had a number of other burning questions that were causing me to scratch away at the red raw skin around my elbows: The first - was the BMX Kid killed? And if so – was it because of him rumbling the rituals on Brooklands Park? What had happened to that memory stick of his video of the ritual filmed from his phone? Was something incriminating on there? The search that I had ordered for the memory stick bore nothing, and it officially became "lost in the system." I contacted his parents about his phone. Maybe the footage was still on there, but that too was never found.

The next question had been overlooked because of spiraling events. Someone had tried to frame Roger Farrady for the first murder. Was that Mallard's doing or his accomplices? Was that by someone who knew about the weirdo filc?

Did the killers also put Ramona up to come to us with that bogus story of Daria's Polish ex-boyfriend?

Which brought me to the final question, and most troubling of all. What has happened to Ramona?

The more I thought about it, the more I convinced myself that Mallard was not the real instigator of these crimes. There was a man pulling the strings, clever enough to deflect away any suspicion or evidence. Turning it around in my head it became more and more obvious. Until one night I sat bolt upright in bed staring ahead of me. It was now so clear. It's Karl King. The Teflon pimp. The self-proclaimed Albert Schweitzer of prostitutes.

I know there will be legions of armchair sleuths reading this going – "Duh? I could have told you that on page 68!" But that's all easier said than done. You want to try getting off your arses and doing some of this stuff for real. When you're spending every waking hour chasing a collar, and a very plausible explanation starts forming – you go with that. You don't start looking at other suspects just because you don't like the look of them.

But let's now look at Karl King. Karl King was the man sitting at the top of the ring. He instilled fear into his girls. He lets them keep 60% of what they earn. What a fucking saint. Cassie the woman lying next to me in bed would never respect or love me again, but if someone like Karl King – all smug and manipulative – walked into her orbit, she would immediately turn her head and look longingly at the life of luxury I could never give her as a humble cooper.

To me Karl King represents evil greed in its vilest form - a man of undeserved wealth, a crook, a banker, a TV presenter, a member of Take That. Even if he wasn't behind these killings. Even if I could only get him for pandering or prostitution, or failing to report a shaving accident, I was taking him down – for whatever I could get on him.

I wasn't becoming obsessed or anything, but I often found myself reading and re reading Karl King's form. Born in 1981 he comes from Tilehurst, a middle class suburb of Reading, and his rackets had been robbery, burglary, obtaining money by menace and drug dealing.

Most criminals either come from a family with a tradition in crime or from a dysfunctional broken home and very often both. But not Karl King. He went to a fee-paying school, paid for by respectable wealthy middle class parents, who had no criminal record.

His first offence in the record was not actually an offence at all, for which he wasn't charged. It still went on his record to provide a shaft of light onto how this young enterprising crook's mind worked. At the Reading Festival of 1995 – a 15-year-old Karl King hung outside the main gates selling ecstasy pills to the festivalgoers. His line was that security was so strict, there was no way they were going to score inside or take anything in – so they may as well buy the pills off him and take them now and come up inside the festival. The pills were all duds, but by the time this had become apparent to the festivalgoers, they were inside with no readmission.

Looking at the rest of his regular criminal activity, clearly we had here someone with a strong commitment to crime. But with no form for the last four years, Karl King had obviously got smart.

Friday 1st May 2015

I met with Bremner at our usual caff in Addlestone. We were now one of their regulars, and the girls knew our orders before we'd given them. Bremner – a cappuccino and croissant. Me – a bacon sandwich and a mug of tea. Bremner was still on the wagon but struggling to get proper paid work. He had been on some panzified Zero hour contract for a security firm. But the work, when he did get it, paid fuck all. So he was grateful to earn himself a monkey from me doing proper work. I gave Bremner a slip of paper with King's home address in Weybridge. "I want him tailed. I've heard that since the raids at the Percy Arms, his CarPhone Whorehouse operation has shut down. So find out what's he doing for money now. Find out what he does for kicks."

Monday 8th June 2015

Now for all my misgivings about the truth about the Slaughter On Thames case, I daren't dare ask top brass for the case to be reopened. That would have been about as welcome as finding Chris Evans' autobiography in your Christmas stocking.

Besides, there was no concrete evidence to justify reopening the case. That was up until this day when I got a phone call from Kenneth Marks grandfather of Ramona.

"Have you heard about the skull they've found by the river in Essex?"

I hadn't.

"We'd like you to find out if it's Ramona."

Apparently a dog, who may have been called Pickles, dug up a skull in the muddy banks of the river Thames over in Grays, Essex. It had been identified as a young woman's and this had made some of the newspapers, which is how it had come to the attention of Ramona's grandparents who had been scouring the media for possible reporting's on Ramona.

I drove over to Essex where the pathologist told me that he had a partial skull just the top half (*calvarium* is the medical term). The entire face below the ridges was missing, so it was impossible to build a picture of who this woman might be or even what she looked like. There was no identifiable DNA on the skull as it had been washed away by the river. All he could say was that the woman had a malformed sinus on the left hand side. There were no other remains from the body, indicating that the skull had been dumped there. No determination was possible of how long it had been in the river.

So in summary it could be Ramona, but there was no way of telling for sure. I felt I should go and tell Ramona's grandparents personally about this frustrating state of affairs.

Their living room was now adorned with pictures of their granddaughter. I recognised the one taken in Zara's flat with the two kids. Her goofy smile frozen in time. This fuzzy focused party snap now gave Ramona a saintly martyred glow. This cozy quiet retirement home, so far removed from the howling chaos of modern life, had been transformed by the energy and mischief of young JJ. From watching Kenneth Marks playing with him it was apparent that bringing up JJ had now become their priority in life.

"It's heart breaking when he asks about her mother." Isobel told me as Ken kept JJ occupied "We now tell him she's gone to a better place."

Isobel went on – "Ramona was such a lovely girl. She just chose a bad road. She had a wonderful sense of humor. We still have her last telephone message on our ansafone. We will never delete it. It's our only recording of her voice." I thought there may be a clue there that I missed first time around, so I asked to hear it again. We both listened to her voice, me for clues and her for a reminder of her lost granddaughter. Isobel smiled ruefully, her eyes teary.

We sat in silence as her message ran onto the mechanical voice – "message was recorded at Eleven-Hour-Fourteen on the Eleventh-June-Twenty-Thirteen."

I checked the calendar on my phone, my heart racing as Isobel and Ken stared at me. "What is it?"

The date Ramona left the message was Tuesday the Eleventh of June. Mallard had been taken into custody the day before. **There was no way then that Mallard could have killed Ramona.** There was no way either that Becky could have been involved.

Instead of telling them that and adding to their suffering, I gave them my word that I would do my best to get to the bottom of what happened to Ramona. They were not impressed. I had said exactly the same thing on the steps of the courthouse six months ago.

Monday 8th June 2015

Mallard must have felt like a patsy. He did not want to grass up his colleagues and yet he took the fall for the two murders. Maybe Mallard was writing the letters to me to drop hints about the others involved – but making them deliberately weird and hard to understand so it wasn't obvious he was trying to tell me something.

This sent me back to the MISC CRAP file to re-read

those letters. I needed some fresh eyes, so I called eagle eyed Matt the Stat down to join me in the dark, cobwebby archives deep in the bowels of our basement in the nick. The first time around those letters read like random images from the brain of an LSD Spazz Monkey – and they weren't any different the second time.

"You're still looking for the Beaver in the river. Gone underwater. The **Boatman** and the Chutney Ferret know. Much cleaner work after Andrea P. "

Andrea P? Is that a reference to Andrea Perry – the unsolved river killing in Maidenhead from 2003? We had looked at that case when trying to find other murders with a similar MO. Why would Mallard specifically mention that killing?

So Matt and me took a trip up the river to Maidenhead.

Tuesday 9th June 2015

The officer in charge of the case was one Ed Brooks now retired and living in an orbital village to Maidenhead called Burnham. I called him up and insisted on seeing him. He was a small balding man with watery eyes and a strained expression. I got the sense he was desperate for someone, other than his wife, to talk to and he readily let us into his cottage and was only too willing to talk about the case.

"I was sure Nick Shoosmith was the killer. But he was acquitted because of the fucking DNA."

"What fucking DNA?"

"The DNA under the victim's fingernails was not his."

"Whose was it?"

"No cunt knows. Sorry." He immediately apologised to his wife who was in earshot.

He went on: "Nick Shoomsith was Andrea Perry's pimp operating in the Slough area. Nick Shoosmith was a very violent man, his record was a long list of brutality and a lot of it was directed against women. He terrified his girls, but all of them were too scared to say anything to us. That was until his drug problems got the better of him, he started losing his grip on his business, and the girls started a mass exodus."

"Who was the pimp he was leaving them for?"

"Er ... some woman."

"It's Karl King. Isn't it?"

"Who?"

"A Reading man. A pimp who has been operating on my patch. It's Karl King isn't it?"

"Never heard of Karl King. No they were leaving for a Madam. Madam ... fuck if I can remember. She ran her operation from her house like a co-op. All the girls got treated proper, kept most of the money. So it's no wonder they were all leaving him. Unfortunately for Andrea Perry she was going around thc pubs of Maidenhead laughing about him."

He offered to take us over to the Maidenhead nick and look at that case file which we readily accepted. Doubtlessly he wanted some time away from the trouble and strife so he could swear as much as he liked, and talk some more about this case that was obviously still playing on his mind. At the station I got to see the police interview videotape of Nick Shoosmith then aged thirty-nine. The accused was not giving the usual No Comment and there was no brief sitting next to him.

A less round Ed Brooks with a fuller head of hair was firing the questions. In the hot seat was a mountain of a man, domed forehead, swept over by long lank greasy hair. He leaned forward on the table, exposing his tattooed forearms. But I could not make out the illustrations on the video. I didn't envy Ed Brooks alone in that interview room with him. I swear I could hear his voice falter as he asked the questions.

"Mr. Shoosmith How do you know Andrea Perry?" "That slag was not my girlfriend if that's what you're driving at." His voice sounded like gravel from the furnaces of hell. "I'm not driving at that at all Mr. Shoosmith. She used to work for you. You used to be her pimp."

"Never pimped in my life guvnor. But I do know she was a bit of a slapper. I hear she spent last night sleeping with the fishes." And he laughed. Laughter can be such an ugly sound. It certainly was listening to Nick Shoosmith's spiteful guttural cackle.

"And it was you who put her in the river. You killed her."

"You'll never make it stick!" He said – and he cackled again.

"That laugh has haunted me ever since. " Said the present day Ed Brooks staring at his adversary on the screen.

"When he got acquitted, I made him know that I would be breathing down his neck for the rest of his life, and as soon as he did anything that wasn't double legal I would be all over him. I tried to make his life hell."

I tried to offer him hope – "Maybe that DNA under the fingernails was that of an accomplice. Maybe we can match it to somebody now?"

"I fucking wish." He replied despondently. "That DNA sample was lost."

"Lost?" I joked, "and I thought the Surrey police were clowns."

We drove the old codger back to his home in Burnham, as he continued to gas away about the case. It was like he had been dying to get it all off his chest, and until we had come along, had no one to talk to about it. And yet all this off-loading brought him no respite. Instead it just perpetuated his torment.

Nick Shoosmith may be dead but he was still very much haunting this man. He directed me to drive him over the railway bridge and asked me to stop the car. He got out and walked over to the bridge – we followed. He looked over the thick steel railings down onto the railway track thirty foot below, and we did the same.

"This where he committed suicide. Three months after he was acquitted, three months of me breathing down his neck. One night he climbs over these railings and throws himself off onto a passing train. He escaped me. But to me by jumping off this bridge he was as good as admitting his guilt."

A train clattered underneath us at frightening speed. "I just hope he felt severe pain before he died." He added.

I looked at this retired cop haunted by the murderer who got away. I hope to God I wasn't looking at an image of me in twenty years' time. Fuck – let's avoid that at all costs. Let's get this one solved.

Tuesday 9th June 2015 – Afternoon

He has an art gallery that is most likely a money-laundering front. He meets with a series of men who appear to be wealthy businessmen. It has not been determined if he is pimping again or what his main source of income is now.

That was Bremner's super brief report on Karl King. I paid out £500 for 46 words. Over a tenner a word. He was on a better word rate than J.K. Rowling and Dan Brown put together.

We sat in our usual place at the Addlestone Caff, speaking in hushed tones, but by now the staff must have twigged we were coppers. We weren't exactly subtle. I said: "okay. What I want you to do now is make contact with him."

"What?" This came with a large intake of shocked

breath from Bremner. "Introduce yourself and say that you knew Mallard. Knew about what happened to the CarPhone Whorehouse because you used hang out there after you got sacked as a copper and if King is looking for a new trustworthy lieutenant to start up a new operation – then Bremner's yer man."

Bremner got up to leave – "Fuck Off."

I pushed him down.

"Come on. What's the worst thing that can happen?"
"I get killed. I get beaten up. I get nicked for setting up a prostitution business."

I put on a bit of a speech: "It's always the worst case scenario with you. We're just trying to find out a bit about him. Come on Bremner you're a cop. You're still a cop. The best cop I know." After Matt of course, but I didn't tell him that. I pressed on "Don't you want to help collar a big time crook? You should want to do this. By the way – how's the zero hour contract going?"

Being reminded of the indignity of his job-not-job, Bremner agreed to take my self-funded undercover operation to the next stage.

Wednesday 10th June 2015

So I was continuing to hire Bremner out of my own funds. (Don't tell the trouble and strife!!) I never told anyone else – not even Matt. He and Bremner of course disliked each other intensely when they shared office space in the King Edward Suite. But just because they are beasts of different colours I did not see any reason why they shouldn't get on. Because even though they did not realise it, they were working for the same team. My team – and I was working them to their strengths. Matt with his analysis and Bremner with his nose. They are opposites that work together – rough and smooth, sweet and sour, mild and bitter, ying and yang. Once this case was cracked I would

bring the two together make them sink their differences over a celebratory drink. Back at the nick I was playing an audiotape. I winced at the sound of my own voice. I always do. My wife Cassie especially winces at the sound of my voice. I was playing back Ramona's interview tape.
Me: "So don't you want to get away from the K Ring?"
Ramona: "No. No way. The K Ring are cool people to work for. They let me take a whole two weeks off for my sinus operation."
Me: "Wow! That is cool. That sound like brilliant people to work for. Do you think they would hire Matt and Me?"
Ramona: "Hey I know you're being sarcastic, but Zara tells me in all her time working in this game, nobody had ever allowed anything like that before."

I stopped the tape with a violent clang. Sinus operation! The skull found at Grays had sinus problems and Ramona went to the health service for a sinus operation! That would mean that the NHS would have an X-Ray of her skull on their records.

I called up the Essex pathologist. "Listen –if I managed to get you an X-Ray of a skull with a sinus problem, would you be able to match it up with the calvarium you have, and tell me if it's one and the same?" The pathologist responded brightly. "Yes! By matching up the sinus cavities I could do that."

I got the sinus operation X-Ray biked over to me and then couriered it straight over to Essex.

Hours later I get a call from my favorite Essex based pathologist.

"Have you got something nice for me?" I asked. He had sent me an email of the X-Ray and the Calvarium. I went to the PC while still keeping the pathologist on the phone. This is what he was showing me:

"On a normal skull – the sinus cavities are butterfly shaped. With this calvarium the right wing of the butterfly is malformed. On your subject's X-Ray the right wing of the butterfly is also malformed in exactly the same way. They are one and the same." The Pathologist pronounced with reassuring and thrilling certainty.

Thursday 11th June 2015

Bremner reported that Karl King was often seen at the Byfleet golf club, and so at the bar Bremner made his approach. He went up to him and introduced himself.

Just like that.

He told him he was an ex-copper and knew Mallard. Apparently Mallard had mentioned Bremner to Karl King and described him as "a good sort." Karl King is by nature wary of ex-coppers and even ex-coppers with a beef against the force. But according to Bremner he played his role well, and convinced King that he genuinely wanted to put one over on the law.

They had a few drinks – Bremner stuck to the Red Bulls and towards the end of the night King turned to him and said "I am moving up market. I need girls – classy girls. If you can bring them to me, then we can talk."

I knew just the girl for the job.

Chapter 18

Ferdy the Fucker

Thursday 11th June 2015

HER NAME IS MEKISHA Lavelle and I refer to her as the Ministry of Sound girl, on account of her scam involved the famous nightclub and a bogus night that she was raising investment for. Ingenious it was, and I even felt slightly bad for nicking her. I marked her out as a young woman of great promise.

So Mekisha the Ministry of Sound girl was out of prison just six months. She had been living with her Mum, and like everyone out of the nick these days was struggling to get any sort of proper paying work to set her on the straight and narrow. This was a real shame because a woman of her intelligent deviousness could make a killing in the city. So Mekisha was game for a bit of proper paying undercover work.

Bremner introduced her to Karl King at the golf club, and the beauty of this undercover operation was the fake story was based on the real story. She used her real name and her real past – she was Mekisha Roland who had just come out of prison for fraud and was looking to earn some serious wedge. She's glamorous and sexy and so would make a perfect high-class prostitute.

Karl King locked his sights onto her, brought her a drink – and Bremner left them to it.

Thursday 11th June 2015

Jane Barrow at the *Surrey Star* had continued running her *Find Ramona Marks* campaign. I called her up to tell her that the skull found in the Grays, Essex may be hers. But I did not tell her definitely. Why is that? Bear with me armchair sleuths, all will become clear.

I also told Jane that I was on the verge of finding out the identity of Ramona's killer – *and it wasn't Mallard.* I told Jane that the killer had messed up and had deposited DNA on the skull, which we were able to trace with new scientific advances. I considered telling Hinty what I was playing at, but after a long discussion, Matt and I decided against it and to just press on. I had spotted Matt acting rather strange of late, distant and troubled. But I thought it best not to pry.

Friday 12th June 2015

On this day the *Surrey Star* published the slightly fake story that the skull that had been found and we were on the verge of finding out who killed Ramona – and it wasn't Mallard. I did not have Karl King down as a *Surrey Star* reader but I was anticipating that this story would reach him. Hinty was straight on the blower demanding to know what I was up to. I fobbed him off by telling him I was investigating the death of Ramona Marks and I was annoyed that the *Surrey Star* had got with the story. I said it was possible that people other than Mallard or Taylor had killed Ramona, but I was not reopening the Daria and Angela case.

Saturday 13th June 2015

The next unexpected development in this investigation came in the form of a harsh vulgar female voice calling me on my home landline. "He's gone missing." She said.

I recognised the coarse London accent as Bremner's wife. She had never been my greatest fan. "Bremner?" I said in a reflex reaction.

"THAT'S NOT HIS NAMEYOU BASTARD!" She

screeched.

I forgot momentarily what his real name was. I mentally scrambled for it - William Naismith.

“When was the last time you saw William?” I asked with genuine concern.

“I am not calling to ask you to investigate. I am calling to tell you it’s your fault he’s drinking again. I HOPE YOU’RE PROUD OF YOURSELF.” And with that she hung up.

I had my mobile on silent. I picked up my phone to find three texts had been sent to me over Friday night going into Saturday morning:

I AM HAVING A DRINK ...

FERDY THE FUCKER!

YOU BASTARD. YOU RUINED MY LIFE!

All from guess who?

Now I remember Bremner showing off his Iphone- an anniversary present from his lovely wife. Now you can locate those phones if you have the password. I picked up the phone and put my head inside the mouth of the beast. “Listen, Jenni,” – that’s Bremner’s wife’s name – “I am going to find Brem ... I mean William for you. I am going to get him sober and bring him home to you safe and sound. It’s the least I can do. I am going to try and find him through the Find My Phone application – do you know what his password might be?”

And so she passed it on - *apophenia23*.

And so from the comfort of my living room and the domestic PC I found a location near Kempton Park Racecourse. The graph took to me a pleasant pub, popular with racing enthusiasts. I drove over there and walked in to see a group of middle aged paunchy men all looking up at the racing on the TV screen. One of the men ran towards a broom cupboard beside the bar and shut the door behind him. I went to the door and knocked gently.

"Bremner. It's Ferdy. Come Out."

The slurred voice from the behind the door drawled "FUCK OFF, FERDY, YOU FUCKER."

"Come out, Bremner – let's discuss it."

"I wouldn't want to discuss the colour of my underpants with you."

"Well, actually neither would I." Not sure what he meant by that.

I felt him release his grip of the door, and I quickly pulled the door open and led him out. The racing enthusiasts were now glued to our spectacle instead of the TV screen.

I sat him down and got him a mineral water.

"I've just had the biggest fright of my life – and it's all because of you!"

"What happened?"

"He cornered me in the bogs, pushed me against the wall and grabbed me by the knackers and said, 'I had you checked out with my people – they say you're not undercover.' He then twisted my balls, I howled in pain, and he said – 'Because if you were, you would die in excruciating pain.'"

"You're talking about Karl King?"

"Of course, I'm talking about your Karl King. He's connected – he has people in the force."

"You know Bremner, gangsters say these things to give the impression they are all powerful. He probably knows fuck all. What are you scared about anyway? I am paying your green gages, not the force, so there's no record of you doing any undercover work."

"You better get that Mekisha out of there. Pronto." "Nah! Mekisha can handle herself. She'll be just fine." Bremner however was off undercover detail indefinitely. I sobered him up and took him back to his adoring wife.

Monday 15th June 2015

Late at night and still at the nick I went back to the MISC CRAP to pull out each one of Mallard's letters. This time I was going to type each one out and, by searching on random words try and find clues or patterns. Yes I was turning into an apophenia-head.

As I dropped the letters out of the folders onto the desk I felt something two inch long lodged inside the cardboard flap of the folder. I pulled it out. It was an unmarked USB memory stick. It must have been tossed in and got stuck. My heart did a pirouette. Could it be the BMX Kid's mythical video of the ritual?

I put the memory stick into my PC, licking my lips in anticipation. Yes! The opening image was of a Park at night. It was pitch black and very little was visible apart from a collection of swaying trees in silhouette. Then the BMX Kid's whispered voice was unmistakable from behind the camera.

"Okay, we are in Brooklands Park at just gone midnight. Those Satanists are out again. They come out here about once a month. What the fuck are they playing at? Let's find out."

He points the camera at nothing in particular in the distance.

"That's them over there."

I couldn't see fuck all.

"Let's get a closer look."

Please do.

The camera glides towards some black shapes. His camera-phone is evidently balanced on the handlebars of the bike. Now I could see something but it wasn't clear what it was. Were they wearing masks? Yes. I think so. But maybe not. Was the blond girl on the altar naked? Not sure. Was she even blonde? This footage was just a collection of fuzzy pixels that could be of something – but could be of anything.

Then I heard a roaring male voice. I turned up the volume on my PC, I couldn't make out every word but I got this: "Crackle, crackle, more crackle service. Crackle, crackle, two rules. Crackle, crackle ... must have his toll. Crackle, crackle, crackle cannot leave crackle.

He repeated louder "Once you have served the devil – you can NEVER leave." The BMX Kid's bike got closer. But still no one is visible. No one could be made out. Not even a description. That man behind the mask might be Karl King, it could just as easily be Bernard Manning or Sid Little. The BMX Kid didn't get close enough. There's no decent zoom on his camera phone. They are just 6 shapes. "Okay, time to break up the party." Whispers the BMX Kid. The camera shakes – I hear a rock being thrown and the shapes turn their heads in the direction of the camera. "FUCK YOU, SATANISTS!" Bawled the BMX Kid and the chase is on. The shapes run towards us. The camera turns in the opposite direction and races towards the viaduct in the wall. I can hear the BMX Kid cry of elation as he sped up the wall. I thought I could hear the running footsteps of the angry Satanists behind. Not a bad way of getting your kicks I thought, the BMX Kid obviously thought so. The kid sure could ride. Out of the viaduct and into the open area he raced towards the car park, he turned the bike to face the running Satanists now just faint distant shapes.

"Too slow. Satanists. Too fucking slow." And he rode way. I played the clip right through till the very end, and I am glad I did. The BMX Kid's bike rattled through a car park and gave me a glimpse – just one fleeting frame – of a complete car license plate.

I pulled up the database on my PC and punched in the license plate and what did it give me? One Jeffrey Findlay. Remember him? The am dram guy who likes a drop of the dark stuff.

Tuesday 16th June 2015

I went to see him the following morning in a police van and a couple of uniforms. We spotted him in among the grey commuter parade on their way to the train station. To give him maximum indignity and shame we pulled him out and slammed him into the police van.

"I am investigating the murder of Alex McNaught." He adjusted himself and looked at me with haughty indignation"I don't know who that is."

"Well nevertheless you are involved. He's the kid that ruined your ritual in Brooklands Park last year."

Jeffrey thought on this "The kid on the bike?"

"So you were there?"

"Yes I'm not denying that. He wasn't killed. We didn't even touch him. He rode off and we went back and got on with what we were doing."

"And what was it you were doing?"

"No one takes it seriously. Well I can't speak for anyone else. I actually don't know who anyone else is. But it's just a bit of fun."

"And what were you doing?"

"We were initiating a girl."

"Initiating her into what?" I wanted him to say the K ring but I didn't want to plant words.

"I don't know – probably nothing at all. We do the ritual and then we all ..."

"Do what?"

"Do what we wilt. Look I don't know how perceptive you are. I just pretend. That's all we are doing is pretending. No one was hurt. I didn't even fuck her in the end. And I paid for it."

"How much?"

"None of your business. Right!" He got up with sudden resolve "I've had enough of this harassment. I shall be making an official complaint to ...."

"Shut it – you tart." I interrupted him, perhaps ill advisedly, recalling his Masonic connection. "Answer my questions, or I'll give you something to complain about ...." Jeffrey protested and moved to leave, I blocked his exit and tried to reason with him.

"Sir, I would not be asking these questions if it wasn't serious. That boy on the bike was killed. So who organised the ritual? Who did you pay the money to?"

"A woman I met at an S&M Parlor."

"Might this S&M lady have a name?"

"I only know her as Madame Headlock."

Wednesday 17th June 2015

I was not expecting a joyous welcoming parade when I returned to the flat of Madame Headlock a/k/a Zara Campbell.

"Hello Zara – still working for the K?" I said.

"No I'm not. And it's none of your business." She looked at me like I was a recently discovered tumor.

"When it comes to murder, it is my business." Crap cliché detective line number 7. I love it. I pressed on and barged in "So you organise those rituals in Brooklands Park?"

"No I don't. I wasn't even there. I send some of the girls over and sometimes find the johns."

"Who organises them?"

"I don't know."

"Fuck Off Zara. Give me a name, or you're getting nicked for obstruction."

"You can't send me back there."

"I can – and I will – if you don't give me the people behind the K ring."

"You have him – Mallard."

"Who else?"

"I don't know who else."

"So who ordered you to paint over that satanic mural?"

"Nobody did. Like I told you I did it because it was creeping me out."

"You painted it out just before we searched the place. You didn't want us to see it because you didn't want us to know what a creepy satanic whore party ring you are running here."

"Do not talk like that in front of my son."

And so I turned to young Cody staring at me from behind the kitchen table – I'd known him a year and he'd shot up in that time. His big innocent eyes, his fleshy cheeks – that scar had healed slightly but was still visible. If I can't get the truth from an adult, I'll ask a child.

I knelt down to him "Cody. Who cut your face?"

Zara jumped straight in. "Don't you dare you talk to my child!!"

I persisted "Cody Who cut your face?"

Zara pulled Cody away from me. "He doesn't want to relive the trauma."

"I think he wants to tell me the truth about who cut his face. Don't you Cody?"

I knelt down and addressed him directly "Did a bad man cut your face?"

Cody nodded and looked tearfully. I hated to make him mentally reenact what happened, but I was onto something.

"Which bad men cut your face? Was it this man?" I pulled out my picture of Karl King conveniently placed in my top jacket pocket.

Cody shook his head. "He was hairy – and smelly."

I got up from my crouching position, creaking and without much dignity and turned to Zara "Don't protect these people Zara. Don't give in to people that would hurt your child to try and control you."

I uneasily lumbered myself down again to speak with Cody. This active detective work is playing hell on my joints. "Don't worry, Cody. We'll get that hairy, smelly man for you."

Friday 19th June 2015

Big day today. I had leaked to the *Surrey Star* yet another fake story. This time the wheeze was that the skull could not be verified as Ramona's, and even worse, the DNA lead had proved to be inconclusive. My direct quote in the paper – "We now have no reason to believe that anybody other than Mallard and Taylor were behind the death of Ramona."

Mekisha's instruction was to meet with Karl King today and at some point bring out the latest copy of the *Surrey Star*. She was to watch and register his reaction as he saw the article.

Saturday 20th June 2015

So in the morning I got the call I had been waiting for from my girl out in the field. She was calling from the street and extremely agitated.

"I am quitting your operation. I am leaving the country."

"What? What happened?"

"He's locked into me, that's what he's doing. Telling me I can't escape him. He's an evil creep."

"I know that," I said perhaps a little flippantly. "How did he react when he saw the paper?"

"Fuck you..."

"Come on. I need to know. What were his exact words and how did he say it?"

"FUCK YOU!" She howled at me. "You have put me in serious danger. I have just had to run away from him. He was trying to ply me with all sorts of drinks and drugs. He now knows where I live."

"How?"

"He's been following me. He's stalking me." Mekisha gave every impression of not being a girl that scares easy, but she was clearly terrified of this man.

"He's been sending me creepy texts."

"Saying things like what?"

"Saying things like – 'You are mine.' 'You can't escape the K.' 'I have chosen you.'"

"So come on, this is real important, how did he react when he saw the paper?"

"Yeah – he punched the air and ordered some drinks."

This would not be admissible in any court, but vital in convincing me that this is the man to go for.

"Anyway – I'm out. I'm not doing your fucking job any more. I'm leaving the country."

"You're leaving the country?"

"Yes – but first you owe me my fifteen hundred."

Thursday 2nd July 2015

Something was definitely up with Matt the Stat today. He had been working on his PC as usual but instead of that mask of squinty-eyed concentration, he was furiously tapping away and every so often looking up to glare at me, and then looking away.

So I went out of the office and came back, telling him that his mother was in reception asking about him. Matt tore out of there, which gave me the chance to take a sneaky look at what he was up to. And what I saw chilled me to the bone. It was addressed to HR and it read like this:

"I cannot work with DCI Colin Ferdinand any longer. I have reached the end of my tether. He disrespects me and takes me for granted. He frequently mocks me in

front of other policemen, the public and even criminals. I am the constant butt of his unfunny jokes and demeaning remarks.

DCI Ferdinand's police methods go beyond unconventional. In fact he has a cavalier disregard for proper procedure and regulation and he is constantly making me party to many practices that could severely undermine the investigation.

Furthermore I am routinely excluded from any social gathering. I am often left to work alone while Ferdy and his cronies enjoy a drink without me. I have NEVER been invited to join them. So far I have suffered in silence, but I cannot suffer any longer..." I was still reeling from what I had read when Matt returned. I turned to him, looked at him straight in the eye – "Matt I am so sorry. I had no idea you felt this way." "You lied to me. My mother was not in reception."

"Matt the reason I never invited you to the pub was because I thought you didn't want to go. I thought you were better than that, sitting listening to Gaffney trying to be funny. I thought I was sparing you."

"It would have been nice to have been asked once in a while."

"Come on let's go for a drink now."

"No. I can't go for a drink with you now – that would be too weird."

"Listen. I can't imagine being a cop without you by my side. If I can't work with you, Matt, I don't want to be a police officer."

There was a big pause as Matt looked away. I went on, "I'll change. I won't do those things anymore. I'll be respectful to you – and I will not take you for granted. I will turn over a new leaf."

"You can't change."

"I will change. Matt, give me a chance. One more

chance. I can do it. I promise."

Matt looked unmoved. This was far more shocking and upsetting than Cassie leaving me or having an affair. With Cassie I knew she disrespected and despised me – but with Matt - all those hours we'd spent alone in cars talking about the case, I had no idea that all the while he'd been harbouring thoughts of resentment towards me. And he said my jokes were unfunny.

"Look let's get to the bottom of this Ramona Marks Karl King case. If you still feel the same way after that, then...well then just put your complaint through, and I will not appeal or stand in your way.

"You're Matt – my partner. I can't be me, without you."

Matt the Stat softened, he was as keen to collar Karl King and avenge Ramona as much as I was. We nearly hugged but we didn't. That's not the done thing in the Surrey Police.

So how was it going with this Ramona/Karl King case? Not good. We had every reason to think that Karl King was involved – but we had nothing solid. With Mekisha's anecdotal testimony I may have been able to persuade top brass to put a surveillance operation on him. But now she had fucked off, I had nothing.

I needed a break. That chink in the armor of evil that lets in the daylight of the truth.

It's coming dear readers. It's coming.

Chapter 19

The Laughter Identity Parade

Tuesday 23rd July 2015

THE BIG BREAK CAME in the form of an early morning feverish phone call from Versago, the ex-Vampire who now loved his Mum.

"The guy who kidnapped me just spoke to me." "When?"

"Just now."

"Stay where you are. We're coming over." Like the clappers I drove over there with Matt to the roadside caff where Roger was waiting.

The caff itself was a hut on wheels in a lay bye off the main road by a thickly wooded area. It's popular with lorry drivers who like to get some grease in their stomachs before taking their cargos to the West Country.

Roger was sat at the wooden bench and took us through what happened. "I was sitting here having a coffee with a bacon sandwich. This bloke came over and threw a coffee cup in the bin next to me. I had my back to him and I didn't turn to look at him. I then got a rough tap on the shoulder and this bloke said 'I thought you preferred cat food.' He laughed and dashed off."

"Did you get a look at him?"

"No he was away too fast."

"Did you see the vehicle he got into?"

"He got into a van, but I didn't see it properly. I told you before, my eye sight is a bit ropey"

"Get some glasses mate. Which direction did his vehicle go? Can you at least tell me that?"

"He didn't go towards the main road, he went into the lane that went into the woods."

"So how do you know this is the guy who kidnapped you?"

"The laugh. I remember that laugh. I'd recognise it anywhere."

We asked the bloke who owned the caff if he knew who the man might be, but he was blanker than a Big Brother contestant on Mastermind.

"He wasn't a regular...."

"Would you recognise him if you saw him again?"
"Who? I've served a dozen geezers in the last half hour" I was on a merry dance to nowhere with this fellow.

Matt chipped in – "Ferdy what about the bin he threw the cup into?"

"Yes but they'll be dozens of dodgy geezers' DNA floating around in there."

"Yes but then we would have a shortlist. If the abductor has previous and is on the DNA database, then he'll be on our shortlist."

Brilliant! I immediately ordered the bin to be taken in as evidence. The caff owner protested vigorously but sod him, we're the Surrey police we can take any bin we want.

Friday 24th July 2015

The DNA results come back! And they were strange and fascinating, and more than a little perplexing. From four DNA samples we had five DNA matches. Yes, five from four.

Cup 1 DNA Sample 1 – (*No match* on the database)
Cup 2 DNA Sample 2 – (Match to *Ray Meredith* 12.3.63)
Cup 3 DNA Sample 3 – (Match to *Brian Donnelly* 15.11.66)
Cup 3 DNA Sample 3 – (Match to *Nick Shoosmith* 23.1.66
Cup 4 DNA Sample 4 – (*No match* on the database)

Note that Cup 3 has two DNA matches against it. What are the chances of that? As remote as Bremner being let back into the force and being made Commander, it's just never going to happen. And wasn't Nick Shoosmith supposed to be dead? His DNA had been taken when he had been accused of murdering Andrea Perry. The person sharing his exact same DNA was taken from a conviction of four years prior. A Brian Donnelly nightclub bouncer who had been arrested for taking advantage of some of the out-of-it female clientele.

Further scrutiny of Brian Donnelly threw up another oddity that only came to light when we cross-referenced all our available databases. Brian Donnelly with that same date of birth, born at the same hospital, born to the same parents, died from Leukemia aged four.

So we have two dead people in our DNA bin. What conclusions can we draw from all of this? I'll give you a minute or two.

Okay – so Nick Shoosmith faked his death and assumed the identity of a dead child. In the conman fraternity this is common practice. The Old Bill also do it to create the identity for an undercover operation. But never assume, always verify we sent two uniforms over to the parents of Brian Donnelly to establish that he really had died at the age of four.

Saturday 25th July 2015

While that was going on, Matt and I looked closer at the circumstances surrounding Shoosmith's "suicide." His battered body was identified by one Andy Mallard. The pieces of track were starting to click into place like a Scalextric train set.

From delving into his records I discovered that Shoosmith was head of security at the infamous, since closed down, Jolly Boatman Nightclub in Hampton Court –

he was known as The Boatman. Wasn't there a reference to the Boatman in crazy man Mallard's letters? The Boatman got form from drug dealing, pimping and grievous bodily harm.

I got a courier to send me over the interview tape of Nick Shoosmith from Maidenhead nick, and I watched the whole two hour police interview performance from start to finish.

I know this sounds silly coming from a grown man, but playing it back gave me the willies. Not something I'm used to you understand. That large frame that took up a quarter of the screen and those burning eyes got me fearing that he would come out at me from the video screen like one of them Japanese horror films.

I reached the bit with the laugh that had so chilled Ed Brooks, the officer in charge of the Andrea Perry case, and was most likely the laugh that taunted Roger Farrady. I played that laugh over and over.

I then collected a sound sample of four other laughs from assorted people around the station and invited Roger in for a laughter identity parade. Yes that's not a misprint I was going to have a laugher identity parade.

I knew it wouldn't stand up in court. In fact I knew it would quite literally make this Ferdy a right laughing stock, but it would establish in my own mind that Nick Shoosmith was still alive and behind the abduction of Roger Farrady. We sat Roger in the interview room and in solemn silence he listened to all five laughs. Without any doubt he went for Laughter Number 3. The distinctive guttural ack-ack of Nick Shoosmith.

I then went to see the houseboat resident, the riverside bohemian who heard laughter and splashing at 2 a.m. the night Angela was killed. I played him back the audio of the five laughs from my phone. Did he recognise any of these as the laugh he heard that night?

He looked at me like as if he'd just caught me in the laundry room sniffing his underwear. "Is this your idea of a joke?" He snarled. Time to leave.

Monday 27th July 2015

So the riverside bohemian was giving me nothing, but nevertheless I now had a person clearly in my sights. This Scalextrix track was leading me all the way to the door of Nick Shoosmith. I pulled out the mug shot of Brian Donnelly and placed it next to the freeze frame of Shoosmith's police interview. The flickering cathode rays revealed an undeniable truth – these two men were one and the same.

Three months after "Brian Donnelly's" release from his too brief prison sentence, he had registered with the police as of No Fixed Abode. Not at all helpful.

So where was he residing? I thought back to Roger Farrady and his encounter with the man. The myopic Roger did not see the vehicle properly – but he was at least able to point in the direction that the vehicle went. And it was away from the main road, and into the slip road that led to a smaller road into the wood.

I got out the Ordinance Survey map of the woods and looked at the businesses and residencies three miles along that road. A cluster of rural businesses here, and a collection of houses there. What jumps out? Let's go back to the first two murders. Remember the horse snaffle bits that were used to fasten the two victims to the riverbed? So let's take a look at anything connected with horses. Some stables – a farm. What about Macken's Knackers Yard? A place where horses are slaughtered and their carcasses sold to the glue factory.

It was owned by a Peter Macken. Very possibly another fake identity.

I looked at the records we had on the Macken

Knackers Yard. They had lost their incinerating license when the residents complained about the smell. Apparently their incinerating business had been dormant for so long, when it started up again, the magistrates sided with the residents who had lived there peaceably for five years without the unpleasant smell of burning animals.

Further investigating in these affairs revealed the owners were in big trouble with the bank for nonpayment of the mortgage. They had started defaulting in November 2014 – at the same time that the CarPhone Whorehouse finally shut down. Southern Electricity had served a final red bill in February 2015, and cut off the supply in March 2015. So whoever was residing there now was doing so without the luxury of electricity.

I then turned to the Enviro Crime incident reports. The complaints of smoke and the smell of burning that shut down the knackers yard business took place in the first three months of 2014.

But there had been another complaint of foul smell and smoke late at night on Wednesday the 11th June 2014. That day Ramona had called her grandparents. The day that she was most probably snatched and killed. Could it be her body that was being burnt that night? This murder was to silence her, and to make her disappear, which is why we did not have the ritualistic overtones of the previous two murders.

According to the Enviro Crime report, the neighbours had descended onto the yard to complain and to point out that their license to incinerate had been revoked. The man that came outside was very rude and threatening, and so the neighbours called the police. By the time the police had arrived the rude man had fled the premises.

The police returned the following morning to speak to the man and in the short interview he denied everything.

He gave his name as Brian Donnelly.

I put down the report and looked out the window. The sun was low in the sky – not much of this highly productive day left, but for Matt and I there was an urge to squeeze yet more out. We couldn't turn in for the day now; we were aching to find out what was going on at that Knackers Yard. Was Brian Donnelly staying there now, and are we looking at the murder scene for all three killings? The repossession notice was dated for Thursday the 30th July four days' time. If I did not act fast I would lose my crime scene to the bank. I needed to raise a warrant to search that Knackers Yard.

So I hastily put the warrant through. The high profile case I had been working on closed last year, so I had no fast track now, so I marked it URGENT! In double-thick red biro.

In the meantime we were going to go over to this Mackens Knackers Yard. Hoping to observe from a safe distance this "Brian Donnelly" going in or leaving.

It was my turn to drive and we remained silent all the way there – our minds simmering with anticipation, the brilliant afternoon sun shining in our eyes.

I considered breaking the silence by cracking some wordplay joke about having him by the knackers, but bearing in mind Matt's recent memo, thought better off it. So in silence we remained. We drove into the slip road that Farrady had pointed down, which took us into a thick wooded area, tall trees on either side and the occasional charming half timbre cottage. After three miles and about 20 minutes of driving I worked out that we had just driven past one of the cottages that would have complained of the incinerating smell. This was when I got a call from Hinton. "What's this warrant for? Your covering note isn't very clear."

"It's about the Ramona Marks murder, Sir."

"Yes, but what actual evidence do you have to justify a search of the premises?"

"We have reason to believe, Sir, that the person who is a tenant there is using a fake ID. I believe him to be a Nick Shoosmith who is supposedly dead but has a connection to the deaths of Daria Lipsinksi and Angela Ashdown." I still remembered their full names, despite all my other cases, even after a year.

"Why do you have reason to believe that - on what grounds?" barked Hinty.

Matt tapped my shoulder to indicate that the knackers yard was now twenty foot away. I braked the car directly outside a two-story cottage.

"DNA evidence, Sir. A sample from a nearby bin from two men who are supposedly dead with the exact same DNA. It would indicate one has faked his death and taken the identity of someone who died as a child."

"And what's that got to do with murder?"

On this I started realizing that my case was rather tenuous so I resorted to a "Sir, please trust me on this one."
"I trust you, Ferdy, but I can't dish out search warrants willy nilly."

Go on, you silly old git – I thought, but didn't say.
"It's not willy nilly, Sir,"

"It *is* willy nilly."

"It's not, Sir – willy nilly."

"Listen, I am not going debate with you the meaning of willy nilly. You will need to come to the magistrate and fully demonstrate your evidence on why you need this warrant."

"Whatever it takes, Sir. I am convinced of the validity of this investigation." I think that came out sounding unintentionally sarcastic.

We got out of the car. The sun was setting. More shadow than light. A curtain twitched in the neighbouring cottage's window but we stared ahead at the suspected building. From the distance all you could see was a high spiked metal fence, topped with barbed wire. They obviously didn't want anyone stealing their dead animals. We walked tentatively towards it, no sign of habitation, but of course the electricity had been cut off. Getting to the metal gate I peered through, to see unruly and overgrown vegetation with a worn down vehicle track passing through the middle. In the far right corner was a rusty metal cylindrical structure with a chimney which corrosion had turned to a nasty faded orange. This I had to assume was the incinerator that they were banned from using. At the very back was a flat roofed concrete bunker. I assumed this to be the slaughterhouse and in the far left hand corner was a tumbledown shack. This had to be the living quarters. No vehicle to be seen, so whoever was staying here was most likely out. The layout of the premises looked like this:

The temptation to look around inside without waiting for a warrant was overwhelming, but the metal spiked fence topped by barbed wire made that a very painful proposition. "Let's go round the back and see what else we can see," I whispered to Matt and we pushed our way through the thick unwelcoming undergrowth to get behind the grounds.

"They've hop wired the electricity from the next house," remarked the ever-observant Matt as I peered through the metal fence from behind. He pointed out a thick black cable that went into the ramshackle hut via a broken hole, about one meter in circumference that had been drilled into the metal fence.

"That's got to be against the law!" I said.

I sized up the hole. It was big enough for me squeeze in if I breathed in hard. I'd had a light lunch so I might be all right.

"I'm going in." I declared to Matt and throwing down

my jacket pushed my way through head first, praying not to get electrocuted by the cable.

"Ferdy!" gasped out Matt – doubtlessly distraught by yet more of my "cavalier disregard for proper procedure and regulation."

Ever seen a mouse push their way through a hole the size of a pencil? That's me folks. Mind you it was an almighty eye-poppingly tight squeeze. Going through the hole was just the first part of the squeeze. With my body halfway through I found myself wedged inside a two-foot gap between the metal fence and the shack. I continued to push my way through, scraping my hands and face in the process, ripping my shirt and cardigan.

I was in. I walked to the center of the yard, the vehicle track running through the dirt and vegetation revealed that a vehicle was regularly using the premises. Debris cluttered against all the walls of the metal fence – a cooker, a fridge, a television. To the left of the presumed slaughterhouse was a pile of rocks stacked four foot high. Is that where the weapons came from?

I made over to the incinerator and opened the small metal door. It creaked in rusty agony. Blackness Inside. Perhaps against my better judgment I placed my hand into the abyss. In amongst the ash I felt a plastic melted object, which could be a burnt out mobile phone. With a shiver I pulled my hand out again. This incinerator was not used to burn the first two victims. But it may have been used to incinerate clothes, purses and other possessions. With Ramona they probably tried to burn the whole body because they wanted that to be treated as a disappearance, and that's why they got the complaints from the neighbours and they then took her remains as far afield as possible. Hence the skull winding up in Essex.

I moved from the incinerator to the slaughterhouse. I opened the metal door and reached around the walls for a light switch. I flicked on a switch and the strip lights came on line by line in a left to right sequence. The interior air here was musty. I fancied I detected the underlying smell of death, putrid organs, and blood that no quantity of cleaning products could ever remove. The floor was tiled and had obviously been cleaned, but traces of blood would still be found between the cracks.

Hanging from the ceiling and in the middle of the room were two straps. Consistent with the two ligatures marks on the victim's wrists. You wouldn't need to hang a horse or a cow up by the wrists would you?

I looked around at the walls – there were padded with that perforated egg box style coating you see in recording studios. So they had soundproofed the walls. Why would you sound proof a slaughterhouse? In the far corner was a guitar and amp. Battered and half destroyed in keeping with everything else in this environment. I walked out and turned right to the living quarters shack next door.

I swung open the door and pushed my head in, looking around in the dusky interior half-light. A camper bed in the corner, a small fridge in the other. Portable TV, dirty plates and cups strewn everywhere. The smell was of stale milk, rotten food and semen. Not even the most slovenly of rats would live in this hovel. There was a door to a toilet. No way was I going in there. Instead I turned to the wall opposite covered by a faded red bed sheet that acted like a curtain nailed from the top. I pulled the sheet back to reveal a series of pinned up photographs. Polaroid images of sadism, women tied up, bruised and bloody. Though repelled, my eyeballs attempted to run over them for any polaroids of the victims. I could not identify any of them. On the facing wall was painted a large black K. I tried to the picture the man staying here. What appeared to me was ugly beyond belief. He must sit here and sing to himself "are you loathsome tonight?"

This is where the man would keep his trophies – mementos of the killing. I badly needed to come back here with that warrant and my silver haired forensic friend to search this place properly. For now better get out of here and share my findings with Matt.

But before negotiating the push through the fence I looked back at the slaughterhouse. It gave off a sense of foreboding, as if it was challenging me to go back inside. So I did, and shut the door behind me. I stood in the middle of the room. I put my hands through the hanging straps and closed my eyes, unseeing like Daria and Angela before they died. I listened hard. I could hear traffic from the road outside. I blocked that out and focused on the room.

I don't want to get all mystical on you, but against the black screen of my shut eyes I swear I could see flashes of the murder, mutilation, fear and excruciating pain that had taken place in this room. My eyes tightened shut and the visions I saw filled me with dread. I knew I was in the killing place.

I opened my eyes to find a man standing before me. He was unshaven with scraggly hair and a face like a starved hyena. This is the man I had seen in mug shots and interview tapes. It's as if he'd really had come crawling out of the video screen like one of those Japanese Horror films. He was an angry beast who had found someone messing with his lair.

Before I could loosen my hands from the straps, my eyes were blinded by a white flash. This came with a sting across my eyes and I was sent swinging in the straps. Still with my wrists looped into the straps and unable now to see my attacker I attempted a sprawling kung fu kick that was more Hong Kong Phoey than Bruce Lee. I next felt a stabbing pain in my kidneys and the impact knocked me out of the straps onto the hard tiled floor.

I looked up at my attacker, helpless as I anticipated more vicious pain and ultimate death from his sucker punch. A cruel smile played upon his lips, he was savoring the moment. This was an encounter with pure sadism.

Then a figure with a familiar bespectacled face grabbed his neck from behind. Matt was no match for this ox but he was at least able to surprise and unfoot him, which gave me the chance to get up and knee this fucker in the nuts. He gave a loud howl and lashed out – but Matt and me both rushed him and he fell down from my very unfair and most irregular rugby tackle.

The man got up with frightening stealth and made a dash towards the wall where the guitar and amp lay. He grabbed the guitar by the neck and swung it about like a demented axe man. We backed off, the guitar swung again whistling past my ear – and we backed off some more.

Then Matt and I ran out of the room and slammed the door shut. Outside Matt fished out his phone and called the nick as I attempted to hold the door shut. I clung to the handle for dear life but he was too strong, he pushed the metal door open ripping off several layers of skin from my palm.

At the count of three we rushed him. I drove my head down and butted him in the stomach sending him back and crashing against the door, he fell to the ground and Matt swopped down to put on the handcuffs.

But the struggle did not end there. Matt pulled his jacket over his head as the man wriggled around like a giant blinded crab. His phone fell out of his pocket. He then charged at us, still with his jacket over his eyes. I tripped him up and he fell to the floor with a loud thud which gave Matt the chance to put a second set of bracelets on his legs. All good cops must go out prepared with two sets of handcuffs, and Matt was one hell of a good cop.

It had been a wordless fight – a symphony of grunts

with a percussion of pained howls. Pulling his jacket away from his face, I read him his rights: "I am arresting you for attacking a police officer. You do not have to say anything, but it may harm your defense if you do not mention when questioned something which you later rely on in court. Anything you say may be given in evidence."

"Where's your fuckin' warrant?"

He had a point there. So without saying another word I dragged him by the leg towards the entrance to the compound. I noticed now his vehicle – a white van – and the open gate. He wriggled free and I motioned for Matt to help – each of us taking a leg.

"You have the right to remain silent. I suggest you fuckin' use it," I said.

"Or what?" As we dragged him through the grass by the legs. We stopped halfway across the yard – he was just too heavy.

We handcuffed him again. This time with my handcuffs and to his vehicle and we called for a meat wagon. I said nothing more to the arrested man – I had done enough protocol breaches and did not want to push my luck. I would next speak to him on the record and under oath, hopefully by which time the boys in yellow would have found some damning forensic evidence.

I was still regaining my breath and nursing my bloody palm when the wagon turned up twenty minutes later. As they took him away I saw that Matt had been studying the arrested man's phone.

"Found anything nice?" I asked.

"Very nice." He handed me the phone and showed me this very intriguing text exchange:

I NEED BUNCE.

AM BROKE AT THE MO. BUT DONT WORRY. AM SETTING UP SUMFINK & YOU WILL BE INVOLVED.

WANT PAYING FOR LAST JOB.

WOT LAST JOB?

THE SCATTY ONE

THAT WAS LIKE THE OTHERS. FUN. NO PAYMENT.

FIRST 2 WAS 4 FUN. 3 WAS A GAGGING. IT WAS A JOB. I WANT PAYING.

CAN'T DO IT. WILL WEDGE YOU IN FOR OTHER JOBS WHEN I HAVE SOME DOUGH.

The text messages had stopped in April 2015. I knew I had to act fast – because the person on the other end of these text messages would soon find out his litigious colleague was in the nick.

There was no time to waste. I had to arrange to get this place searched immediately, and thinking of procedure I needed to make sure that we stayed out of hot water for this entering without a warrant thing. Even though no one was around, I whispered this to Matt.

"By the way if anyone asks the fight took place <u>outside</u> the knackers yard."

"That's a lie. I can't do that," Matt said with an air sickening sanctimony.

As we got to the station Hinty was in the car park waiting for us. Instead of being elated, which was how I felt he should be, he had his stern face on.

"Your suspect has made a serious allegation that you entered his premises without a warrant." I played it cool "Well he's a crook. He would say that wouldn't he?"

"Before I allow you to interview the suspect or search the premises I have to investigate this."

"What?" "I need to take official statements from the both of you. I need to convince myself that this is regulation, and if he does take this to the courts, we'll come out on top." I did not get a chance to brief Matt as he was led away into an interview room by Hinty and a support officer. I waited outside with my stomach in knots. By trespassing I had comprised an enquiry, and not just any enquiry a murder investigation. This was ultra-serious.

My future was in the hands of my estranged colleague Matt the Stat. If he wanted to undermine me, if he wanted me sacked, if he wanted promotion for himself – this was his chance. Was he going to tell the truth to the makeshift tribunal – or was he going to do the decent thing and lie?

I looked around the corridor; this could be my last day as a police officer. I couldn't imagine myself doing anything else. I'd spend my days having croissant and cappuccinos with Bremner bitching about how the force had changed for the worse.

I was in agony, scratching at my ringworm like no tomorrow. Eventually the door opened, Matt looked at me blankly, and then turning his back marched down the corridor. I felt sick. Then Hinty appeared at the door and summonsed me in.

My head was swimming as I sat in front of him. What could I say in mitigation to soften the blow? Would I be thrown out of the force? Or could I take demotion instead? I would take demotion. Just so I could stay in the force. I couldn't not be a copper. Please Hinty – at least let me stay a copper.

I was about to start my pleading when Hinty spoke. "Matt told me everything."

Long Pause.

"This man did you a favor by attacking you outside his premises because now he is arrested you have the right search the premises. It's obvious this man has something to hide. " "So I don't need to add anything?"

"No Matt was quite comprehensive. Now get to work on this man Donnelly ... Shoosmith whoever he may be, and let's see what we have on him."

I leapt out of my seat and gratefully shook Hinty's hand and walked straight out of the station. Matt had come through and lied for me. I wanted to buy him chocolates and flowers, take him to a fancy meal and a show of his choice in the West End. Whatever he wanted. I breezed out the station and when I got a safe distance from any cooper I dialed.

He did not pick up.

The clock had hit seven when I returned to the nick. Matt was at his desk. I smiled – he did not smile back.

"I really appreciate this Matt," I offered.

"You put me in an intolerable position. I will not do that again for you," he said staring at his PC and avoiding eye contact. I stood there with my head bowed momentarily, trying to look suitably guilty and humble.

"I will not do that again, Matt. I promise," I pronounced solemnly.

More silence until I eventually said "Okay, now we've put that behind us. We have a case to solve. Now give me the accused's phone, and let's get this fucker nailed."

Chapter 20

Ferdy's Goal Late Into Injury Time

Monday 27th July 2015 – Evening

I LOOKED OVER THAT TEXT correspondence again – they could only be talking about one thing. The Scatty One must be a reference to Ramona. How dare they call her that? How dare they do what they did? Once again I became seized by a wave of anger.

I decided I needed to ambush this other man. Make him come out of his hole. I was still stinging from my injuries from my fight with Shoosmith and did not fancy another scrap, but if I was smart, this time I could get others to do the scrapping for me. I called the front desk to order that under no circumstances is Shoosmith/Donnelly to have any contact with the outside world for the next four hours. I then arranged for five uniforms in an unmarked van to immediately take Matt and me back to the knackers yard. In the van from Shoosmith's phone I knocked out this text.

I WANT PAYING PROPAH FOR THE RAMONA JOB AND ... YOU'D BETTER GET DOWN TO MY GAFF FOR 10 TONITE TO TALK ABOUT IT ... OR ELSE I AM BLABBING TO THE OB!

Showing my text to Matt, he shot me his look of disapproval "you really are pushing your luck," he said shaking his head. "But this is regular ... Okay, maybe this text correspondence would not be admissible. But we can arrest him on it and search his premises and something will come from that."

"That text is entrapment. It will not be admissible. It's a big risk."

"What else can we do? I need to smoke this guy out; otherwise he'll just go to ground and destroy that phone the minute he hears we've got Shoosmith. Come on we are going to find out the person pulling the strings behind all of this. You should be excited."

In the van I got a call after call from that number. Naturally I did not pick up, but each time the caller declined to leave a message. Instead he eventually texted back C U @ 10.

It was Nine O Clock and now dark on this balmy late July evening. As we reached the knackers yard we parked the unmarked van out of sight and some distance away. We walked through the gate still open from our previous fun and games, the white van was still there parked in the middle.

So Matt and two uniforms hid in the shack. I couldn't go back in there myself, so three uniforms and I hid in the slaughterhouse.

So who was it going to be? Now of course my money is on my man Karl King. But in fantasy detective land that would be much too obvious because I'd had my eye on this fellow since the beginning of Part 3. So who else might show up as the string puller? Let's run through some the suspects we met earlier:

> **Jeffrey Hindlay?** The am dram guy who likes the dark stuff. I'd love to hang this on him.
>
> **Terry Bowell and Vince Machin?** The satanic cult experts, dubbed Hinge and Bracket by Bremner. Likely suspects with their unhealthy obsession with the satanic.

Bremner? Et tu Bremner? He knew about the weirdo file, and he knew that Roger Farrady was in it.

Mr. Montgomery? The free mason magistrate. I doubt a plumy mouthed magistrate would send texts worded like that. But you never know.

Hinty? "This is coming from the very top." Detective novel cliché #9. We can rule him out. He knows we've arrested Shoosmith so he wouldn't fall into our trap.

Slimy Simon Todd? Could Bungle the Bear be the killer? I doubt it.

That sandy haired git who runs the pub? He's a bit of a nonentity but he could have a dark side.

Zara Campbell? Coming out of leftfield. I would not like to tackle her with those biceps. Would she cut her own child?

Ann MacLean? The Cat Sanctuary lady. Come on – now you're being silly.

Anyone else? John the john? Ahmed the taxi driver? Jack the hair gel student? The batty houseboat resident? Roy the Silver Fox CS Guy? Who are you betting on?

We waited in the darkness in total silence, playing anxiously with our torches and listening out for a vehicle to arrive. Presently we heard a mechanical roar from a powerful engine getting louder, getting closer. I peered through the crack in the door.

Too dark. I could only see shades of black.

"Come on Nick. Let's sort this out." I heard an impatient male voice shout out. I saw a black shape moving twelve feet away.

I pushed open the door and marched towards the

figure "You're nicked." I shone the torch in his face as rudely and as intrusively as possible.

It was Karl King. His jaw dropped open as he clocked the rest of the uniform appearing around him. He was supposed to look daggers at me as the five uniforms swopped on him from either side and whisked him away. Instead he charged towards me and held his head back. In a split second I registered that he was about to head butt me. In police training we are told to lower your head if you see this happening. That way your forehead will hit his nose – and you will head-butt him.

Crack! An explosion of blood over his face as the uniforms seized upon him and did their business.

Phew! That was close. If I'd lowered my head a split second later I would have lost my nose. It took me a good few seconds to recover my composure but I eventually managed to stand up over the restrained Karl King and say what I had been dying to say for a very long time:

"Karl King I am arresting you on suspicion of murder. You do not have to say anything, but it may harm your defense if you do not mention, when questioned, something which you later rely on in court. Anything you do say may be given in evidence. Take him away."

Tuesday 28th July 2015 – Morning

Now in your traditional detective story the main bloke is nicked and it's curtain down and big applause. But this isn't how it is in real life. The arrest is just the beginning of a whole new chapter that could take ages. This is when the lawyers take over and things are never straightforward with them around.

Now as everybody knows, the smarter and richer the suspect, the better his solicitors and the better his chances of beating the rap. I think we had enough on Shoosmith – the fake identity – but there was a real danger that Karl

King could wriggle out of this.

I don't know if it was the throbbing pain in my face or my racing heart that kept me from sleeping that night. I knew the suspect interviews would give me nothing – so everything would hang on what forensics found at that Knackers Yard, and the premises and vehicle of Karl King. So first thing this morning I head to the Knackers Yard where the CS search had already begun.

"Who's in charge of this case? I bet it's Charley Cairoli." Bellowed Roy – the Head Canary surrounded by his team in yellow. This is what greeted me as I arrived at the Knackers Yard early in the morning. For the younger readers, Charley Cairoli was a popular children's entertainer – a clown. So he wasn't paying me a compliment.

I walked into the crime scene singing "Be A Clown." "Guilty as charged," I then said, stepping forward.

He was not the least bit embarrassed by me overhearing him and seemed quite prepared to insult me to my face. "This crime scene has been contaminated," he declared, looking at me distastefully.

"I am sorry about that. You knew when the murderer attacked me, I should have asked him to step outside first so we could have our fight there."

"What fight? I thought that did take place outside." Damn! When you lie you've got to have a good memory. "Yes, it did. Sorry, you mean the ambush then?"

"Yes. Why didn't you set it up outside the crime scene?"

"I had to do it in this space because by him driving into it, it proves that the murderer knows this place and knows that the other murderer is based here."

"The alleged murderers. We haven't found anything on them yet. So keep away from the site. You've contaminated the crime scene enough already."

I walked away and grabbed a coffee from the police van outside. Nasty brown liquid that was coffee in name only. I remembered the roadside caff three miles up the road and drove up there.

The man recognised me and was about to give service with a smile when he remembered what happened. "Where's my fucking bin?"

"We haven't finished with it yet. I'll have a coffee and a bacon sandwich. Thank you."

"I tell you what – you bring me back my bin and then I'll get you a coffee and a bacon sandwich."

I was about to pull out my badge and order he serve me, when my phone rang. The canaries were twittering with excitement about something to show me. When I got there they opened up the doors to the slaughterhouse to reveal an interior with the room lighting off and under UV lamps. The glowing purple Luminal had showed up blood splattering all over the floor, all over the walls and the ceiling.

"I wouldn't get too excited, you'd expect to find blood in a slaughterhouse," said Roy trying to piss on my parade. "Yes but if it's human then we're in business. And if it's the blood of one of the victims, we are in cigar city." Now that I had something to bait my suspects with, I headed back to the nick.

When I got there Hinty was waiting for me in reception. "Karl King's solicitors have been hounding me nonstop this morning. They say you attacked him."

"Leave it out. He attacked me – he tried to head butt me and I remembered my police training and lowered my head. The other officers will bear me out."

"They are also saying you have nothing on him and you must release him immediately."

"Nah! Let him stew."

"Ferdy you can't do that unless you have proper evidence."

"I need my top CS man Roy to lead the search of Karl King's place and vehicle and he is currently at work at the Knackers Yard. We've already found blood and I am sure we'll find more before the day is out. As soon as he's finished I'll get him transferred to search Karl King's premises and vehicles."

"Listen you need to get them searching Karl King's place now. I am not having my day ruined by his lawyers calling me, and I will be most displeased if my force faces a lawsuit over this. You need to find something, and find it quick – or you'll have to let him go."

What a jerk. I'm on the verge of cracking this case and finding the real villain and he's worried about his day being ruined by some nagging lawyer.

Our resources were stretched so I had to split my CS team in two. Roy would go straight over to Karl King's place in Weybridge, leaving two junior CS behind to carry on at the Knackers.

Meanwhile Matt had been going through Karl King's phone and apart from the previously seen text exchange with Shoosmith had found nothing incriminating.

I dragged Donnelly/Shoosmith out of his cell and with his brief by his side showed him the Maidenhead nick video.

"Remarkable likeness don't you think?"

"No comment."

"Another remarkable coincidence. You have the same DNA as that fellow."

"No comment."

"Brian Donnelly born 15th November 1966"

"No comment."

"We've been searching your gaff. Nice place you got there."

"No comment."

"So why do they call you the Boatman?"

"No comment."
"I heard it's because you like a sailor."
"No comment."
"You'll get to meet plenty of sailor boys in prison."
"No comment."
"I bet you're looking forward to spending the rest of your life in stir."
"No comment."
"And you will get life, on account of your so called mate Karl King grassing you up good and proper."
"No comment."
"According to him you're the one who did it all – everything. He wasn't even there."
"No comment."
"Some friend that Karl King. He has you living in that horrible shack, while he's living in luxury."
"No comment."
"He owes you for the third job."
"No comment."
"And now he's trying to get you sent down for it."
"No comment."
"He's laughing at you."
"No comment."
"Don't you want to have a laugh on him?"
"No comment."
"Come on give us your nasty laugh."
"No comment."
"Have you stopped shagging sheep?"
"No comment."

I came out for a break from this revelatory stuff to run into Matt with yet more developments. CS had taken a swatch of the soundproof wall cladding to the lab. The blood had not been identified yet but it was definitely human. I just hoped it wasn't mine. Next they had found shards of DNA in the straps hanging from the ceiling. Again I hoped it didn't turn out it to be mine. The lab technicians were now attempting to match the samples to any of the three victims. So I could now formally charge Nick Shoosmith, but the big worry now was Karl King.

To add to my worries, Hinton came into the office. "Have you found anything on Karl King?"

"Give us a break," I said for the first time showing a bit of petulance – "we only spoke about this half an hour ago."

"Listen if you don't find something on him soon I am releasing him. Understand? He's walking."

"Hang on Sir we can't do that. Karl King is an associate of this man Shoosmith, who we do have stuff on." "That doesn't justify keeping him in custody. Get on the phone to CS – find out if you have anything. If not – Karl King is walking."

Suddenly the office down the corridor erupted into cheers. I ran in. CS had called in to say that in the shack in a draw wrapped up in a bloody handkerchief they had found a pair of eyes. So Shoomsith had kept a trophy and that was to be his undoing. We had him. But how could I link this to Karl King? The eyes have it. We have the eyes. But not on KK. The ever-helpful Matt had drawn up a chart of what we had found in the knackers yard :-

- Human blood residual DNA on the floor – as yet unidentified ...
- A melted mobile phone
- Skin in the straps
- Gaffer tape ... saliva ....

In the corridor I called Roy for news on the Karl King search. Two people passed me. I looked away to concentrate on my phone call. Wait. One of them was looking back and leering at me. Fuck. It was Karl King out of his cell and walking free alongside his power dressed female solicitor. I was disappointed to see that Karl King's nose had not been broken by my defensive head butt – there was only mild bruising around his forehead.

"See ya!" he said raising his hand in a mocking wave as he proceeded to the door.

"Your parents let you get away with murder, but I will not," I called out to him. He waved me away like an annoying fly and was out the door. Meanwhile Roy had answered his phone.

"Have you thoroughly searched the boots and back seats of all Karl King's vehicles?" I immediately asked.

"Yes – nothing. Nothing on the passenger seat, or the driver seat. Not even the trace of any cleaning products." My case against Karl King was about to collapse. I was going to have to let him go.

"There must be some DNA of the victim's in the boot. Search again."

"We've searched thoroughly already, there's nothing more to do here." And with that he hung up. I put my head in my hands and shut my eyes tight wishing the earth would swallow me up.

The man I had spent the last year chasing was going to be let loose on the streets. Free to come back at me in revenge, free to start up another prostitution racket and free to kill again. This man is guilty I know it. Matt the Stat is right – my police work is shoddy, a mess and as a result my case was slipping away. I sat down in reception just next to a cardboard cutout of a TV celebrity promoting road safety. I cradled my head and held it in my knees. I squeezed my eyes shut and in the black I thought. I thought hard. Harder than I had ever thought before.

Think Ferdy. Think. What am I to do? What can I do? Can you help me out reader? Do you want to take a minute? But don't make it any longer mind, Karl King is outside and his taxi is approaching.

Wait! – I opened my eyes and dialed.

No time for pleasantries.

"Have you run Luminol over the car's front bumpers?"

"No."

"Do it. Do it now. I'll hold"

I looked out the window and saw Karl King and his solicitor standing outside, they were apparently waiting for a taxi. Karl King was laughing, raising his voice, jubilant. Silence on the other end of the phone. A taxi cab pulled up. King was vigorously shaking his solicitor's hand still with that sickening oily smile.

More agonizing silence at the other end of the phone. Karl King was now sat in the cab.

"Yes we've found blood on the front bumper." Get in! This was my goal deep into injury time. In my excitement I punched off the head of the cardboard cutout TV celebrity promoting road safety, and I raccd out of thc door and in a desperate dive placed myself in front of the cab as it was pulling out. The taxi broke against my shinbone. With the cab stationary I scrambled over the bonnet to the passenger door and pulled Karl King out. I pushed him violently against the wall. In a flash two coppers grabbed hold of my arms and were holding me back.

"I've got you now you scum." With the police still holding back, I got to say: "Karl King I'm arresting you on suspicion of the murder of Alex McNaught otherwise known as the BMX Kid. You do not have to say anything but it will harm your defense if you do not say something which you later rely on in court."

The uniform let me go and now pulled King away to reacquaint him with our police cell. His solicitor said something to me which I was too pumped to hear. I later learnt that she was declaring that she will be putting a full and formal official complaint about my conduct.

Hours later it was confirmed that the blood on the bumper was that of hit and run victim Alex McNaught a/k/a The BMX Kid.

I called Karl King into the interview room with his brief to try out one big bluff. With the video rolling I asked:

"So I expect you want to know about the DNA we have on you?"

"No comment."

"It's not just the blood on the bumper. We've also got your DNA in a place it shouldn't be."

"No comment."

"Your DNA was found under the fingernails of Andrea Perry."

This obviously threw him. His "No comment," was delayed.

"Remember the caution – you have the right to remain silent, but it will harm your defense if you do not say something which you will later rely on in court."

Long pause. His solicitor was about to shut him up, before King said "We had a row that night. That's all."

I turned to the camera "Did you get that folks? Karl King knew Andrea Perry and had a fight with her the day she was killed."

This was in fact one big bluff coming straight out of Lieutenant Colombo's book of tricks. You will recall that the baboons that are the Maidenhead police had lost the sample of DNA under Andrea Perry's fingernails. Because of this I probably would never be able to prove King's implication in Andrea Perry's murder, but at least I got to give the bastard something to worry about.

Thursday 30th July 2015

"I've heard you've arrested Karl King and his goon. I am so relieved. Well done." The voice on the phone was Zara Campbell's. She sounded very different – relaxed and pleasant. Almost like she actually liked me. Don't get carried away now.

"Why thank you." I blushed, "You know I'd really appreciate you coming in for a chat about all of this." She came in that afternoon. Because of her aversion of police stations, she put the call to meet her in the pub car park across the road.

She got out of the car, and it was immediately noticeable that her tension had eased and that the wall of hostility had lifted. We talked by the car while Cody played noisily in the back seat.

Zara wanted confirmation that the two men were behind bars, even wanting to know the actual nicks they were in. I showed her pictures from my phone of the two men in their cells. As you can imagine I had loads of questions to fire at this new friendly faced Zara.

"So Zara give me all you have on Karl King."

"It's truc what I said before. I only ever knew that man as K, but it was him backed up by the man we knew as the Boatman. Those two got us doing the rituals round mine once a week. K is into mind control, and the rituals were all part of it. They've been terrorizing me and the girls for so long."

"So okay, you might have been too scared to speak up, but why didn't at least drop some hints?"

"We were so terrified. When they were in power, they were all powerful we daren't question, daren't speak up. All we could do was keep up the wall of secrecy." "So what was the story with Mallard?"

"Mallard was just the odd job man. He got paid a pittance – like me. The lion's share went to the K."

"And how did you get the money to him?"

"The Boatman was the man that came over and collected. Most of the time no violence or heavy stuff was needed. Most of the time." She looked over at Cody.

"And what about the Devil Tarot Card?"

"When we did the initiation ceremony we got given the devil tarot card and they made us carry it at all times. It made us feel we were part of something we could not escape from.

"So when Daria was killed with the Tarot Card in her mouth that was supposed to be the signal to the girls that it was one of them that was killed, but the rest of the world wouldn't know because only people within the K ring knew about the Devil Tarot Card. That's why you fucked them up but not telling the press about the tarot card in their mouths."

I smiled proudly.

"So why was Daria killed? Was she going to leave the K ring?"

Zara shook her head.

"Becky had been sleeping with K and she was hoping that he would give her a ticket out of there. But after a while it was obvious this was never going to happen. Then K started showing an interest in Daria. Becky hated that, and so she told K that Daria was planning to escape the K Ring. So K decided to make an example of her and it was Becky who lured Daria to get killed.

"I overhead Becky say to K 'She's playing you.' And K was getting all angry and calling The Boatman over. Then I heard K say 'If she was to go no one could trace her. Her parents are far away.'

"I also overheard K say, "It's time to take another one." I knew what that meant and it made me sick to the stomach – but you got to understand I felt powerless against them."

"So why was Angela Ashdown chosen as the next victim?"

"To take the police spotlight away from the K ring. K ordered Becky to entrap a random non-sexworker. So you would think you were after a serial killer with no links to the K Ring. But Becky's such a vindictive bitch she picked a girl she had a beef with since primary school,"

I said. "And that vindictiveness led us to her. If she'd chosen someone totally random we probably would have never have solved this."

Zara nodded and proceeded.

"Even the evidence she gave against Mallard was a way of getting back at him for all the bad things he'd done to her."

"So what's the story behind Mallard and his dream?"

"K and the Boatman's mind control is done through rituals and drugs. They got Mallard tripping and planted the idea of telling the cops the story. The two angels in his dream were K and the Boatman. They wanted to sacrifice him and close up the investigation

"Mallard was there at the two killings – he's guilty and deserved everything he got. But the real men behind it are K and the Boatman."

I had a burning question "So when Karl King came to see me the first time, I am assuming that was to announce himself to me. Because if I had thoroughly investigated the K ring and found out that he was running it, he would have been suspect number 1."

Zara shook her head – "I doubt that. K is so clever, so powerful. You would have never figured out he was behind it. None of the girls would have given him up."

"Well, he ain't so clever and powerful now. I can tell you."

Zara went on, "I am so ... relieved. I hate them – I was too scared to even think it – but I hate them."

I felt vindicated. Zara's words had validated everything that Matt and I had done, and I was proud of Zara summonsing the courage to finally come forward.

"Zara, this is wonderful you coming forward. I just need you to say all this on the record."

Zara shook her head and moved towards the car.

"Now the K ring is finally shut down. I can leave the country, start a new life somewhere far way, but I can't testify."

"But you MUST testify. This will make sure they go down."

"For all I know this doesn't end with Karl King. It's not me I'm scared for. It's for him," she gestured towards her Cody in the back seat – now howling impatiently.

And with those words she was in her car and gone.

Friday 31st July 2015

My next stop was Holloway prison to see Becky Taylor. Her testimony that sent Mallard and herself down was now the biggest problem in my Shoosmth/Donnelly Karl King case. Mainly because these two new killers were totally absent from her story.

The stark visiting room of Holloway prison stank of disinfectant and menstrual blood. I sat there not sure how to play this. Do I play it tough – or do I play it nice? Or maybe tough but nice? I wanted the truth. I decided to play it straight.

So I greeted Becky with a big smile. Her hair was shorter, less black. How is that possible? Is she dying it now? Or was she dying it before? A crucifix dangled conspicuously around her neck.

"How can I help?"

"It's about Daria Lipsinski and Angela Ashdown. We've discovered the place where their murders took place. The slaughterhouse. Ramona Marks was also killed there."

"Yes. And?"

"We know that you could not have been there when Ramona was killed because you were in custody then. But I wanted to find out what you can tell us about Daria and Angela."

"I said what I had to say in court."

"Well now we have two more perpetrators – and two men who instigated the killings. I am of course talking about ..." I wanted her to give me the two names. "You know who I'm talking about right?"

"The Good Lord wants me to put the whole sorry episode behind me and never to revisit it."

"Look I can understand that you did not want to name these men before because you were scared. But both these men are now behind bars and awaiting trial. You're safe."

"I've said what I had to say and I'm doing my time," she repeated.

"I just want you to tell the full story – the whole truth. Testify against these two evil men."

"I was in a dark place then and I must never revisit it."

"I need you to help me to put these men away, so that they never do this again. This is justice for Ramona your friend."

"I don't want to get involved. I just want to do my time and forget that whole horrible time."

I looked at her crucifix – "I've been told about your conversion to Christianity playing the model repentant prisoner. I know your game."

"I'm not playing any game."

"Yes you are – the get-out-in-four year's game. Well listen right. When I prove there are more people involved you ain't getting out in four – you'll be seeing a charge for perjury. You'll be doing your happy clappy routine in here for another twenty."

"The Lord does not want me to go back to where I was. He has spoken and I must listen." And she called over to the warden to take her back to the cell.

So much for trying to be the nice guy. When I got

back to base I went through Karl King's file yet again. By now I pretty much knew it word for word. For one crime of assault for which he was not finally charged, a girlfriend named Mary, then 18 years of age, had provided him with an alibi.

I looked her up on my grand database and discovered she was married, and divorced, and now living in Claygate. So I was taking a drive up my favorite road the A3.

Mary Clarke nee Madigan met me at a Travellers Rest just off the A3. She was a brunette in her early 30s with fleshy cheeks and pouty big lips. Her eyes slanted downwards as if someone had grabbed hold of her eyes on either side, and pushed them down. Maybe her ex Karl King had done it.

She did not register any surprise when I told her that her ex was involved in some murky business. But to offset that she said: "I was only with him for six months. He was a very sweet guy."

That's not I wanted to hear. She went on "He just fell in with a bad crowd."

"Like who in particular?"

"That creep – Nicky SixStars. He was the guy who got him into the drugs and other stuff."

Nicky SixStars? "Describe this Nick SixStars to me."
"Big man – bad breath, tattoos."

I pulled out my picture of Nick Shoosmith. Her eyes froze.

"That's him." Still staring at the photograph.

"His real name is Nick Shoosmith," I informed her. Going through the records of Shoosmith would reveal that Nicky SixStars was one of his nicknames before The Boatman.

"It was him that got him into...."

"What?"

"Like I said drugs...."

"What else?"

"The orgies...." I sat forward. Now she's talking.

"He was always staring at me ...those eyes ... put that picture away please." I obliged, then went on, "That's why we split up. He tried to persuade me to get involved in this kinky stuff. He called it my initiation. I said No. He kept insisting. I kept on saying No. Then he offered me money. That was the end. I broke up with him. I went to college and he tracked me down saying 'You Can Never Escape Me.' But he had to let me go, because he needed me to vouch for his whereabouts the night that girl got attacked."

"And he wasn't with you that night?"

"I can't remember."

"Yes you can – he wasn't with you."

She reacted angrily – "I told you I can't remember." She looked out the window and fell into a reverie – "Such a shame – he was my first love."

She then turned to me, "I would like to write to him. Just to see if he's okay."

"Well, he's not okay, is he? He's up for murder."

Monday 5th October 2015

Karl King's legal team requested a separate trial from Nick Shoosmith. They wisely wanted to distance their client as much as possible from Shoosmith. The forensics in his knackers yard, especially the eyes, and the stolen identity made Shoosmith a dead cert for going down. And they got their separate trial. Damn!

But I did not need Chapman Bendy to point out that the case against Karl King was looking well dicey. Yes I had evidence of Alex McNaught's blood on his bumper, but a clever lawyer – which King had - could turn that into a manslaughter hit and run. I still had nothing to link him directly to the murder of the girls.

When Nick Shoosmith faced the crown court in the autumn he pleaded Not Guilty to all charges. Sociopaths like Shoosmith always do – just to be difficult, just to drag out their time in the limelight. He still didn't take the stand though, hiding behind his pathetic weasel of a brief. He had no explanation for the eyes being found in the shack. The brief suggested that someone staying there before Shoosmith had put them there. He even hinted that we had planted them. Their main – in fact only - thrust of the defense was reasonable doubt. The jury had none – and he was found guilty of the killings of Daria Lipsinski, Angela Ashdown and Ramona Marks.

Justice for Andrea Perry would have to wait for another trial.

He was also found guilty of various identity theft crimes, the legal jargon of which are too boring for me to remember. In all he was giving three life sentences for murder – making the identity theft charges as redundant as Ross Kemp's hairdresser.

Next came the big one. My career was hanging on this. If Karl King walked, his solicitor was threatening a very costly law suit against the Ageing William – and targeting yours truly in particular. Nervous? It's safe to say I was giving birth to several kittens over this one.

I was outraged to discover that Karl King was granted bail. I thought homicide cases were always kept in custody, but I was wrong. In Surrey bail is granted under certain stringent conditions. King's wealthy parents had put their large house up as surety. So I guess if he skips bail, at least the Surrey Police would get a nice four-bedroom house in Berkshire.

To make matters worse, Chapman Hendy then told me they wanted to drop the case. I stood firm and insisted, staking my increasingly shaky reputation on it.

So I needed more evidence. Up until his release on

bail, I had been intercepting his post in prison in case he admitted guilt anywhere or any of his associates would write anything that would incriminate him. Nothing.

In amongst the post I was disappointed to discover that ex-girlfriend Mary Clarke had been writing to him. I then heard that she had gone to see him in prison.

Monday 2nd November 2015

November the 2nd was set as the big date for our Karl King Crown Court showdown. Like a Berni Inn opening at the top of the BT Tower – the stakes don't come any higher than this. So this story is not a whodunit any longer, it's become a is-he-going-to-get-away-with-it.

Because KK was such a hit with the ladies I wanted our legal team to push for an all-male jury. But apparently that is unconstitutional and we were stuck with a jury of six men and six women. King's brief was a different class from Shoosmith's. She set great store on his client's reputation as a legitimate businessman, his good parents, his good education. Distancing him as much as possible from the obvious low life that is Shoosmith. And Karl King looked the part of a successful entrepreneur in the dock – neatly groomed in a Hugo Boss suit.

We were legally not allowed to mention his extensive criminal record. So his barrister was allowed to make all sorts of false claims about Karl King and we were not allowed to counter these lies with the truth. The law really is no end of an ass. Now of course Bremner's and the Mekesha girl undercover work was all inadmissible. But we got served a severe blow when the judge ruled that the text messages between KK and Shoosmith, which I had jumped in on to lure KK to the gaff, was also ruled inadmissible.

The barristers were trying to dismiss the BMX Kid's murder as a mere hit and run. Blaming the accident on the BMK Kid's reckless riding. The barrister said, "My client is offering a donation of a substantial sum of money to a road safety charity – to help communicate the importance of riding carefully. Once the accident had happened there was nothing my client could have done."

She went on to dismiss everything surrounding the death of the women. She also made great pains to try and make out that I "had it in for his client." That I had a personal grudge and it was colouring my treatment of the case..

I got to tell you at this point it was looking majorly bleak for the prosecution, and Karl King was wearing his smug face in the dock. That was until we called in the next witness – Becky Taylor.

Chapter 21

Revenge of the Crazy Cat Lady

Thursday 12th November 2015

NOW, DEAR READER, for this entire narrative I have kept you informed of everything relevant that has happened in the investigation. However for dramatic purposes, I held back one very important nugget. Leading up to the trial I called in my final blackmail favor.

I got Jane Barrow to go to Holloway Prison and tell Becky that she had a number of book publishers interested in Becky's story. Jane was confident she could get her a very large advance, on the one condition that she told the court in the Karl King trial what really happened.

So enter Becky Taylor, walking slowly to the stand. She obviously knew that every eye in the room was on her and she was milking it. She sat down in the dock, that large crucifix dangling round her neck. Our prosecuting counsel began the questioning:

"Now Becky. You are serving a prison sentence for your participation in the murders of Daria Lipsinski and Angela Ashdown. You gave evidence in that trial against Andrew Mallard. But today you want to give new evidence?"

"Yes."

"You do realise that if your new evidence contradicts or is radically different from your previous evidence, that makes you liable to a charge of perjury?"

"Yes I understand that. I just want to tell the truth."

"Why did you not tell the truth before?"

"Because of fear. Because I thought I would be killed."

"By whom?"

"By Karl King. I need to tell the truth – and unmask the evil man behind these terrible murders. Before I was in the service of the Devil. Now I am the service of God." That bit sounded rehearsed.

"Mallard was still guilty of these crimes and I am still guilty of the part I played. As before, I stress it was under extreme intimidation and duress. But the real instigator is Karl King and his right hand man is the person I now know to be Nick Shoosmith – but then we all knew him as the Boatman.

"My motivations were jealousy and spite, and I am so sorry. I can only thank God who has shown me a better way...." Leave the God stuff out, I thought, we need the jury to buy this.

Our counsel steered her away from that nonsense and towards what we all wanted to hear. What REALLY happened over the killings? Let me give you the highlights of her testimony.

Daria was chosen to be killed by Karl King because she was planning to leave the K Ring. (Contrary to what Zara said). Becky was summonsed to join K and the Boatman at the kitchen table round Zara's, while everyone else was partying. She recalls the Boatman saying to K - "We are going to have fun with this one." Becky was ordered to arrange a meeting with Daria alone and was given the night off in order to do it.

Becky explained that K enjoyed killing, but he can control it. He can plan it so that no suspicion falls on him. He had a good life – and did not want to lose it. But The Boatman on the other hand is just vicious and can't control his urges to inflict pain.

The method of killing - the eyes gouging and the stones throwing - was done to prolong the pain and increase the suffering. The fixing of the body to the riverbed was a way of revealing the body 12 hours after the body was dumped to create the maximum impact and shock. She heard K and The Boatman laughing about it.

Becky still claimed that during the murders she sat in a van, but this time the vehicle was The Boatman's white van. Both killings took place in the knackers yard – and she was ordered to burn the personal effects – clothes and mobile phones – of the two victims in the adjacent incinerator.

Ramona had been ordered by K to come forward with the anonymous tip about the Polish ex-boyfriend to throw the police off the scent. When that was rumbled, Ramona was put in danger – and further heat came when the police found out about the weekly satanic rituals round Zara's that were used to control the girls. So in order to steer the police investigation away from the K Ring, the murder of Angela Ashdown was hastily brought forward.

Becky said she knew that Ramona would be killed because of her failed attempt to give the police false information. Once the police realised that her information was bogus, they would have figured out that the killers had put her up to it, and put pressure on her. Becky explained that through the brainwashing ritual, all the girls in the K ring were so scared that they daren't keep back any of the money or even think about leaving, speaking to the police or even bad mouthing the set up.

In her own words "It was their way of putting a chicken wire around us – a mental chicken wire – so we daren't even think about escaping. Like the Cat Sanctuary. But the big difference is, while the K Ring was based on hate and fear, the Cat Sanctuary is based on love and compassion. I guess that's why we liked going there so much." She went on – "The K Ring set all the girls against each other, put them in competition, but you can see in the Cat Sanctuary, even though they are prisoners, they are as one. That's how it should be."

Our solicitor said to her – "you do realise that all you have said is unlikely to get you an early release from prison."

"I am not interested in an early release. My life story is a history of abuse by men and there are no men in Holloway."

Then our solicitor came in with the set up question to lead us to the really good bit "do you have any physical evidence to corroborate any of this?"

"I do. Outside the slaughter room Karl King gave me Daria's clothes and phone to burn in the incinerator. Before giving me her t-shirt he wiped his face in it, covering his face and neck in her blood. It obviously gave him a thrill. I took all the items to the incinerator, but I hid and kept the t-shirt. "I took the t-shirt home and put it in a Jiffy Bag. I then put it in my mother's garden shed. I told my mother to never open the bag until I tell her to and if I died suddenly to send the bag to the police."

"And what were your reasons for doing this?"

"For security. If I thought that Karl King was going to bump me off because of what I know, I could tell him I had this evidence that would prove his guilt and send him to prison.

"I also thought at some point I could blackmail him with it for a lot of money. That's the sort of person I was back then."

"And is that Jiffy bag now in court?"

"Yes."

The jiffy bag was handed to her by the usher. After putting on plastic gloves, Becky opened the bag and pulled out the T-shirt. Becky unraveled it and showed it to the court. Which drew loud gasps followed by frantic murmuring.

Though the shirt was covered in dried blood – the

legend was still visible – **Crazy Cat Lady.**

"I put a covering note in the bag." She took out the note.

"Would you mind reading out the note to the court?"

"To whom it may concern. This is the T-shirt that Daria Lipsinski was wearing when she was killed. She was killed by Karl King and his accomplice. Karl King wiped his face with this shirt so you will find Karl King's DNA on it. This will prove his guilt. Signed Becky Taylor."

More gasps and murmurs from the court. Inevitably all eyes eventually drifted over to Karl King – he wasn't looking so smug now.

His barrister leapt up and demanded an adjournment to consider this evidence. The judge agreed, and with a knock of the hammer, court proceedings were finished for the day.

In an interesting example of lies turning into real life, Jane really had actually secured a book deal for the Becky Taylor story, and Becky was smart enough to know all along that legally she could never personally gain financially from the book. So she was signing off all her royalties to Ramona's son JJ – via the grandparents and to the Cat Sanctuary. So after years of doing nothing but wrong, Becky finally managed to do the right thing.

Friday 13th November 2015

I was looking forward to seeing Karl King turn up at court this morning. So much so, I got to the court a good half an hour early and grabbed a coffee and stood by the entrance. I was going to enjoy this. But something was up. Panic at the courthouse. Headless chickens running all around.

Karl King had absconded! He was supposed to be at his parents' home at 8.00 a.m. to be taken in the van to the courtroom. But he was a no show.

I needed to take control of this, so I drove straight over to the parent's place in Berkshire which of course, because of the skipped bail, was now property of the Surrey Police. I went with this gag when I got there. "I've come to look over our new home," I told the parents, who were defiant refusing to take any responsibility "It's because of you he did this. He knew you were out to get him and he knew he couldn't get a fair trial."

So where the hell had Karl King gone? Well I had a pretty good idea of where he might be holding out. Where do you think he may have bolted? Are we on the same page here?

Now I couldn't take any chances on this one. If I requested a warrant, the mysterious secret networks might tip King off – and besides I was acting purely on a hunch and generally speaking magistrates don't give out search warrants purely on hunches. But this hunch was a golden one.

So me and a team of six uniforms, supportive of the Ferdy cause, took a couple of unmarked cars on a drive up the A3 to a residential estate in Claygate. We parked up at the opening of a cul-de-sac and fixed our binoculars on the two-story house at the end.

We are deep in the heart of dreary suburbia here. For miles and miles and miles nothing but houses, and the exact same type of houses, no pub, builder's caff, petrol garage or corner shop to break up the residential monotony. According to our records Mary Clarke lived there with her ten-year-old daughter. We couldn't see any evidence of anybody else staying there. Though we were unlikely to, as all the curtains were drawn in broad daylight.

Now you will already be familiar with Ferdy's hide-outside-their-house-and-tell-them-I'm-coming-over-in-a-couple-of-hours ruse. So I dialed –

"Hello, Mrs. Clarke. Ferdy, Surrey Police."

"Yes, what do you want?"

"You may have heard that your ex, Karl King, is giving us the Mike Reid."

"Mike Reid? What do you mean?"

"He's giving us the run around."

"Yes and –?"

"I need to talk to you. You may be able to give me some insight into where he might be. Would it be convenient if I came over in a couple of hours?"

"Well, it's not convenient."

"Well, I'm sorry, Mrs. Clarke – I must insist. This is a very serious matter. I will be coming over in a couple of hours."

"Well, I can't guarantee I'll be in."

"Make this easy for everybody, Mrs. Clarke. Be sure to be in when I come over." And I hung up and raised my binoculars. No movement nothing. But then again with the curtains drawn there would have been very little to see. Ten minutes later the garage is opened by Sarah Clarke and she drives the car out to the front of the house. Then she brings out a large suitcase – which she puts in the back seat. Why not put it in the boot? Is that because somebody was in the boot?

I got out of my car and marched towards the house. I got there just as she was locking the front door. "Hello, Mrs. Clarke – I've come over early. Hope you don't mind." Mary Clarke's sloping eyes lifted as terror seized her face. She then spun on her heels and made a dash for her car. "Mrs. Clarke – are you fleeing the interview?" I called out in reference to one of my favorite films. The speeding car only got as far as the police roadblock at the entrance of the cul-de-sac.

I calmly walked over to the stationary car and said to the red-faced Mary Clarke, "Hello again, Mrs. Clarke. Would you mind opening the boot for me please?"

She obliged to reveal Karl King cooped up and sweaty.

I had tried to plan a revenge of poetic justice. Something that involved stringing him up, throwing stones at him. Something that reflected what he had done to those women. I had also planned to give him a chance to run, which would then give me the opportunity to stick in a few kidney punches.

But instead, collaring him like this, squeezed up in a car boot would have to do. Nevertheless I was mightily pleased with this.

As they pulled him out the car Mary Clarke came howling at me, "You should be ashamed of yourself – persecuting an innocent man."

I laughed so hard I nearly forgot to charge her with aiding and abetting a fugitive.

So the next day Karl King was back in front of the judge and jury. Still maintaining his innocence. But his whole run away thing straight after Becky's testimony was as good as an admission of guilt. The jury might be fucking stupid – but they are not THAT fucking stupid. I hope. Nevertheless, a week later, I still had a bellyful of butterflies as the jury came back into the room to announce their verdict.

The convictions were rattled out.

Karl King was convicted of the killing of Alex McNaught, the BMX Kid.

He was also found guilty of the murder of Daria Lipsinski, Angela Ashdown, and Ramona Marks. Big cheers and loud sighs of relief. This time I felt that the backslapping was justified.

Monday 16th November 2015

For the first time since seeing Daria's body fastened to the riverbed in May of 2014 I felt I could truly celebrate. I could have a drink and smile without feeling guilty. But I didn't want any of the other free load coppers around – I just wanted to celebrate with my two real colleagues – the loggerheads Matt and Bremner.

So we sneaked out from the official celebration to another riverside pub and found ourselves a quiet table. Matt and Bremner may never be friends, but today I made them know they were on the same team. I got them to shake hands and we raised a glass to Alex McNaught, the BMX Kid who cracked the case for us. And in his honor we sank a few.

Friday 20th November 2015

The following Friday I had booked the day off to relax and recover after my last year and a half of intense work. I got up especially late for me – 8 a.m., and I drove Luis to school. It was nice to remind him that I was still around. The scars of thc borough sports final had healed for Luis, and he was back to his football crazy self. I told him we were going to Brazil in the New Year to see a couple of football matches. His eyes lit up and I gave him something to tell his friends that day.

When I got home I opened my post box to find the latest edition of the *Surrey Star*. The headline story by Jane Barrow read: "HOW FERDY THE FOX CRACKED THE SLAUGHTER ON THAMES MURDERS." Ferdy the Fox? This may catch on folks. Watch this space!

❊ ❊ ❊

Thank you for reading.
Please review this book. Reviews help others find New Pulp Press and inspire us to keep providing these marvelous tales.

If you would like to be put on our email list to receive updates on new releases, contests, and promotions, please go to NewPulpPress.com and sign up.

About the Author

Paolo has worked in media sales, as a journalist, a film-maker and a promoter of raves. His debut feature film, the black comedy horror The Toybox, was released on DVD to some critical acclaim, and is available for viewing for free (and legally) on www.hulu.com .

Recent work includes Everyone's Wally a biographical documentary about Wally Hope the founder of the Stonehenge free festivals, who died under mysterious circumstances in 1975.

The BMX Kid & the River Cult Murders is his first crime novel, based on a real life murder case and drawing on his experiences of working at the court house of Walton-on-Thames.

Paolo lives in West London with his wife, Sarah, and two cats – Dougie and Tallulah.

www.ingramcontent.com/pod-product-compliance
Lightning Source LLC
Chambersburg PA
CBHW060522260626
47161CB00003B/734
* 9 7 8 1 9 4 5 7 3 4 0 0 7 *